Dead DETECTIVES Society

MONSTROUS
BOOKS

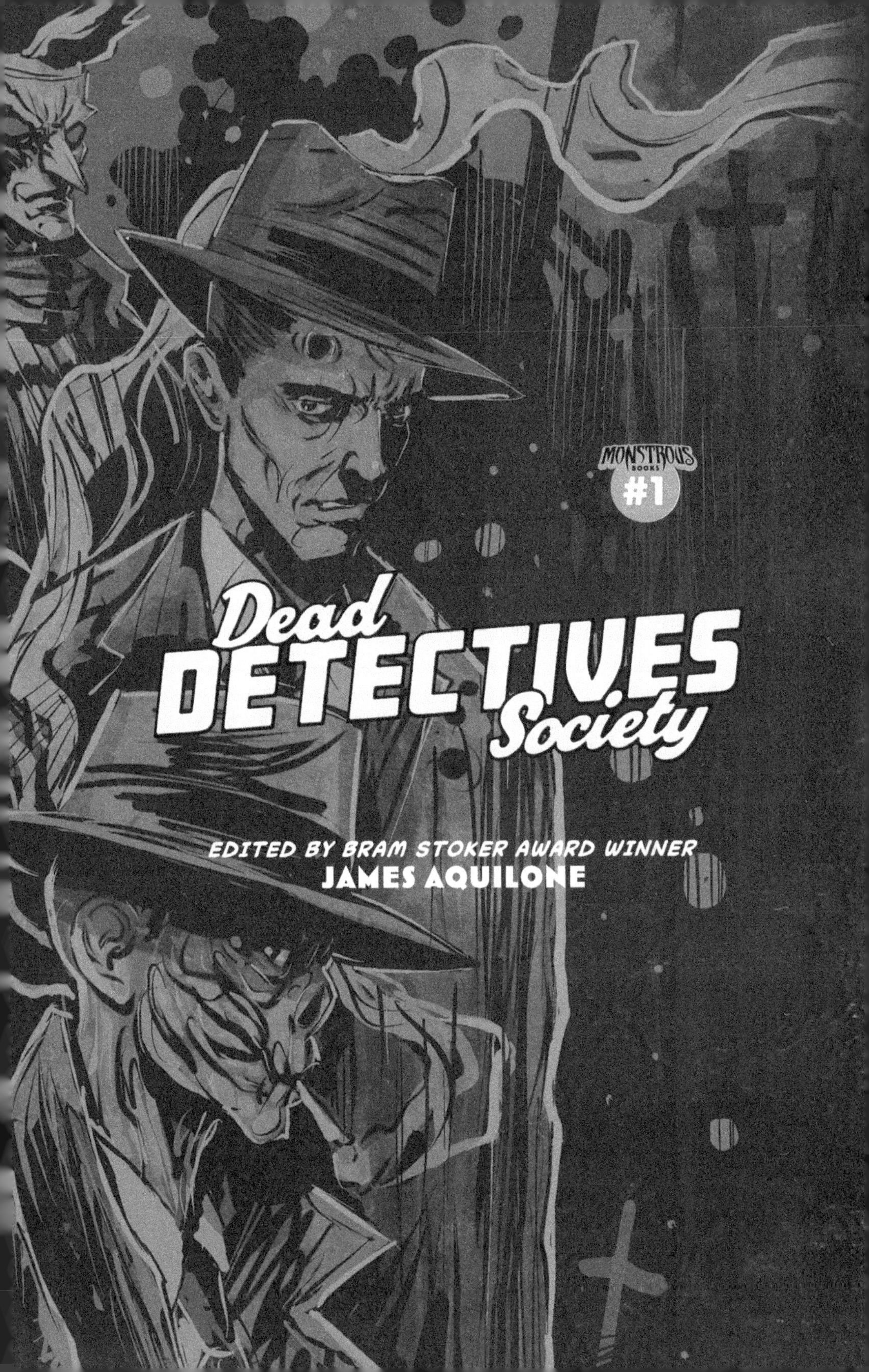
MONSTROUS BOOKS
#1
Dead DETECTIVES Society
EDITED BY BRAM STOKER AWARD WINNER
JAMES AQUILONE

DEAD DETECTIVES SOCIETY #1

Editor: **James Aquilone**
Cover Illustration: **John Jennings**
Interior Design Layout: **Qamber Designs**
Interior Illustrations: **Zac Atkinson** (Dan Shamble, Nick Carter, Thomas Quinn, Jin G. Fox, Mr. Cricket, Sonja Blue), **J.K Woodward** (Dead Jack), **Paul McCaffrey** (Matt Richter, Monk Addison), **Sean Von Gorman** (Snippy), **John K. Snyder III** (Johnny Fade), **Russ Braun** (Cal McDonald), **John Jennings** (Saul When)
Proofreader: **Kenneth W. Cain**

eBook ISBN: 978-1-946346-22-3
Hardcover ISBN: 978-1-946346-23-0
Paperback ISBN: 978-1-946346-21-6

Worldwide Rights 1st Edition
Published by Monstrous Books

MonstrousBooks.com

*Dedicated to the Founding Members
of the Dead Detectives Society*

Tarhan Kayihan
James Johnston
Emily Rousell
remlub.navi
Rena Mason

ALSO AVAILABLE FROM MONSTROUS BOOKS

Shakespeare Unleashed
Monstrous Magazine

Dead Jack and the Pandemonium Device
Dead Jack and the Soul Catcher
Dead Jack and the Old Gods

CONTENTS

THRILLING MYSTERIES OF THE MACABRE!

WHAT IS THE DEAD DETECTIVES SOCIETY?

Throughout history and infinite dimensions, there exists a secret group of supernatural investigators operating on the fringes of society, lurking in the shadows, working strange cases with little reward. They are hardboiled zombies and ghosts, mythological creatures, ass-kicking vampires, tortured humans, and uncanny sleuths whose normal is the bizarre and weird.

Rumors about the establishment of the Dead Detectives Society abound, but so-called experts tend to agree that it began with three zombie detectives. When and where it was founded are difficult questions to answer. When? In the distant past, according to some. The near future, to others. And they're both correct—because it happened out of time. Where? Again, there are many conflicting stories, but it certainly didn't occur here, in the world in which you exist. Each of the original zombie P.I.s reside in an alternate dimension, where time runs differently. Their meeting, as far as I can tell, took place in an extra-dimensional nexus upon which each stumbled, their meeting purely an accident. That story will be told one day, but not now.

Over the years, more investigators—not all of which were zombies or the undead—joined the society. It is an inclusive group. Alternate universes, after all, are infinite in number. These are a sampling of their cases....

—*Kilgore Birch, Dead Detectives Society Historian*

NICK CARTER:
RECALLED TO LIFE
THE MASTER DETECTIVE RETURNS IN A THRILLING NEW STORY
BY DAVID AVALLONE

Nick Carter regarded the ring of ugly metal muzzles pointed at him and wondered, not for the first time, if he could be killed. *Or more to the point*, he thought, *would I stay dead?*

The Shpagin, which he had always thought of as the ugly stepbrother of the Thompson, was not a particularly accurate weapon, but the six men holding them were only two yards away at most. The clumsiest, most poorly trained marksman couldn't miss. The Shpagin is a garden hose for bullets.

It had been a few months since Nick, like old Professor Manette, had been "recalled to life." A busy few months. Acclimating. Learning the lay of the land. Adapting old skills to a new world. A new world he was relieved to find still had a use for him.

While he'd slumbered in suspended animation, evil hadn't gone anywhere. If anything, it had become more ambitious. Global. Plenty to occupy a man like himself, in this new world.

Since his return, so far, he had been in a couple of tight spots, but this was shaping up as the tightest.

He had some aces up his sleeve, quite literally, but he was struggling to picture an outcome where he wasn't thoroughly ripped up by 7.62 millimeter slugs.

"Well, Mister Carter," said the silken voice in the darkness, beyond the ring of ugly metal muzzles, "what have you to say for yourself?"

Heroes die.

It comes with the job description.

That's not always convenient for the Powers That Be.

The Powers That Be need heroes. Heroes keep the machine going because heroes by themselves aren't quite enough. You need the little guys, and gals, to run into machine-gun fire and barbed wire, to storm the beachhead and plant the flag, and that takes some persuading, as you might imagine. Heroes can inspire the little guy to slap a helmet on his head and go Over There, or clip on a badge and a gun and Protect and Serve. And die. Ugly? Sure. But that's the system. That's the history of the world. Without Jason you don't have any Argonauts…and then who brings home that Golden Fleece?

Once upon a time there was a man named Nick Carter, back when he was still just that—a man. In the late 19th century, his father Sam trained him to be the greatest athlete, the sharpest mind, the world's preeminent detective. By the '30s it seemed like everyone was working on a superman of some kind, but old Sam Carter got there first.

Nick was not a big guy. To look at him, you wouldn't know he had the strength of ten men. You wouldn't know about the gadgets and disguises. He didn't have the airs of a great intellectual. He didn't have a certain English gentleman's air of superiority, but his affable, handsome face belied a brilliant mind. And for a good few decades, he cut a swath through criminality like a one-man police force.

Nick Carter had died, as heroes inevitably do, in the combat chaos of the Second War to End All Wars. Those aforementioned Powers That Be had been ready, though. They hadn't told Nick about it—top secret stuff, hush-hush, need to know, you understand—but they were ready.

Ironically, it was Carter's longtime enemy, the vivisectionist serial killer and psychotic genius Dr. Jack Quartz, who was the key to his rebirth. The madman Quartz had been a prolific inventor. His cabinet of horrors also contained wonders unseen outside of the pages of the science fiction pulp magazines. They were, in a word, astounding. When Carter finally defeated him one last time, the Powers That Be had taken those wonders into their possession and spent decades trying to understand them, so as to turn them to future use.

One of the many Quartz Gizmos was a suspended animation system. So it was that when Carter fell in battle, he was tossed in the Quartz Tank before his body was even cold.

In his first life, Carter had been frustrated that the maniacal Quartz had this neat trick of coming back from the dead. Repeatedly. He'd been to the electric chair and the gallows, and somehow there was always a new Jack Quartz, like some monstrous, murderous jack-in-the-box.

The Quartz Resurrection Gizmo was harder to crack…but the Powers That Be have a lot of money, and nothing but time.

It took them a couple of decades. In the end…they figured that one out, too. And in due time, Nick Carter opened his eyes once again, for the first time since 1944.

Carter hadn't questioned the miracle. Maybe it was superstition, maybe he was afraid to find out what unholy combo platter of Dr. Frankenstein, Dr. Moreau, Baron Samedi and/or Anubis had been involved. Maybe it just seemed ungrateful to ask. Whatever the reason, he didn't ask, and nobody else broached the topic. The Powers That Be didn't get to be the Powers That Be by volunteering such information. Naturally, he remembered the seemingly endless line of ever younger, ever stronger Quartzes he had faced, and he shuddered to think. So he didn't think long, or deeply.

When the fog of two decades in the Quartz Tank wore off, Carter found that he did, after all, recognize the face in the mirror. The body, he noted, was about six inches taller. *New and improved*, he thought, but he chose not to question that, either.

In his first life, he'd been his own man, run his own shop, done things his own way. In the new world, he found himself a cog in a much larger machine. Much to his surprise, he also found he had no objections to being led. That could change, in time. For now, guidance was appreciated, and he was happy to have tasks, complex and dangerous tasks, just like the good old days in the good old world.

Like any well-dressed secret agent in this new world, he was provided with new weapons. Some were pleasant echoes of his old tools. He had to admire the more streamlined profile of the Space Age arsenal, though they did let him keep the Luger he'd picked up back in the ETO. His preferred handgun, functional and stolid like a Dusseldorf hausfrau. Depending on the mission, the Luger found herself at home in his armpit, his waistband, or a simple leather holster.

The razor-sharp stiletto was the literal ace up his sleeve. Silent and sure and you never saw it coming.

Then there was the steel globe, little bigger than a marble. The most innocuous, and the most terrifying, once you knew what it contained. Nerve gas, released with a twist of the sphere—the most impersonal and the deadliest of all the toys, and used with the greatest care.

And so it was that in the year 1964 he was back in the field, doing the job his father had so strenuously trained him for in the late 19th century, with his ever-sharp mind, his murderous toybox, and his "new and improved" body. *Seems a shame*, he thought, regarding the Shpagins, *to let these low-level punks drive a bunch of holes through it.*

"Step into the light, Professor Citrine." Nick Carter spoke in his calm, even baritone. "There's no need for the cheap theatrics."

There was a dry, throaty chuckle, and Professor Citrine emerged from the shadows. She was pale and, one had to admit, lovely, in a severe way. She wore a light yellow sheath dress with a matching, well-tailored jacket. The color scheme continued to a bell of hair framing her face and was reflected in her eyes. *Cheekbones sharp enough to cut oneself on*, thought Carter. *And surely a few men have.*

Citrine regarded him closely, circling him from safely outside the protective ring of machine pistols.

"I suppose I can hardly be surprised the great detective saw through me so quickly. And you are him, aren't you? A little taller, maybe…"

Carter smirked at her. "You noticed. I'm flattered."

"We are in an age of marvels, Mister Carter. Rockets and missiles and supersonic jets…wonder drugs and organ transplants and…resurrection? Bringing a man back from the dead and adding a few inches in height seems like showing off, wouldn't you say?"

"Perhaps I'm just a tall ghost."

Citrine laughed again. "I think a ghost wouldn't be so wary around machine pistols. Whatever you are…it won't save you in this moment, as we lay all the cards on the table."

"Choosing as your alias a variety of quartz was just one touch too cute, Professor. You're not surprised in the least to find me here. You very much wanted me to figure out you were the joker in the deck."

She laughed. "I'm the queen, Mr. Carter. The joker is the fellow who walked willingly into an obvious trap and finds himself surrounded. The fly in the spiderweb."

Nick Carter sighed. "If I had a nickel for every criminal *mastermind* who employed that metaphor in similar situations, I could retire to the South Seas…and I wouldn't have to spend so much time breaking and entering remote lairs. There's nothing original about you, Citrine. I confess to some curiosity as to your motives. That *nuclear device* on the table is a cheap suitcase full of wires, old transistor radios, and just enough radioactive material to make a Geiger click. If that's a bomb, I'm Audrey Hepburn."

"Well, you have me there, My Fair Lady. It's not a bomb, so much as…"

"A worm on a hook? I eagerly await your next cliché."

Citrine reddened. Even worse, one of the Shpagin-men snickered. Her head whipped about to see, but the errant trooper successfully went stone-faced before getting caught.

It was Nick Carter's turn to laugh.

"So you wanted me here. If the purpose had been sending a half-dozen magazines worth of Warsaw Pact ammunition through me, that would have happened the moment I entered this room. If this is just your moment to gloat…I can't imagine it's going as you expected."

Citrine regarded him impassively. "You're the great detective. Reason it out."

Carter looked around the dimly lit room. Not much to see, beyond the worthless prop bomb and the gunmen. The dull greenish light of a single overhead fluorescent bank made an ugly scene as ugly as possible. He looked back to his slim antagonist.

Citrine had taken her name to arouse his interest and suspicion. There was no plan for global domination here. No nuclear blackmail or targeted population. The target was the man he saw in the mirror every morning while shaving. All those blunt Soviet-made machine-pistols were there to restrain him, but they wanted Nick Carter as intact as possible. For study. That might give him an edge, when push came to shove. At this point, shove seemed imminent.

"My guess is, you want to know how Sam Carter's little boy gets from Gilded Age to Space Age."

Citrine nodded.

"Which means, evocative name aside, you're as in the dark about Doctor Jack Quartz as you are about me."

He could see her stiffen. That one hurt a little. Time to turn the knife.

"So you're not a daughter, or a true acolyte…just a fan borrowing a little sinister resonance from the real thing. A poseur. A fake."

She turned blazing eyes on him, but the rest of her face was perfectly calm—a mask of self-control.

"Mister Carter, what you're about to experience will feel excruciatingly real, I assure you."

She clapped her hands, and Carter heard some sounds in the darkness. Metal sounds. Creaking. He had some ideas what they were.

"So you do share the good doctor's fondness for vivisection, then?" Carter offered, dryly.

Three lab-coated and surgical-masked underlings pushed a gurney into the light. Citrine ignored his jab.

"We have theories, of course. We know you're not Carter's son, or some distant relative. You are some…version of him. But what? A cyborg? A clone? Something more…exotic? We shall soon see."

The Shpagins parted for the gurney, and Carter realized he didn't have much time left to make his move. He also knew that Citrine was no fool. She'd have to know, too, that this was the moment he could seize.

Carter made eye contact with her. Her face was still an impassive mask. There was no sign of tension about her.

Carter hadn't had much time to take her measure. Dr. Jack Quartz was customarily undone by hubris. Failure was unthinkable to him. Surely, a world of puny mental insects could never thwart the amazing super-genius of Quartz. Did Citrine suffer from the same arrogance?

Conversely, a great detective is always imagining the ways in which things may have gone, or can go, wrong…and so Carter had always beaten Quartz, in the end. Carter knew, in his bones, that the history of the world is the history of things going terribly, terribly wrong, and heroes tend to be those who can most swiftly adapt to that inevitable turn in human events. Ulysses Grant, a childhood hero of Carter's, didn't win because he had the better plans. He beat Lee by knowing how to react when those plans fell apart, and improvisation was the only way to victory.

Nick Carter did not have the Army of the Potomac to help him out, just then…as one of the lab-coated anonymous underlings stepped toward him, with a syringe.

With only seconds to choose, he settled on his target—the fluorescent light.

Carter raised both hands with great casualness, until his right arm was pointed directly at the overhead fixture.

The lab assistant with the syringe said, "Roll up your sleeve."

Carter complied, reaching over with his left hand to his raised right sleeve. As his fingers started to turn back the cuff on the black commando sweater he wore, he flexed his right bicep, triggering the mechanism which shot the stiletto into his right hand.

"Grab him!" yelled Citrine, but she was entirely too late. A flick of the wrist sent the stiletto skyward, right into a fluorescent tube. Carter was counting on the sudden plunge into darkness to create just the right amount of chaos, but he also knew the shattering tube would supply a gunshot-like *pop* to add just one more element of confusion. It did not disappoint.

Carter grabbed the unfortunate fellow with the syringe before Citrine's shout had finished echoing off the bare walls and tossed him easily to one side. In the darkness, he could see no target, but given the circumstances, he knew the hapless lab assistant was very likely to collide with one of the gunmen. And trigger, literally speaking, a response.

Citrine's heels could be heard clicking swiftly toward the door, as the lab-coated missile collided with a machine-gunner. His Shpagin burped twice in the darkness, the muzzle flash illuminating the room like lightning. In that momentary blaze, Carter saw the startled trooper's burst catch one of his comrades across the chest. One down. Five to go. Carter was already pulling the Luger from his belt with his right hand and snapping her toggle with his left.

It must have been the squad's non-com—if there was any kind of rank system in place—who barked the order to back toward the door. In the dark, Carter grinned. Their incompetence and inexperience was making this part easier than he expected. But he had to keep moving, and moving fast.

The door opened, and a thin slice of light split the room. Carter could see the uneven line of confused gunmen squinting into the dark, the panicked lab assistants, the dead man on the floor. He was moving toward the nearest wall, while their eyes readjusted.

Silhouetted in the door light, the gunmen were shooting gallery targets. Carter knew that after his first shot popped off, the muzzle flash would let them know where he was, but he had no choice. His marksmanship, always excellent, had not been negatively affected by slumbering in the Quartz Tank, or whatever arcane process had brought him back. His speed, if anything, was even greater.

He aimed and fired, moving toward the line of gunmen. The man in the middle's head snapped back and he went down, even as Carter fired again, taking down the next gunman over. That left three, and they could see him, out from the shadows, but it was already too late. He was within inches of them.

Carter grabbed the closest man with his free left hand and threw him into his nearest comrade. They went down in a heap, as the last gunman standing, confused and terrified, fired point blank at Carter. He felt a distinct sting but didn't flinch as he shot the man directly in the face with the Luger. Carter imagined that sting had been a bullet graze. Nothing serious. *Astonishing to think the man could miss at such close range,* he mused, *but panic is a saboteur of intention.*

Carter was out the door before the two downed gunmen could regain their feet. Maybe they weren't in such a rush to face him again, and he felt sure the cowering lab technicians wouldn't follow.

But where was Citrine? She was the whole mission, now. She had said *we* a few times. Nick Carter intended to find out who comprised that *we*.

Carter fully understood that following her was diving deeper into her trap. It did not cause him to hesitate, just an angle to consider. She had expected the first trap to work. That in no way precluded further traps, of greater complexity and danger.

It did not cross his mind to look at his left arm, to investigate the source of the dull ache which had replaced the initial sharp sting.

Carter was moving quickly down a bland concrete corridor, lit by the same ugly green fluorescence as the first trap. He stopped for a moment to listen. No more clicking heels. She was either beyond his hearing, or waiting somewhere ahead. It struck him that no alarm was sounding. Citrine was not alarmed. Can't play chess without losing a few pawns. Carter was still in her maze, and under her dominion. He looked forward to disabusing her of that notion.

Carter turned a corner, and saw his own rope, trailing down from a skylight overhead. *A smarter man might just exercise the better part of valor,* he thought. Out there in the moonless night was a boat with a radio. That radio could summon a platoon of Marines to storm this facility…or a B-52 to wipe it from the face of the Earth. While attractive, neither of these options would solve the mystery of Professor Citrine. That was not an acceptable outcome. He was not that desperate. Not yet.

Up ahead, the corridor terminated in a large metal door. Carter raised the Luger and approached slowly. Wherever she had ended up, Citrine had gone through this door. As he got closer, he noticed a small homey wooden plaque, which simply said DAMON in large block letters. He reached out with his left hand for the door handle, glancing down as he did so. What he saw froze the blood in his veins.

His left arm was a shattered bloody mess. Multiple rounds from the Shpagins had ripped it to pieces, and while it was responding to his mental command to reach for the handle, it was jerky and spasmodic. The fingers twisted in a rictus of wrecked nerves.

Carter stared at the arm, wondering. He had already lost a lot of blood, but aside from the visual shock, and the dull ache, what he was feeling didn't correspond to what he was seeing. He holstered the Luger, and with his right hand, ripped the remains of the black sweater's sleeve off his left arm. It should have hurt like crazy, but it didn't. He carefully tied the sleeve into a tourniquet around his left bicep, above the savagely torn and bleeding flesh. He hoped that would keep him from losing too much more blood and passing out.

Maybe he wouldn't pass out. Maybe this new, improved body didn't need the blood. Either way, better to be safe than sorry.

After drawing his Luger again, Carter reached for the door handle with his bloody left hand, and slowly turned it.

The new room was well lit, soft tungsten instead of buzzy green fluorescence. Almost cozy. Bookshelves lined the walls. There was another metal door set between two bookshelves. A loudspeaker hanging from above the door. A large armchair—oddly large,

Carter noted—sat with its back to the door. There was a blackboard with incomprehensible scribbles on it, and on the tiled floor, incongruously, a stuffed giraffe. A small pile of wooden blocks. Carter's eyes were drawn to a framed portrait on the wall. A face he hadn't seen in half a century. The smug visage of Doctor Jack Quartz.

Citrine's voice filled the room, crackling from a loudspeaker.

"There you are. Welcome, Mister Carter. I really wanted you to meet, Damon. Please rise and greet Mister Carter, Damon."

There was a grunt, and the comically large armchair shifted, its feet scraping the floor. Something got up out of the chair and turned to face Nick Carter.

Damon was a man. Or he had once been one, at least.

Carter estimated his height to be close to eight feet. Massive shoulders and chest. Muscles bulging from biceps, under a utilitarian jumpsuit.

The face, though. Carter couldn't take his eyes off the face. *Like a Picasso*, he thought. All the features were there, but they were in the wrong place, or they were the wrong size.

"It's impolite to stare, Mister Carter. Damon, why don't you take Mister Carter's toy away from him," Citrine purred.

Before he knew what was happening, one of the titanic arms shot forward and grabbed Carter's right hand, immobilizing it. With his left, Damon snatched the Luger. Carter had no time to get a shot off. He had not expected the monstrous creature in front of him could move so swiftly and with such control.

Damon looked quizzically at the Luger. A new toy.

"So," said Carter, "you've been hard at work. Experimenting on human beings. And you've failed. That's why you wanted me."

"Failed? Hardly. Damon has your gun."

"I have the distinct feeling Damon isn't all you'd dreamed he would be, Professor."

There was a pause, and then the loudspeaker crackled again.

"Damon, give Mister Carter a nice big hug for me."

The nightmare turned toward him with a slack-jawed grin. Damon tossed aside the pistol and wrapped Carter in its steel cable arms. Carter could feel Damon's hot breath on him, his arms pinned to his side.

"There now...you see, Mister Carter? Damon is a kind and loving soul. Can you not feel the warmth of his embrace?"

"Glargh," burbled Damon.

"Squeeze him, Damon. Squeeze him as hard as you can."

The embrace tightened, and then tightened again. Carter had the absurd thought that the tourniquet had hardly been necessary, for there was surely no blood flow in either arm right now. He could feel Damon's *hug* starting to force all the breath out of him. Unconsciousness wasn't far off.

The Luger lay on the floor—a few feet away. But enfolded in the iron grip of Damon, it might as well have been on the other side of the world. His stiletto was stuck in a ceiling, equally distant. Carter was so immobilized that he could make no kick, no punch, no chop to free himself. All that was left were his rapidly fading wits and his fingers. And Damon's weaknesses. *What were those, again?* he thought, his head swimming.

Carter could reach his right front pocket with his hand. He pawed at the small globe until it was in his palm...and then, eyelids fluttering, he took his hand out of his pocket and dropped the globe.

Carter didn't have enough strength left to twist the globe and release the nerve gas. He wasn't sure, in his current condition, if he could have managed to hold his breath while it filled the room. He was counting on a child's curiosity.

Luckily, the globe made a sharp *ping* when it hit the tile... and a little rumble as it rolled away.

Damon turned sharply to see it. The deadly embrace relaxed ever so slightly. Carter gasped, then choked out, "My last toy, Damon. You like it?"

"Now, Damon, don't let him distract you!" the loudspeaker commanded. Citrine was trying to maintain her controlled purr, but Carter could hear the concern creeping in.

"It's my special toy. Very special," Carter goaded. "You can have it. I don't mind."

Damon dropped him and turned for the ball. Nick collapsed for a moment. He knew he needed to move fast, get his hand back on that pistol...but that wasn't going to happen without some oxygen back in his lungs.

"Put that down, Damon. That's not for you..." Citrine entreated.

Damon looked up at the sound of her voice, his jaw slack, frustrated. Damon then turned his attention back to the globe. He shook it. Glared at it.

Nick was on his knees, regaining strength quickly. "You have to twist it," he said, making a twisting gesture with his right hand. "Twist it for the surprise."

"Damon!" She was stern now. "Do not twist it! Mister Carter is trying to make a fool of you! You are not a fool, are you?"

Nick was on his feet now, walking cautiously toward Damon, smiling his friendliest smile. "She never wants you to have any real fun, does she? But it's okay. You can twist the globe. You don't need her bossing you around."

Damon looked intently at the globe, and twisted the top, as carefully as his clumsy hands could manage.

"Damon, no!" Citrine fairly screamed.

The hiss was so low as to be undetectable. Carter held his breath, and his right hand shot out...slapping the small globe directly into Damon's mouth.

Damon looked at him in complete bewilderment, and for a moment Carter feared he would spit it out too quickly. Then Damon slowly tried to chew it, as the compressed nerve gas shot directly down his throat.

Carter hadn't tested the ability in a while, but last time he did, he had been able to hold his breath for seven minutes and ten seconds. It didn't take half that long. Damon's eyes quickly glazed over, and he stiffened.

The large body hit the tile with a heavy thud. If Citrine had anything to say about this disappointment, she didn't bother broadcasting it into the room.

Carter scooped up the Luger and crossed to the door with all possible speed. Once it was safely closed behind him, he drew a deep steady breath, and regarded his new surroundings.

That's when the alarm went off, and the lighting around him turned red. He was in another concrete corridor, but he could see a handful of doors and intersecting corridors ahead of him. A few lab-coated men and a trooper with a Shpagin crossed the intersection ahead at a run, not even sparing a glance in his direction. Their pace could be described as *headlong*.

Evacuation order, he thought. No announcements over the loudspeaker. The sound and the red light were enough to send the message. Carter considered that he might have lost Citrine's trail for now, but he wasn't quite ready to give up. He made his way to the corridor intersection and took a careful look around the corners.

To the left, the direction the running men came from, Carter could see another handful of scientists and soldiers heading the same way as their comrades. A quick glance to the right showed an open door with a couple of guards in front of it. The open door seemed to lead to darkness. Night.

Carter weighed options in a split second and choose right. He turned the corner and moved steadily toward the door, raising the Luger. He had used only two rounds. Six left.

More than he would need here, if he was careful and precise.

The guards, unprepared, peered at him down the corridor and slowly raised their Shpagins at the figure in black closing in on them. Too slowly. Uncertainty doomed them.

Carter fired twice and they went down. The second man had managed to get a finger on his trigger, but he was no longer alive by the time his death-spasm pulled it, sending half a magazine thudding into the concrete wall beside him.

Carter heard a voice behind him cry out, "Stop!" as he reached the bodies. The man on the right had fired, so as he holstered the Luger he picked up the Shpagin on the left and spun around, dropping to one knee. It had been a good guess, as the pursuing trooper was firing and the stream of rounds screamed just over his head.

Carter fired a sharp burst, taking out the two troopers coming up on him. The men behind them flattened to the floor, but Carter was already on the move, out into the dark night. Over the sound of the clanging alarm, he heard something else. The distinctive heavy bass *whup whup whup* of a large helicopter, immediately accompanied by the hard wind of the downwash.

It was a Sikorsky CH-53 Sea Stallion. Unmarked, of course. And it was leaving the ground.

The helipad was cross-lit for takeoff, and in the glare of the spotlight, he caught Professor Citrine looking directly at him through the helicopter's heavy glass cockpit window. She noticed his look, and her mask slipped just long enough for a crooked smirk before the CH-53 picked up speed and throttled into the sky.

Carter raised the Shpagin and took careful aim at the rotors.

He had seconds before the helicopter would be out of the submachine gun's limited range. He ran through outcomes, desirable and otherwise, and let the seconds pass.

Carter looked back through the open door, into the facility. The alarm was no longer ringing. The red lights snapped off.

An instinct made him run at full speed away from the door. The blast wave hit Carter as he reached the lip of the helipad. It knocked him over the edge, and he took a few bounces on the surrounding hill before coming to a stop thirty feet below, battered but alive. Instincts had saved him, once again. Watching the fire and smoke billow into the sky, he wondered if the blast wave had spared him from the unpleasant experience of being burned alive. Regardless of the mysterious powers of his new, improved body, he had no interest in testing its flammability.

He stood, brushed himself off a bit, and made his way slowly down to the beach and his boat.

Even with his mangled arm, he was able to pilot his boat back out into the dark sea and rendezvous with the sleek yacht he'd come from earlier that night, a few hours or a thousand years ago. To Carter, it could have been either. He was met in the forward stateroom by the tall, gray figure with the trim beard who'd been his tour-guide and taskmaster in this new world. He looked like Uncle Sam and sounded a little like John Huston. Sometimes Carter wondered if his appearance and demeanor were a piece of theater for his benefit. What would a man born in the 19th century, who died during World War Two, respond to best as an authority figure. At least he eschewed the top hat and red, white, and blue cutaway coat. He was in a perfectly normal brown suit. The old man's eyes were immediately drawn to Carter's bloody left arm.

"Looks like they got you pretty good there. Doc?"

A pretty young woman in a trim professional outfit entered the room with a small bag. Carter vaguely recalled having seen her before, but he couldn't quite identify where or when. That bothered him. He wondered if her tight bun of hair and conservative spectacles were more theater. *Trustworthy, attractive doctor.*

"Doc here'll put you under and we'll get you fixed right up."

She was reaching into her bag when Carter said, "No."

"What's that?"

"No. I don't want to be put under. I want to see what she does to me."

The old man looked genuinely surprised. He didn't surprise easy, in Carter's experience. The doctor watched in silence, holding a hypodermic needle.

"Well now, that's not...I mean to say..."

Carter regarded them with a level gaze. "I have been a good boy. I have played ball. I have asked no questions. Tonight, on the mission, my ignorance put me at a disadvantage. I won't have that again."

The old man nodded. "I can certainly see that. Did they...?"

Carter didn't like interrupting. That wasn't how he'd been raised. He did it anyway. "You'll have my full report after the good doctor has done her work. Scout's honor. First things first. Exactly what is going to be done to *fix me right up?*"

The old man looked at the doctor and nodded. She replaced the needle in her case and came out with a small box. She opened it. Three smaller needles inside. The liquid inside was colored—one red, one white, one blue. Yet more theater. So they'd been prepared even for this. One day, if not tonight.

"Patriotic," said Nick Carter.

"This will hurt," said the doctor, flatly. "Secrecy isn't the sole reason we put you under."

"But it is a reason." It wasn't a question.

The old man smiled at him. "Isn't it always?"

The red needle went in while the old man was speaking. Carter was reminded of how you distract a child before you give them a shot.

The doctor was right. There was a sharp sting, and then every bullet wound woke up at once. Carter winced.

"Number two," she said, plunging in the white liquid.

Now his arm was on fire. Pulsing. The flesh turned bright red. The flames were invisible, though. They were a signal from his nerves to his mind. His training, his mental discipline, could help his mind ignore those signals. Slowly, they ebbed away. Carter had no way of knowing if that was his doing or the natural course of the treatment.

"Last one," she said.

This time the pain hit him squarely between the eyes. Watching him, you might have seen the slightest rock backward, weight moving from toes to heels and back again. But even that passed, and he dared to look down at his arm again.

The flesh was bright red. The wounds were now flowers. Blooming. As the petals of flesh pulsed, dull gray slugs were pushed out by them. Carter watched in wonder as one dropped to the floor. Then another.

He looked at the doctor and she allowed herself a smirk.

"Better than penicillin, huh?"

The last slug dropped out. His bright red arm had some welts. It ached badly. The nightmare of torn flesh seemed like just that. A bad dream. Now over, and soon forgotten.

Carter regarded the old man and the doctor, their satisfaction. Magicians before a stunned audience of one.

"Thank you. For the wonder drug, and for letting me see it in action. I might not have believed it otherwise. Even so, you took a bad risk."

The old man and doctor exchanged a look. Carter picked up the last hypodermic.

"This," he said, "is what they wanted. There was no bomb, no real threat. All a trap to get me. And to get this." He placed it back on the table. "We face an enemy that has a dim understanding of what I am, and how I'm kept alive. They want that secret. Badly. I suspect they'll do anything to get it."

Carter closed the box, and placed a hand on it for a moment, before turning his gaze back to them. "I appreciate you keeping it handy to patch me up, but it's far too dangerous to bring this into the field. At least until Professor Citrine is caught or captured, and her mysterious organization destroyed…this formula, whatever you call it, needs to be under lock and key, in a vault, surrounded by every guard you've got."

The old man frowned, "That might mean some bad times for you."

"That's my risk to take, and I take it gladly, sir. I'll try to avoid getting shot again." Carter smiled at them. "You forget, I've been dead before. I barely noticed."

NICK CARTER WILL RETURN

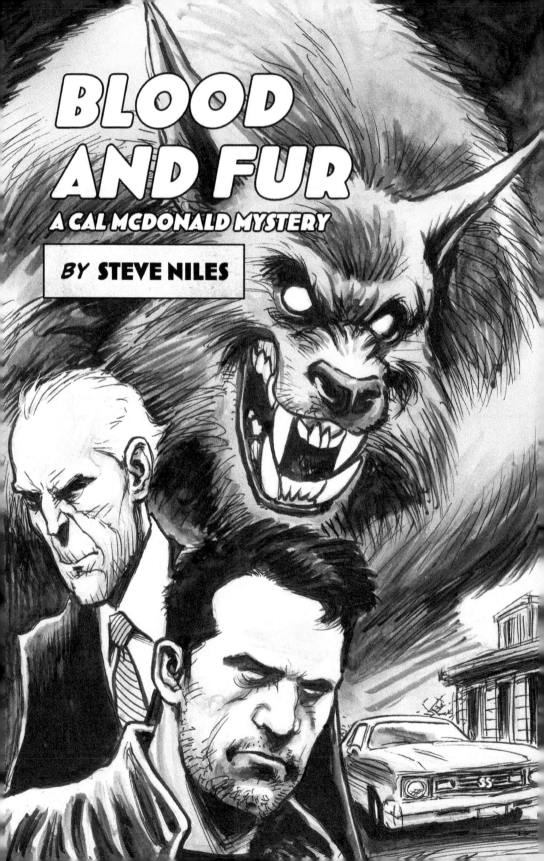

I woke up at 3 a.m. on the can. I was beaten and bloody and in no mood for trouble. I'd spent the previous day getting an exorcism for my cop friend, Wheatley. Suffice to say, it was no fun. Every bone and muscle in my body hurt.

It took all my strength to get myself off the toilet.

As usual, Mo'Lock was lurking in the living room. He stood in the corner like a creepy hat rack.

"How long was I out?"

The ghoul looked at the clock. "Around five hours."

I opened a new bottle and drank down a few good glugs. It burned, but it was a good burn. Woke me right up. Things were not really that great. I was broke as hell. I owed rent and a bunch of other bills I'd lost track of. My desk had a pile of last notices. My last gig was helping a priest with some demon trouble, but it was one of those non-paying gigs.

"Did I get any calls?"

"The landline hasn't worked for weeks."

I checked my cell. Nothing. Not even a thanks from Wheatley for removing that demon.

I looked at the ghoul. "I guess we need to find some trouble. You up for a ride?"

The ghoul nodded. That's about as excited as he got. I took a couple more swigs and then headed out to the car. Mo'Lock followed me.

Outside, it was a hot August night in Los Angeles. Had to be at least eighty in the middle of the night.

We hopped in the Nova. It started after a couple tries and roared to life. Mo'Lock got in the passenger's side. As soon as he shut his door, I hit the gas and burned some rubber. There was no one around in Studio City so I headed over the hill and scoped out Hollywood. The only action there was some drunken street fights outside the clubs.

We drove around for hours and came up with nothing. I spotted a couple vampires skulking around, but I was in no mood. I needed a paying gig. I headed onto the freeways and enjoyed some high speeds. Eventually, we wound up on the 14 North and started heading away from the city.

It's one of the impressive things about California. You can drive from beach to mountain to desert in a matter of hours. Out in the desert, things were different, spread out, flat. At 6 a.m., things were starting to happen. People were starting to wake up. Trucks started filling the vacant back road. And by filling, I mean three or four. It was quiet out here. I kind of liked it. It was like being on another planet.

I glanced over at the ghoul. He looked out of sorts and out of place. His pale skin against the rising desert sun seemed as unnatural as he was, a dead man out of place.

"You okay?"

"I am fine."

"You don't look fine."

The ghoul adjusted in his seat and looked right at me. "I am fine."

I backed off. Who knew what was up?

In the near distance, I could see the San Gabriel Mountains surrounding the desert valley and decided to head toward them. The scenery changed a bit. More juniper and Joshua trees littered the landscape.

As we drove on and reached higher altitudes, my ears popped. The roads started to get rough, and we saw very few people. We passed by homes and ranches, but they were spread out and far from one another.

We came to a point where the roads became dirt and I just kept driving. The Nova wasn't made for off-roading, but it powered along. Mo'Lock was fidgeting next to me, which was odd. He was usually as still as a fucking statue.

"Seriously, you wanna tell me what's wrong?" I asked.

The ghoul shifted and looked at me. "There's something out here. Something bad."

"Like what?"

"I cannot tell what it is exactly."

"Well, that helps exactly zero."

The ghoul was usually right when it came to detecting trouble, but I didn't give a shit. Maybe we'd stumble on some work.

After some bumpy driving, we found ourselves in the middle of nowhere. There were no homes or ranches in sight. All we could see were mountains and desert. As the morning crept, the heat started creeping right along with it. It was 8 a.m. and around ninety degrees. Even the breezes did little to cool and of course the Nova's AC had been broken for a while.

We drove for a bit down the dusty dirt road when something came into view ahead. At first it was like a mirage, a wavy image beneath the rising heat. Then as it came into focus, I saw a ramshackle building on the horizon. Then another and another. We'd discovered an old ghost town sitting in the middle of the desert.

I came up on the town. It wasn't more than a dozen dilapidated buildings, had an old-timey feel, complete with tumbleweeds. It was very out of place, almost had a movie set vibe, like a town in an episode of *Mannix*.

I pulled down the "main" street dividing the buildings, six on either side and that was it.

"What do you make of it?" I asked the ghoul.

"I think we should leave."

I pulled over and stopped in front of the largest building, an old hotel from the look of it. I got out and then leaned in the window.

"I'm going to look around. You coming or staying?"

The ghoul looked at me with grim disapproval. "I am coming."

It was hot. Just blazing as the sun pounded down on us. I could see Mo'Lock was uncomfortable. I scanned the street and spotted something odd… There were piles of shit everywhere and it looked human. Too big to be a coyote or bobcat. I doubt bears ever came down to the desert. Very strange.

We stepped up the two stairs to the front of the hotel and I tried the door. It swung open. Inside was dark. It took a moment for my eyes to adjust. When they did, I saw more shit piles all over the place. This town seemed to be somebody's personal toilet. It stunk like hell. Nothing worse than superheated feces to brighten your day.

"I do not like this," said Mo'Lock.

"What's to like? A bunch of dilapidated buildings filled with turds."

I was about to turn and leave when I heard a sound come from upstairs. Somebody was up there moving around. I started up the stairs. The ghoul didn't budge.

"You coming?"

"I'll wait here."

I sighed and pulled out my gun. The ghoul got me spooked. I slowly walked up the stairs, stepping around turd piles. At the top I just saw a long hallway with doors on either side. One door was open.

I crept along the hall to the door and jumped in front, gun ready. I froze.

Inside, stood a little boy, dirty, with no shoes. He looked petrified. I slowly put my gun away and raised my other hand. "It's okay. I'm not going to hurt you."

The kid ran at me, slid under my legs, and then sprinted down the hall at an incredible speed. At the end of the hall, he turned and disappeared.

Then a hand touched my shoulder. I spun, pulling my gun back out.

It was Mo'Lock.

"Don't do that shit!"

"I apologize. I heard a noise and came up."

"Some weird wild kid just ran by me."

"Wild?"

"Well, he was dirty."

The ghoul looked down the dark hall then into the room. He furrowed his brow and stepped inside. Something caught his attention. He walked to the end of the filthy bed and leaned over, picking something up off the floor. He turned and held up a glimmering gold nugget. A large nugget at that.

"Is that what I think it is?"

The ghoul nodded. "Gold."

I walked over and took the rock from his hand. It was gold. Real gold. Heavy and valuable.

"Shit. This could pay some bills."

"Then why don't we take it and leave?"

The ghoul was anxious.

I fumbled the rock around in my hand. It felt good. The way I saw it, there had to be more. Maybe I could pay all my bills if I found more. The ghoul was glaring at me. He knew what I was thinking, and he wasn't happy. Fucking ghoul.

I told him I wanted to look for more. Maybe there was a stash around the hotel. He looked at me deadpan, turned away, and headed back down the stairs. I followed him.

At the bottom of the stairs, he lumbered right out the door. I was right on his heels.

Outside, we both stopped cold on the rickety porch. The hood of the Nova was open. The battery was gone.

"Son of a bitch!" I yelled. "Now we're stuck out here."

"I told you we should leave."

"Thanks. That's a big fuckin' help."

We both just stood there a moment. I was sweating from the heat. Ghouls don't sweat, but Mo'Lock looked pretty uncomfortable in a suit and tie. I looked up and down the street. Except for a lot of shit, I didn't see a thing.

I jumped down the stairs and went to the trunk of the Nova, where I kept supplies. I grabbed a shotgun and a belt of shells. Then I went back to the porch and Mo'Lock.

"I'm going to search the hotel and see if I can find more gold."

"Greed kills, Cal."

"So does not eating."

I headed back inside the hotel. After hesitating, the ghoul followed. We walked up the stairs and at the top we stopped.

"Room by room search," I said, looking down the hall.

At the first door, I held up the shotgun and Mo'Lock opened it. Inside was clear—just a bed, dresser, and a bathroom. The second door was the same. The third door, however, was anything but empty. It was filled with bones.

"Holy shit."

There were human bones mixed in, but it mostly looked like animal skeletons, probably coyotes. On closer inspection of one of the human skulls, there were scrapes and scratches in the surface, deep grooves. These bones had been stripped clean by teeth. I couldn't tell what kind, but they weren't human.

"Do you think the child did all this?" Mo'Lock asked.

"By himself? Jesus, I hope not," I said. "Let's keep looking."

We went side to side down the hallway. Most of the rooms were empty. A couple had shit on the floor. No gold, though, or any sign of the boy. We came to the end of the hall, where a narrow stairway led down to a rear exit. The door was open.

We went down the stairs nice and slow, checked corners, and went outside to the rear of the hotel. The sun hit hard from directly above, beaming down and blinding. I shielded my eyes so they could adjust and looked down. There were footprints in the sand. Small human footprints, so it must have been the boy. I pointed it out to the dead man and we followed.

They stayed human for a few steps. Then they started to change, enlarge until we were following animal tracks, but still only two so they were walking on hind legs.

Werewolf.

I looked at the ghoul. I didn't even have to say anything. We both knew what we were dealing with.

"They rendered the car useless and now they are leading us to a trap," Mo'Lock moaned. "We should head back."

"Not a chance," I said, feeling the gold in my pocket. "We know how to deal with werewolves."

I cocked the shotgun. Mo'Lock rolled his eyes.

I pressed forward. The ghoul hesitated then followed. There wasn't much out there behind the one-street town. Mostly plants and dirt and some rock formations in the distance. The werewolf tracks were leading us toward the formations.

But oddly, as we got closer to the huge rocks, the werewolf tracks turned back to human, and by the time we reached the formations, the boy was waiting for us by the opening to an ancient-looking mineshaft.

The boy stood, back against the rocks surrounding the shaft. He was barefoot and filthy. Couldn't have been more than ten or eleven years old. I leveled the shotgun at him. Young or not, he was still a lycanthrope.

The kid held up his hands in reaction to the gun pointed at him. I felt bad and lowered it. He lowered his hands.

"Why'd you mess with my car?"

For a second, I thought maybe he was mute, but then he said, "I need your help."

"Weird way to ask for help, kid."

The wolf boy pointed at the mineshaft. "My family. They are trapped in the mine."

"With the gold, I assume?"

The boy nodded.

Next to me, the ghoul leaned in and whispered, "I do not trust him."

I shoved the ghoul away. He was too close.

I looked at the kid. "Okay, show me."

The boy walked to the shaft, and we followed. Mo'Lock hung back a bit. Immediately inside, the mine was dark, and I had to wait for my eyes to adjust again. When they cleared, I saw the boy a few yards ahead, standing at a ledge.

I walked up and looked down. It was a dead drop into darkness.

"You telling me they can't climb as werewolves?"

The boy sighed. "Mother and father are too old. They cannot climb like they once could."

"You ever hear of rope?"

"I tried. It is too far down."

I turned and looked at the ghoul. He was shaking his head side to side. I looked back at the boy beside me.

"Get me my battery back and I have an idea," I said. "And get me all the rope you have."

The kid nodded again and darted off, leaving the ghoul and I alone in the mineshaft. He was giving me an annoyingly judgmental look.

"You're going to help werewolves?" he said. "They cannot be trusted."

"I met a decent werewolf once or twice. They're rare as hell, but they exist."

A couple minutes later, the kid came running back carrying the car battery and a bunch of rope. The kid stayed behind with Mo'Lock watching him. I went back to the Nova, replaced the battery, and then drove it to the mine, where I backed it in as far as it would go. In the trunk, I had a lot of rope and some chain, too. I also grabbed a backpack and a light.

I tied all the rope together and anchored it with the chain, then, tying one end to the Nova bumper, we began lowing rope down the shaft.

The boy leaned over the hole. "Mom! Dad! Can you hear me?!"

There was a long pause and then a guttural howl came roaring up the shaft. It chilled me to the bone.

"This is an incredibly bad plan, Cal," the ghoul said.

He wasn't wrong, but what can I say? I was tired of always working for free and being broke. I had the fever. I wanted that fucking gold. A little windfall would go a long way.

I took out my flask and emptied it, then looked at the ghoul. "When I signal, pull the car forward…slowly."

Mo'Lock shrugged. "What's the signal?"

"Just yelling, I guess."

Mo'Lock got in the driver's seat. I grabbed hold of the rope and lowered myself over the edge. I started climbing down, wishing I had gloves. My hands burned. I climbed down a long way until the light was all but gone, and kept going. It seemed like a long time, but eventually my feet touched ground. I made sure it was secure and then let go.

I was standing in a dark chamber with tunnels leading off on either side. I pulled out a small penlight and looked around. I almost passed out. There were gold chunks all over the place. Pretty much everywhere I shined a light. I immediately took the backpack and started loading it.

That's when I heard the growl behind me.

I spun with the shotgun and light, one-handing each. There stood an old werewolf, rickety looking with gray hair covering its body. It was one of those werewolves with a more human face as opposed to the dog-headed variety.

"Put back the gold," the werewolf said. "It's ours."

I kept the gun trained on the old beast. "I'm here to help. I'm taking some of this as payment. That's all."

The werewolf sniffed the air and then looked to his side in the darkness. "It's okay. You can come out, dear."

From the darkness, emerged an equally ancient female werewolf. She walked on hind legs with a slight limp. She looked at me, and I could see she was afraid. I lowered the shotgun.

But then another werewolf emerged and another, and these two looked pretty fucking spry. I raised the gun again and backed up to the wall with the rope. Above me in the shaft, I heard a ruckus. It sounded like Mo'Lock was fighting. The ghoul was right. It was a trap.

I yanked on the rope and yelled, but nothing happened. I yelled again and this time fired the shotgun in the air. The snarling werewolves were closing in, moving slow on both sides. The elders stood back, but they were salivating. I knew then I was dealing with starving werewolves. The worst.

The Nova roared to life above. I gripped the rope tight with one hand and held them off with the shotgun in the other hand.

"NOW!" I screamed.

The ghoul did not drive slowly like I had told him. I was ripped up the wall at an incredible speed. I lost the backpack and almost the shotgun. One werewolf leapt at me. I fired and took its head off. The other grabbed my legs and was going up with me. I kicked and shot but missed on both.

The werewolf was literally climbing me as we flew up the wall. With only one free hand, I held the shotgun and jammed it into the beast's mouth. Its eyes went wide, and then I fired. Its headless body fell back into the darkness. I looked up. I was heading toward the light way too fast. I hit the ledge and got dragged through the dirt a good fifty yards. It hurt, to say the least, but not as bad as getting devoured hurts, so it was a win in my book.

I looked outside the mine and saw the Nova spitting fumes. I heard the engine cut out and then Mo'Lock climbed out. He looked like he'd been through a shredder. He was scratched up, bitten, and his suit was in tatters. The kid had done a number on him.

I walked up as he stood outside the Nova. "Where's the kid?"

"He ran off."

I tried to look apologetic, but the ghoul just glared at me.

"Well, the good news is ghouls are already dead, so you can't turn into a werewolf."

"I would like to leave now."

"Quit whining. You'll be healed by the time we're home."

"Not the suit."

I started to climb in the car and Mo'Lock was heading to the passenger side when I heard howling coming from all directions. I looked at the cave and realized we forgot to pull up the rest of the rope. A dozen or more werewolves were spilling out of the mine, into the blazing sun, and running straight at us.

"Get in the fucking car!"

Mo'Lock got in and slammed the door right as I was starting her back up. The engine sputtered. I glanced out the front windshield. More werewolves, led by the kid, were coming from there, too. At least six more. The place was crawling with them. In the rearview, I saw the dozen descending on us. We had seconds to escape.

The Nova roared to life. I jammed on the gas, and we shot forward like a bullet. Werewolves leapt at us from front and behind. I didn't slow. I ran down one, then another and another. Werewolves went flying.

I hit the one-street town and a werewolf appeared at my window. Boom! He went flying, and I was sprayed with blood and fur. In the rearview, I saw the boy chasing after the Nova as the others gave up. I kept on driving fast until the town was a wavy blur behind us. We both wanted to get the hell out of there and get back to the city.

I nodded, pulling out the gold nugget I found in the hotel. I held it out. "Not a total loss."

The ghoul grabbed the nugget and threw it so far I lost sight of it.

"Hey!"

"It will only bring you trouble."

"And food and rent, you asshole."

We were silent the rest of the drive.

HALF A MONSTER IS BETTER THAN NONE

A NEKROPOLIS STORY

BY TIM WAGGONER

"Excuse me, are you Matt Richter?"

A woman's voice, tone hopeful, but with an edge of desperation.

I stopped walking, but I didn't immediately turn around to face the speaker. I was in the Sprawl, domain of the demon queen Varvara, and in a city filled with monsters, this was the most dangerous place of all. There could be any number of reasons someone might be looking for me—a former client unhappy with my services, a revenge-minded friend or family member of someone I'd helped put in prison, someone out to make a name for themselves by taking down the great zombie detective... I reached into the outer pockets of my black trench coat to have quick access to any of the weapons I keep stored there, and only then did I slowly turn around. I was nearly due for a new application of preservative spells, and slowly was the only way my decomposing body could do anything.

The woman was tall, lean, and in her early twenties, with short sandy-blonde hair. She wore a long-sleeved blouse the same color, with brown vertical stripes running across it. Her slacks were black, as were her flat shoes. But what caught my attention most was her eyes. They were a deep brown, with rings of rich amber around the irises. Those rings were a sure sign of her species.

"You're a Lyke," I said.

"I prefer *Shifter*. Lycanthropes transform only into wolves."

"It's a slang term," I said. "But if you want to be technical about it, it's no dead skin off my nose."

We were far from alone on the street. The Sprawl is like Vegas, New Orleans, Disneyland, and a medieval torture chamber all rolled into one and cranked up to eleven. It's perpetually packed with revelers in search of some kind of pleasure, usually illicit and deadly, and these seekers come from every species and economic strata of Nekropolitan society: the rich and powerful, the poor and powerless, Lykes—excuse me, *Shifters*—the Dead, Demons, Bloodborn, and Arcane, along with dozens of other creatures from humanity's worst nightmares.

Several centuries ago, Earth's Darkfolk—vampires, werewolves, witches, ghosts, demons and the like—decided humanity was becoming too advanced and too numerous for comfort. The Darkfolk built a vast city called Nekropolis in a dimension of eternal shadow and emigrated there, so they could live their lives without fear of being hunted by humans. The Darkfolk didn't sever all ties with their birth world, though. Passageways between the two dimensions allowed for travel back and forth, and enterprising Darkfolk began importing goods from Earth— especially technology, which was why in Nekropolis you could find a ghoul living in an ancient, crumbling tomb with a flatscreen TV, an espresso machine, and wi-fi. The passageways also permitted tourism. Some Darkfolk had remained behind on Earth when their fellow monsters left, but they and their descendants enjoyed visiting Nekropolis from time to time, and many Nekropolitans made the occasional trip Earthside.

The woman's body language screamed *tourist* to me. Her eyes kept darting back and forth as she continually searched for threats, and she'd stare at some of the Darkfolk that passed by—especially those whose appearance bore only a tangential resemblance to being human. Native Nekropolitans knew better than to stare at anyone. It was a good way to find yourself embroiled in a street fight with beings who could kill you as easily as snapping a twig.

She was currently gawking at a forty-foot-tall, thin-limbed creature with extremely long arms that almost dragged the ground. It had a pair of acoustic sirens where its head should be, and as it stalked down the street—people jumping to one side or another, desperate to get out of its way—those sirens emitted an eerie low-pitched wailing

"Don't mind him," I said. "He's new in town. My guess is you are, too."

An embarrassed smile. "Shows, huh?"

"It does." I decided she wasn't a threat—to anyone other than herself, that is, so I removed my hands from my jacket pockets. "Can I do something for you?"

I tried not to sound weary when I asked the question, but I didn't quite manage it. For the last few years, I had stood in for Edrigu, one of Nekropolis's five Darklords, overseeing the region known as the Boneyard and watching over the city's post-living denizens, helping or punishing them as needed. It had been a challenging time, especially since I didn't possess the power of a Darklord, but I got by with the help of family and friends until Edrigu returned and reclaimed his office, freeing me to resume my own life—and not a fucking moment too soon. Now that I was no longer a substitute Darklord, I was back to being a private investigator, and while I couldn't have been happier, I'd forgotten how busy I used to be.

When I first started out as a P.I. in Nekropolis—after having followed a supernatural criminal from Cleveland as a still-living cop, then dying and being resurrected as a sentient zombie—I had to scratch and scrape for clients. But after saving the city a few times, people began to view me as a miracle worker, and clients flocked to me, all of them wanting me to do the impossible for them. It was exhausting and, during those times when I couldn't deliver, demoralizing.

I'd just finished a case for Renwick Poe—a supposed descendant of Edgar Allan—who was being harassed by a six-foot-tall raven pissed off that people constantly demanded he say *Nevermore!* wherever he went. The raven figured persecuting Renwick for his ancestor's literary offense was a sufficient substitute for getting revenge on the long-dead poet himself.

As a zombie, I don't get physically tired, but when I'm close to rotting completely away—as I was that night—performing even the simplest actions is like moving through cold, thick molasses. It wears on me, psychologically if nothing else. Plus, I was in a hurry to get home to Devona and the twins. Tonight was the anniversary of my death and resurrection, and in Nekropolis, that's the equivalent of a birthday. After all, it was the night I was born into darkness. I didn't know what Devona and the kids had planned, but my wife had made it clear that under no circumstances was I to get home late. *Let someone else save the world tonight*, she'd said, and I'd promised I would.

Now it looked like I was about to break that promise.

"I need your help. I've only been in the city for a few hours— it's my first time here—and I don't know who else to turn to."

I forced a smile that probably looked more like a grimace, given how atrophied my facial muscles currently were, not to mention my utter lack of enthusiasm.

"There's a Scarbucks just down the street," I said. "We can talk there."

On the way, she told me her name was Cathy Peterson. When we reached Scarbucks and stepped up to the counter, she looked over the menu—today's special was a ground-glass latte with two pumps of spinal fluid—and she shuddered.

"Just a hot water, please."

"I'll have a chupacabra heart mocha."

My dead body can't process food or drink, and unlike mindless zombies, I don't desire to eat human flesh. I can only smell or taste something immediately after a fresh application of preservative spells, but I viewed buying the drink as paying rent on the table where we'd sit and talk. The verman behind the counter nodded—the humanoid rat beings don't talk much—and I handed him a couple darkgems to pay for our drinks and told him to keep the change. He then turned around to face the back counter and began working on our order.

Cathy leaned in close. At this point in my decay cycle, I knew I had to smell like three-day-old roadkill baking in the summer sun, especially to someone with a Shifter's heightened senses; but if my odor offended her, she showed no sign of it.

"I've seen a lot of those rat people since I came here. They always seem to be doing menial labor. Is it some sort of racist thing? Like, are they a servant class?"

"There are conflicts between individuals and between different power groups in the city, but overall, Darkfolk view themselves as one people. Vermen just…like these kinds of jobs."

Our furry barista shot me a look with his glossy black eyes then returned his attention to our drinks. I couldn't tell Cathy the truth about the vermen, that they were actually the Dominari, the most powerful criminal organization in the city, and they only pretended to be meek and subservient so they could operate in the open with no one suspecting the truth about them. I'd discovered their secret on a previous case, but as long as I kept my mouth shut, they allowed me to continue existing.

When our drinks were ready, we took them to an open table and sat. A pair of Shifters occupied the neighboring table—a werewolf and a werecrocodile in their humanoid-animal forms, both sporting a number of cybernetic enhancements. The Darkfolk are much stronger and sturdier than humans, and they experiment with surgical augmentation the way humans try on different clothes. The Shifters looked over at us—or rather, at Cathy—and sniffed the air. They wrinkled their noses, scowled, then got up and walked out of the café.

At first, I thought my rot-stink had driven them off, but Cathy said, "They can smell what's wrong with me. It sickens them."

"That's what we came here to talk about. Tell me."

"My mother and father were born in Nekropolis and grew up here. When they reached adulthood, they decided to marry and visit Earth for their honeymoon. They liked it so much that they decided to live there. We have a small farm in Wisconsin. That's where I grew up. They're both Shifters, and they would tell me stories about Nekropolis when I was a child, especially about the Wyldwood."

The Wyldwood is the region of the city that Shifters call home, located next to the Sprawl.

"I promised myself that when I was an adult, I'd visit Nekropolis and see where my parents came from. They tried to talk me out of it, said the city was far too dangerous for someone who wasn't raised there."

"They were right about that," I said. In Nekropolis, the life expectancy of an underprepared tourist can be measured in minutes—if they're lucky.

Cathy continued.

"I was determined, though, so Mom and Dad told me everything they thought I'd need to know in order to survive here—which turned out to be a *lot* more than I'd expected—and they took me to an old antique store whose owner had a special mirror in a small backroom. The mirror was glossy black, like obsidian, and my parents told me it was a gateway between Earth and Nekropolis, the same one they'd used when they were my age."

Only the five Darklords who rule Nekropolis—along with Father Dis, who rules them—are supposed to possess travel mirrors. But there are any number of illegal ones in the city, many of which are unstable and dangerous. Cathy was lucky she'd made it to Nekropolis in one piece, but this wasn't the time to tell her that.

"We paid the store owner quite a lot of money, and I stepped into his mirror. The one I came out of was located in the basement of a bar called Skully's."

"I know it well. The bartender is a frenemy of mine."

"After I came up from the basement, I asked Skully for directions to the Wyldwood, and he kindly gave them to me. It was weird talking to a man whose head is only a skull, but it was also kind of cool, you know? He gave me a glass of brandy on the house to welcome me to town"—she glanced with disgust at my chupacabra heart mocha—"a *real* brandy. After I finished it, I hit the street. Everything was so disorienting at first, so different than Earth. The people, the buildings, the smells…even the light."

Nekropolis lies beneath Umbriel the Shadowsun, which drapes the city in perpetual gloom. Good thing, since so many of its denizens are allergic to actual sunlight.

"After a while, I started getting used to things—a little, anyway. But then I felt something weird. A tingling sensation spread through my body, I became dizzy, and then I experienced… I guess you could call it a *pulling*. It was uncomfortable at first, but it quickly became painful. I felt a tearing then, as if my very soul was being forcibly removed. And then, just as fast as it came, it was gone. I was weak and exhausted, but I didn't hurt anymore. Then I noticed something: my senses were dulled. I couldn't see and hear as well as I'm used to, and my sense of smell was practically dead. I think I understood right then what had happened, but I didn't want to believe it. I tried changing into my wildform, but for the first time in my life, I couldn't do it. I tried again, concentrating as hard as I could, but I remained human."

"You think someone…*stole* your animal side?"

"Yes. It's possible, isn't it? After all, this place is full of magic."

"True. What did you do then?"

"I freaked out. I ran around like a crazy woman, sniffing the air in the hope that I'd catch a scent that would lead me to my other self. I know my sense of smell was basically gone, but old habits die hard, you know? Eventually, my exhaustion caught up with me again, and I stopped running and just stood in the middle of the street, crying. Eventually a guy came up to me, a vampire. First one I'd ever seen."

"They prefer to be called Bloodborn," I said.

"He was nice, but strange, even for a vamp—for a Bloodborn. He had a lit cigarette in his mouth, but it never seemed to grow any smaller, and whenever he exhaled smoke, he became transparent."

I smiled. "That's Shrike. I know him well."

"He asked me what was wrong, and I told him. He said there was only one person in the city who could help me, and he gave me your name and description. He said he didn't know exactly where you were, but he was sure I'd find you somewhere in the Sprawl. I searched for over two hours until I finally saw you. That's my story. Can you help me?"

"Yes."

I had no idea if I could, of course. I'd never heard of anyone stealing a Shifter's wildform. It would take powerful magic to do that, and magic that strong wasn't common. A Darklord could do it, but slumming around the Sprawl to perform a sneak attack on a tourist wasn't their style. If the Darklords want something, they take it. No subterfuge, no hiding. Still, I wanted to reassure Cathy, so I told her what she needed to hear. I just hoped I hadn't told her a lie.

"What is your other form?" I asked.

"A thylacine."

"What's that?"

She looked at me like I was crazy.

"I got a C in Intro to Bio," I said. "Humor me."

"It's a carnivorous marsupial native to Australia and Tasmania, sometimes called the Tasmanian tiger or Tasmanian wolf. They went extinct in 1936. In nature, anyway. My parents are thylacine Shifters like me. I don't know how many of us are left, though. We might be the last."

"If your Shifter form is that rare, it makes sense that someone would want to steal it." I thought for a moment. "I'll be right back."

I rose from my seat and walked to the counter. The verman barista was already standing there, as if he'd been waiting for me. I kept my voice low so none of the other customers could hear me.

"I know you weren't listening to our conversation, you being a professional and all. But my friend has lost something very important to her, and I'd be grateful to anyone who could point me in the direction of where to find it. Grateful enough to provide a favor at a later date. A *substantial* favor."

The Dominari love nothing better than having someone in their debt. The barista didn't say anything, but he picked up a black felt-tip marker, wrote something on a napkin, folded it, placed it on the counter, then turned his back to me and headed to the storeroom. I took the napkin, slid it into my pants pocket, then returned to Cathy.

"Let's go"

She rose and accompanied me outside. We walked to the next block and stopped beneath one of the ever-burning greenfire torches that light the streets of the Sprawl. I removed the napkin from my pocket and unfolded it.

"What's that?" Cathy asked.

"If we're lucky, it's help."

I held the napkin up so we could both read it. Three words, written in thick black ink.

House of Pain.

✝

"Who's Doctor M?"

We were standing in front of a building several blocks away from Scarbucks. The architecture was modern—polished glass and gleaming steel—and mounted above the double doors was a sign formed from red neon letters: *Doctor M's House of Pain.*

"Doctor Moreau. He specializes in genetic augmentation, especially for Shifters. He's always had a fondness for working with animals. Shifters visit him when they want to jazz up their DNA, become something more interesting and unique than just another werewolf or weretiger. Plus, it can give them the edge in combat. Combine a shark Shifter with a gorilla, and you've become an extremely deadly opponent."

Cathy frowned. "Do Shifters fight a lot in Nekropolis?"

I laughed. "*Everyone* fights in Nekropolis! But for Shifters— the predator ones, anyway—fighting is a way of life."

"So you think my other half is inside there?"

"The Dominari might be criminals, but they have a strict code of honor, and they don't lie. The barista sent us here for a reason. Let's find out what it is."

I started walking toward the building, but Cathy grabbed my arm and stopped me.

"Wait, we're just going to go in there? Don't we need some kind of plan?"

"In my experience, plans only get in the way. Just follow my lead, okay?"

She looked doubtful, but she nodded and together we started toward the House of Pain.

✝

"How may we help you?"

A woman greeted us as soon as we stepped inside. She was medium height, with long curly black hair, and wore a long-sleeved emerald-colored dress. She possessed sharp facial features that her open, friendly smile couldn't soften. At first glance she appeared human, but she exuded an aura of power that marked her as Arcane, one of Nekropolis's magic-users.

The House of Pain's lobby consisted of walls painted hospital white, a polished chrome floor, animal skeletons hanging on metal wires from a high ceiling, and a large DNA helix sculpture in the middle of the room. Harsh fluorescent lights illuminated the lobby, rendering it cold, sterile, and lifeless.

I tried to return the woman's smile, but my upper lip chose that moment to become partially unattached, ruining the effect.

"We've heard a lot of good things about this place, so we thought we'd come check it out," I said.

The woman glanced at Cathy, then looked away—too quickly, I thought—and then looked at me, taking in my decaying mottled-gray features.

"I don't know," she said. "We may work miracles here, but even we have our limits."

Hilarious.

"It's for my friend. She feels she's missing something in her life, and she hopes she can find it here."

What can I say? Subtlety was never my strong suit.

But before the woman could answer, another voice—a male's—spoke.

"You've come to the right place."

A pair of double doors on the far side of the lobby labeled *Staff Only* opened, and a stout man in a white three-piece suit stepped out. I say he was a man, but his body displayed only traces of humanity. He was a nightmarish hodge-podge of animals—skin covered with patches of fur, scales, and feathers. His right hand was human, his left a huge lobster claw, and he peered at us with owl eyes. His bare feet were cougar paws, and they allowed him to move with smooth, feline grace. He had a small black mustache and Van Dyke beard which made his overall aspect even more sinister.

Despite all the years I've lived in Nekropolis, I'd never met Doctor Moreau. He had a reputation for being something of a recluse, a man who lived solely for his work and rarely left his place of business.

"Looks like you've done some work on yourself," I said.

He smiled broadly, revealing twin rows of shark teeth. "I'm a strong believer in self-actualization."

He walked over to us and stopped next to the woman in green. "I am, as you've no doubt surmised, Doctor Alphonse Moreau. And this lovely woman is my associate, Lithia. What might we be able to do for you, Mr. Richter?"

"I see my reputation precedes me."

Lithia waved her hand in front of her face as if trying to disperse a bad odor. "Among other things."

I ignored the dig. I wouldn't want to smell me either. Good thing my nose is as dead as the rest of me.

Instead of answering Moreau's question, I asked one of my own.

"So you use magic"—I nodded to Lithia—"as well as science in your work?"

"The two aren't as different as you might imagine," Moreau said. "They both deal with understanding and manipulating the primal forces of creation. But enough pretense. You've come here for a specific reason, and it isn't difficult to guess what it is. You want your friend's wildform back."

Cathy had been quiet up to this point, but she spoke now. "Yes! I want to be whole again."

Moreau showed his shark teeth once more. "People in Hell want ice water, but that doesn't mean they're going to get it."

"That's what Lithia does for you," I said. "She uses her magic to separate a Shifter's wildform from their human body, and then brings it to you. Why?"

"Because I need raw material to work with—especially when that material is as rare as this young woman's wildform. There are no other thylacine Shifters in the city, which means her genetic material will be quite in demand."

"And quite profitable," I added.

"Indeed."

I turned to Lithia. "What do you do? Troll the streets, casting spells to identify Shifters and determine what kind they are, then dividing their two halves and bringing the animal selves here for Moreau to experiment on?"

She shrugged. "It's a living."

Cathy took a step toward Moreau, hands balled into fists, a dark expression on her face. She might have been separated from her animal side, but she still had plenty of fight in her. When she spoke, her words were nearly a growl.

"Give me back myself. *Now*."

"As you wish." Moreau raised his lobster claw and clicked twice.

An instant later, the staff doors slammed open, and a bipedal creature exited.

It was tall and lean, but well-muscled, with tawny fur, white around the eyes and bottom of the muzzle, slightly rounded ears, and a long thin tail. Its most striking feature was its vertical black stripes, which stretched from halfway down its back to the base of its tail. Its black eyes fixed on Cathy and me with pure hatred, and its jaws opened impossibly wide, revealing sharp teeth with prominent incisors. It flexed its sharp claws as it came, as if anticipating rending our flesh with them.

"Tear them apart," Moreau said. "But do try to leave a few pieces intact. I doubt I can find much use for their genetic material—especially the zombie's—but one never knows."

The thylacine growled and came running toward us, claws raised, eager to kill.

I began to frantically rummage through my pockets, searching for something that might prove effective against Cathy's savage half. Silver tends to work on most Shifters, and while I had silver ammo in the 9mm I carry in my shoulder holster, I was reluctant to use it. What would happen to Cathy if I killed her other self? I couldn't risk it.

Instead, I pulled out a pepper shaker.

I quickly unscrewed the lid, tossed it aside, and flung the contents into the thylacine's face. The creature let out a pained howl and recoiled, eyes squeezed shut and watering. It gave a series of barking coughs, punctuated by wheezes as it attempted to breathe.

"Is that the best you've got?" Lithia said. "Pathetic."

She waved a hand and a gust of wind kicked up and blew into the thylacine's face, clearing away the pepper. The creature's eyes still watered, but they were open once more and blazing with fury. It lunged toward me, clawed hands raised and ready to strike.

Cathy darted forward and placed herself between me and the attacking thylacine. Cathy held out her hands, as if in a warding gesture, and when the thylacine swept its claws downward, they raked Cathy's palms. Blood gushed from the wounds, and Cathy hissed in pain and yanked her hands back. The thylacine hissed as well and drew its own hands back, mirroring Cathy's actions. Blood dripped from fresh wounds on the creature's palms, and Moreau stared at the injuries with fascination.

"I had no idea that was possible," he said. "Amazing!"

I realized something then, and I turned to Cathy, who was cradling her bleeding hands to her chest.

"The two of you are still connected! Not even Arcane magic can completely separate you. You just need to remind her. You take care of that while I deal with Lithia."

I knew I was gambling with Cathy's life. What if I was wrong and the thylacine tore out her throat? But my guess *felt* right, and I've lived in Nekropolis long enough to get a sense of how various kinds of magic operate. So I did my best to put Cathy and her furry friend out of my mind. I had a witch to deal with.

Lithia gave me a mocking smile. "What are *you* going to do? Rot on me? I'm Arcane. There's no way you can defeat me."

"I've gone up against your mistress many times over the years, and if she's never been able to beat me, what makes you think you can?"

Talaith was the Darklord who ruled the Arcane, and she hated my undead guts with unrelenting passion. She'd tried to destroy me on numerous occasions, and each time she'd failed. And because I knew she'd try again sooner or later, I'd prepared myself.

I reached into my jacket's inner pocket and took out a small doll constructed from twigs, cloth, and twine.

Lithia burst out laughing.

"A voodoo doll? Seriously? It has to be magically connected to the person you wish to hurt for it to work, and you don't have the power or knowledge to do that."

I risked a quick glance at Cathy. She stood in front of the thylacine, holding her wounded hands out to the creature. The thylacine looked at Cathy's proffered hands for a moment before reaching out to take them in her own. Their combined blood dripped to the floor, and Moreau stood off to the side, watching with interest. I turned back to Lithia.

"You're right. I can't work magic to save my soul—assuming I still have one. But the houngan who applies my preservative spells made this doll for me. It's already charged, and all I have to do to bond it to someone is simply will it. So I'll bond it to you."

Lithia shook her head. "I've never heard anything so ridicu—"

I squeezed the doll—hard.

Lithia gasped as her arms were suddenly pressed against her body. Her eyes bulged in their sockets, and her faced turned red. Her skin began to edge toward purple and capillaries in her eyes burst. She struggled to breathe for a few more moments, and then she went limp. She hung in the air for several seconds, then I lowered the doll to my side, and she collapsed to the chrome floor. She wasn't dead, just unconscious, but I wouldn't have cried about it if she *had* died. When you fight in Nekropolis, you fight rough, you don't fight fair, and when necessary, you fight for keeps.

I turned to check on Cathy once more. She and the thylacine stood facing each other, hands clasped, eyes closed, heads lowered. Then Cathy gently pulled her other self toward her. The thylacine's form wavered and blurred, and then it slipped into Cathy as if it were no more substantial than a wraith. Cathy raised her head, opened her eyes, and grinned.

"I'm me again! *All* me!"

She held out her hands for me to see. The palms were still smeared with blood, but the wounds themselves were gone. Shifters heal incredibly fast, and now that she was whole, that power had returned to her. She looked at Moreau then, and her smile fell away. She ran toward him, and by the time she reached him, she'd assumed her thylacine form. She looked the same as the thylacine had when they were separated, except that Cathy still wore her clothes. She grabbed Moreau's suit vest with one hand, lifted him off his feet, and growled. I strolled over to join them.

"If I were you, doc, I'd apologize—and fast. And I'd promise not to steal anyone else's genetic material again."

Beads of sweat broke out on Moreau's forehead. "Yes, of course! I'm sorry, so very, very—"

Before Moreau could complete his sentence, Cathy hurled him at the DNA helix sculpture. He hit it hard, breaking the thing in two. The pieces fell to the chrome floor with loud clangs, but Moreau made only a dull thud when he landed. He lay there, moaning.

"Now I know why it's called the House of Pain," I said.

Cathy resumed her human form once we were back on the street.

As we walked away from Moreau's place, she said, "Thank you so much, Matt. My parents gave me some darkgems to spend during my visit. There's not a lot of them, but I want you to have them. I won't need them. I'm going to go straight back home and try to forget that Nekropolis exists."

"Keep your money. But there is one thing you can do for me before you leave. I was on my way home to celebrate the anniversary of my resurrection day with my family. Why don't you come with me? It'll give you a chance to see another, less-predatory side of the city. After all, just because we're monsters that doesn't mean we have to act like it."

She considered, then smiled. "I'd like that. Thanks."

We continued walking down the street, and after a time, Cathy asked, "How were you resurrected?"

"That is a *long* story."

And I began to tell it.

My preference was for it to be a beautiful woman who walked through the door of my office. Instead, it was a couple of dudes. Not gay guys—at least then I could've been happy that somebody found love in this cold, cruel world. These men looked like a) brothers and b) douchebags.

"How may I help you gentlemen?" I asked, not standing up.

"We'd like to hire you," said the first one, whose name looked like it should be Benedict or Montgomery.

"Then, please, have a seat."

The men sat. "Are the prices on your website accurate?" asked the second one, whose name looked like it should be Digby or Yates.

I nodded.

"Kind of expensive."

"I'm the greatest detective who ever lived," I said. "I'm better than Sherlock Holmes, Hercule Poirot, and Nancy Drew combined."

"But those are fictional characters."

"Right. I couldn't think of any real-life ones that would be a good point of reference for you. Robert Stack, maybe?"

The brothers looked at each other. "Wasn't his whole deal that they were *unsolved* mysteries?"

"Look, I could rattle off a list of impressive names, but you'd have no idea who they were, and I'd be wasting my time, and I didn't get to be the greatest detective who ever lived by wasting my time. What are *your* names?"

"I'm Blake Smith," said the first one.

"Chet Smith," said the second.

My guesses were close enough. "And I'm Timothy Perkins. Not Tim. Call me Tim and I'll plant evidence in your automobile that gets you arrested for murder." I paused. That line usually got a nervous chuckle, but not this time. "Should we discuss the elephant in the room?"

"You mean that you died a few times?"

"Yes, that elephant. As you can see, I look like a normal, Caucasian, mid-thirties, brown-haired, blue-eyed private investigator. I'm communicating with you just fine. I can do my job better than anybody else. The fact that I died those seven times does not in any way impact my ability to solve your case."

"What about the side effect?" asked Blake.

"I was just about to disclose the side effect," I lied. "As you may have heard, sometimes, without warning, I gaze into the Dark Void, and I either shriek in terror at the nothingness that lies beyond our current existence, or I'm paralyzed with trauma. Neither of these last very long, and then I get right back to work. Sound okay?"

"That's fine," said Chet.

"So what can I do for you?"

"Our neighbor across the street stole our dog."

"You suspect this?"

"No, we saw him do it. Snippy got loose, and while we were out looking for him, I saw our neighbor bribe him inside his house with a treat."

"What kind of dog is Snippy?"

"A poodle."

"I fucking hate those dogs, but that's irrelevant. Please, continue."

"We're pretty much finished," said Blake. "We just want you to get Snippy back."

"That doesn't sound like a case you actually need me to solve."

"Well, I mean, I guess you could pretend you didn't know for sure that he's the one who took him. But we're really only prepared to pay you for one hour of your time, so you'd have to solve the mystery pretty quickly."

I sighed. "It's fine. Why not just call the cops?"

"Snitches get stitches," said Chet. "Really, they get *killed*, but that doesn't rhyme."

"Squealers need healers," Blake said.

"Rats die in combat," said Chet. "Nah, that sucks. Rats get sat...upon."

"Rats go splat," I said.

"Nice!" said Chet.

"Tattletales..." Blake trailed off. "Ummm...tattletales... uh, end up on the cattle trail. I'm sorry. I don't know why I said tattletales. I was never going to come up with a good rhyme."

"You realize that I'm charging you for this time, right?" I asked.

"We just want you to get our dog back," Chet told me.

"Why me?"

"Our neighbor is kind of violent. A bit homicidal. He's not going to give up Snippy without a fight, and if we got a normal private investigator killed, we'd feel terrible. But you've been through it a few times, so it's no big deal."

"Actually, it *is* a big deal. I don't just get killed and walk it off. It's very unpleasant."

"Even the seventh time?"

"Yes."

"Our mom said that childbirth got a lot easier by the seventh kid. Granted, she went from insisting on natural childbirth to demanding that they pump her full of drugs. I assumed that getting killed got easier the more times you did it."

"Reminding you again that I'm charging you for this conversation," I said.

Truthfully, he was right. It did get easier. The first time was like "*Holy fucking shit, I'm dead!*" and the seventh time was like "*Ugh, not this crap again.*" But I wasn't going to share that with these guys.

If I died retrieving their miserable little dog, they were going to pay my full rate.

"Will you accept the case?" asked Blake.

"Yeah, okay," I said.

We drove separately to their residence, which was a two-story home in an upscale neighborhood. I wondered why two adult brothers of seemingly sound financial means lived together, but I wasn't paying myself to investigate that mystery.

"He's in there," said Chet, pointing to the equally impressive home across the street. "The abductor's name is Franklin, but he likes to be called Franky-Z."

"I won't be calling him Franky-Z," I said.

"He has a large gun collection, and a larger knife collection, and an even larger garrote collection. If he asks you to turn around, I wouldn't do it."

"Anything else I should know?"

"Snippy likes to be scratched behind the left ear."

"Noted. I'll be back. This shouldn't take long."

I walked across the street. Hopefully, it would turn out that the brothers were simply cowards, and Franklin wouldn't put up much resistance. I knew how to use my fists, so if he did get violent, I could probably pop him in the nose before he garroted me. I went up the three steps to his front porch and rang the doorbell.

The door swung open, revealing a man who looked as if he really did not enjoy answering the door for strangers. He was a tall guy, kinda bulky, with slicked-back gray hair.

"Unless you're a really ugly Girl Scout selling cookies, I'm not interested," he said.

"My name is Timothy Perkins. I'm here to talk about the dog."

"What dog?"

"Sni—"

Suddenly, the Dark Void revealed itself to me. The infinite emptiness.

"Nothing lies beyond!" I wailed. "Our existence is meaningless!"

I stood there and shrieked for a full fifteen seconds.

The Dark Void closed in upon itself.

"You okay?" asked Franklin.

"Yeah," I said. "It happens sometimes."

"What did you mean by nothing lying beyond and our existence being meaningless?"

"Not important. I'm here to talk to you about a dog."

"The poodle?"

"Yes."

Franklin scowled. "I told them to quit letting that dog take a dump on my lawn. Every single morning I'd sit down at my dining room table with my fresh hot coffee and my newspaper, and I'd look out my front window to watch the sun rise, and every single morning there was a fresh new pile right in my line of sight. So I had to make the problem go away."

"Did you kill the dog?"

"No. Goodness, no. That would make me the least popular person in the neighborhood. Nobody likes a dog-killer. I don't want everybody keying my car as they walk by. No, I simply adopted the dog as my own. I take it for regular walks and I use a pooper scooper to keep the neighborhood clean."

"That's very considerate of you," I said. "But you can't just steal somebody's dog."

"They don't care about that dog. Snippy's a pawn."

"What do you mean?"

"They didn't hire you to retrieve the dog. They hired you so they could send you to your death at my hands."

"I beg your pardon?"

"Did they tell you to call me Franky-Z?"

"Yes."

"I *hate* being called that. It fills me with murderous rage. And I hate visitors who aren't selling Girl Scout cookies. You've been set up, my friend."

It's worth noting that I was lying about being better than Sherlock Holmes, Hercule Poirot, and Nancy Drew combined. I was, in fact, quite a dumbass. Five of my deaths were the result of my own clumsiness.

"But why would they want to do that?" I asked. "And how do you know all this?"

Franklin shrugged. "I guess that's a question for a skilled private investigator."

Could he be lying? Maybe Franklin was just trying to keep me from rescuing the poodle. Why would the brothers have warned me about the potential danger if they were trying to send me to my death?

"I'd like to see Snippy," I told him.

"I don't think so."

"That's very interesting, because I *do* think so. I think so, big-time. Now, are you going to take me to where you're keeping that dog, or do I have to take things up a notch?"

"Are you threatening me?" Franklin asked.

"No," I said. "That was the pre-threat."

"Fine." Franklin turned around and walked back into his house. I followed.

"Close the door behind you," said Franklin. "I don't want the dog to get out."

I closed the door. It made a loud *click* that sounded very much like the door locking behind me. Hmmm.

As I glanced around the living room, I noticed that there were a few human heads mounted on the wall. A garrote was mounted underneath each head. A better private investigator would have noticed this before closing the door.

"Interesting," I said, inspecting the closest garrote. There were a lot of red stains on the metal, along with scraps of what I was pretty sure were human flesh. "Looks very realistic."

Franklin nodded. "Very realistic indeed."

"Where'd you get these heads? They're so lifelike. It's almost as if you could carry on a conversation with them. Not a fun conversation, not with the expressions of pure horror on their faces, but a conversation nevertheless."

"Thank you. It took a long time to get that good at taxidermy."

"Taxidermy, huh? I assumed they were fake."

"No."

"Ah. Well, the skill is evident, that's for sure. I don't know which one I like best. Anyway, you're a busy man, and I hate poodles anyway, so I'm going to leave you to whatever business you were conducting before I so rudely interrupted you and be on my way."

"Aren't you going to ask how I got the heads?"

"I wasn't, no."

"You don't want to know?"

"I'm not one to poke into the private business of others."

"I cut them off myself," said Franklin.

"Is that so?"

"Yes."

I nodded. "Well, I commend you on your technique. Those are some cleanly severed heads, no doubt about it. I'm so clumsy I'd probably make a complete mess of it." I chuckled at my own hypothetical ineptitude. "Anyway, I've taken up too much of your valuable time already, so I'll leave you to it. Thank you for indulging me."

I walked back to the door and turned the knob. It didn't open.

"Whoopsie," I said. "Your door appears to be stuck."

"Why wouldn't you listen?" asked Franklin. "I told you what was going to happen."

"That's right. You sure did. *So* much egg on my face. Yolk galore. Ha ha."

"So, Mr. Perkins, what would happen to you if I cut off your head?"

"You know, that's a very interesting question. It's never happened before, and it's not something I've given much thought."

"But you've died a bunch of times."

"That's right, I have. I sure have."

"And...?"

"When I die, I spiral through the darkness for what seems like thousands of years, but obviously isn't. When I wake up, I'm naked in a cave a few hundred miles from here. I wander out of the cave, try not to get arrested for indecent exposure, find my way home, and try to resume my normal life."

"Is it always the same cave?"

"Yes."

"Then why don't you leave a spare set of clothes there?"

"Not sure. That's a good idea."

"What happens to your other body?" Franklin asked.

"It fades away."

"There's nothing left?"

"Not a speck."

"Are you sure?"

"Well, I'm not there when it happens, but that's what I'm told, yes."

"Dammit!"

"What's wrong?"

"The whole point of killing you was to have your head on my wall. And then I was going to keep killing you, over and over, keeping your head each time. I was going to do this until I had a dozen of your severed heads mounted on my wall."

"Oh," I said. "Why would you do that?"

"Who else can say that they have a collection of a dozen heads from the same person?"

"Nobody, I suppose," I admitted.

"It would've been awesome!"

"It sure would have. But, yes, my dead body would just fade away. No trophy for you."

The Dark Void revealed itself to me.

I stood there, gazing into the nothingness, paralyzed with terror.

"You okay?" Franklin asked.

I didn't answer. When confronted with the evidence that nothing lay beyond our earthly realm, Franklin's words were meaningless.

"Helloooooo," he said, waving his hand in front of my face. "Anybody home?"

I trembled in fear. Oh, how I wished I lacked this bleak knowledge that burdened me so. Ignorance would be such sweet, sweet bliss.

The Dark Void closed in upon itself.

When I returned to sanity, Franklin had a garrote wrapped around my neck.

"Aw, c'mon," I said. "You can't take advantage of me when I'm overcome with nihilism."

"I think you're lying," said Franklin. "I bet that after I pop your head off, it'll drop right onto the floor."

"Untrue."

"I guess I'll just have to find out for myself."

I stomped on his foot. Franklin didn't react.

"I've spent my whole life building up a resistance to people stomping on my foot," said Franklin. "You'll never escape."

He yanked on the ends of the garrote, tightening it even further. It was becoming difficult to breathe, and I felt a thin trickle of blood run down my neck.

"Please, don't," I said. "I'm serious—my body is just going to disappear, and you'll get super frustrated. Do you really want that?"

"Do you think your head will retain its awareness as it hits the floor? Will you look up at me with your dead eyes and know exactly what's happening?"

"Nope."

"Have you been decapitated before?"

"No, but none of my other deaths have worked that way, so there's no reason to think this one will. I wasn't aware of being in my own drowned body, and after the front tires of the semi-truck went over me, I wasn't conscious of the other ones crushing me more. For real—right after you kill me I'm going to vanish."

"We'll see," said Franklin.

"Maybe I'm wrong. Maybe I *will* retain my consciousness. Maybe my severed head will start talking. Can you handle that? Can you handle a severed head taunting you?"

"I'd be okay with it."

"Are you sure? There's a pretty big difference between imagining what it would be like and actually having the head talk to you. And keep in mind that it'll be spurting blood while this conversation is happening. You may *think* you're depraved enough to enjoy the experience…but are you really?"

Franklin pulled the garrote tighter.

"Are you just trying to draw out the suspense?" I asked.

"Yeah," Franklin admitted.

And then he gave a violent tug on the ends of the garrote. My head tilted forward and then I saw the floor rushing up toward me. My head bonked against the tile, which really hurt, and then rolled away, stopping face-down against the wall.

Oh, crap! I'd retained my awareness!

I tried to taunt him, but I was face-down and it came out all muffled.

Then I spiraled through darkness for what seemed like thousands of years, but obviously wasn't.

Suddenly, I was naked in the cave.

Okay, the idea of leaving a change of clothes here was probably a good one. It wasn't that it hadn't occurred to me before, but it seemed too cynical to assume I would get killed again. But if I could get killed eight times, I could get killed nine, so I'd be more prepared next time.

The cave was approximately four hundred and fifty miles from home. Each time I died, I had to hike about five miles to get to a road, in bare feet, which sucked. Then I had to keep walking until I found a driver who would give me a ride. This was a challenge, considering that the only clothing I was wearing had been fabricated from leaves and branches. If I was lucky, the driver would lend me enough money to buy an outfit from Goodwill. Then I'd hitchhike back home.

And that's what I did again.

The old lady who picked me up on the side of the road insisted on driving me all the way home, and insisted that there was no reason for me to change out of my forest attire. "I sure would like to see what's under those leaves," she kept saying, which was amusing the first few times but got progressively creepier as the hours went by. When we arrived at my apartment complex, I repaid her kindness in a way that doesn't need to be recounted here, and then took a nice long hot shower and went to bed. Dying was exhausting.

The next day, I decided to pay Chet and Blake a visit. When I knocked on their front door, Chet answered. "Oh, it's you," he said.

"That's right. Mind telling me what yesterday was all about?"

"We just wanted our dog back. And we still don't have him, by the way. I thought you were the greatest private investigator who ever lived?"

"You set me up," I said. "Franklin is a serial killer."

"We told you he was a homicidal psychopath."

"Yes, but it was never about the dog. You sent me over there to die."

"No, we told you to be careful. Why would we warn you about his guns, knives, and garrotes if we were sending you over there to die? Snippy was kidnapped by a madman and we wanted you to get him back."

"But Franklin said…" I trailed off. Sometimes in the business of being a private investigator, you discover that not every case is filled with twists and turns, and the most reasonable explanation is the correct one. In retrospect, I shouldn't have been swayed by the man with severed human heads mounted on his wall. "Why do you live with your brother?"

"We split the rent and can live in a nicer home."

"That makes total sense. Okay, I'll go get your dog."

I walked across the street and knocked on Franklin's door. When Franklin answered, he frowned at me. "You were right. Your body disappeared. I killed you for nothing, except the thrill of taking a human life."

"I told you, Franky-Z."

"By the way, I'm not giving back the dog, so don't even bother asking."

"Ha! I knew it!" I shouted.

"Knew what?"

"You didn't get mad when I called you Franky-Z. You *like* being called Franky-Z! You were lying all along. The brothers, though douchey, were on the level."

"Then why would I have planned to cut off your head twelve times? How would I have known they were hiring you?"

"Shit!"

"They were playing you like a didgeridoo."

I'd be damned if I admitted I didn't know what the hell a didgeridoo was. "Sorry to have bothered you," I said.

"No problem. Be safe."

"Wait! I think they told you they were hiring me. 'Give us our dog back or we're hiring Timothy Perkins!' And *then* you conceived the plan to decapitate me twelve times!"

Franklin applauded. "Well done. You've figured it out. But I'm still not giving the dog back."

The Dark Void revealed itself to me.

I screamed and screamed and screamed.

When I recovered, Franklin had a garrote around my neck again.

"Seriously?" I asked.

"What were you screaming about?"

"It's just the Dark Void. When I personally die, I wake up in that stupid cave, but for the rest of human existence there's nothing beyond our realm. Just an infinite emptiness."

"I beg your pardon?"

I nodded, which hurt a bit because of the garrote. "No afterlife. This is it."

"But...but...but I assumed I was sending my victims to a better place."

"Nope."

Franklin loosened the garrote. "That's really upsetting. I knew I wasn't a good guy, but I assumed there was an upside for my prey."

I shook my head, which hurt again. "There sure isn't. You owe an apology to every head in this room."

"Wow. I don't even know how to express what I'm feeling right now." He removed the garrote completely. "Obviously, you're free to leave. My killing days are done."

"And the dog?"

"I'm still keeping it."

I punched Franklin in the face. I'm a pretty good puncher, and the blow knocked him off his feet and onto the floor. I glanced around for the nearest weapon, which I decided was one of the mounted heads, so I yanked it off the wall and started hitting him with it. I lost my grip and the head rolled away, so I pulled another one off the wall and resumed the process.

Typing it here, it sounds kind of fucked up that I spent the next fifteen minutes bashing him with the severed heads. In the moment, it seemed like the right thing to do. Eventually, my arms got too tired to continue, and I didn't want to actually kill him with the heads, so I left a bloodied and broken Franky-Z on the floor to reflect upon his wrongdoing.

It didn't take long to find Snippy. I know that many people couldn't care less about the owners of the severed heads or their families as long as the doggie is okay, so I'm pleased to report that Snippy was totally fine. He bit me as I carried him out of the house, but I guess that was his prerogative.

The brothers were delighted to have their pet back. However, they refused to pay me for the time spent riding back from the cave, which turned into a major argument. I'm not proud of myself for threatening to bash them to death with Franklin's heads. We eventually worked it out.

If you're upset about the revelations of the Dark Void, just keep in mind that it means there's no Hell. If you take a good long look at yourself, I think you'll agree that's a win.

DEAD DROP

A JOHNNY FADE STORY

BY **NANCY HOLDER**
AND **ALAN PHILIPSON**

A ghost cop followed a ghost heiress up the staircase of a ghost hotel.

"Lindsey, why won't you tell me what this is about?" Johnny Fade asked.

The heiress didn't reply. She didn't even look at him.

He took that to mean it was about what it was *always* about: the search for the ghost of the father she worshipped—home cleaning product tycoon/banned chemical weapon developer Charles DeVore.

Dear damned Daddy.

On Fade's right, a flaming torch jammed into a no-longer-functional electric sconce revealed peeling wallpaper and threadbare carpet. On his left, beyond the staircase banister, beyond reach of the torch, was impenetrable darkness. Like everything and everyone in Deadtown, the landmark Los Altos hotel was a reflection glimpsed in a grimy mirror.

Dim. Distorted. Decaying.

They turned onto the third floor. The door to Room 323 stood open. Smoke and dancing light spilled into the corridor.

"Osie! Yoo-hoo, it's mee-ee!" Lindsey called as she swept through the pall.

Between sofa and armchairs laden with rags, scrap wood, and cardboard, the once-elegant parquet floor had been ripped up, and in its center blazed a leaping campfire. On the far side of the flames, backlit by rows of candles, a massive figure loomed. Stripped to the waist, his chest, arms, and back were furred like a grizzly bear. He held a long stick over the fire; the tip ended in a glowing gob of cinder. Judging from the bag beside his soot-blackened toes, the cinder had once been a marshmallow.

Lindsey DeVore rushed headlong into a seven-foot expanse of welcoming arms.

"I knew you wouldn't let me down, honey," the hairy giant said, his long, pointed black beard draping the top of her head like a shaggy beret.

Dead peas in a pod.

In his previous life, Oso the Maneater had been a professional wrestler. For years he'd moonlighted as Charles DeVore's bodyguard. After he killed a man in the ring, a death widely rumored to be a mob hit, Daddy had to let him go. But the story didn't end there. Oso's deceased opponent, a gambling addict and notorious welcher, had younger brothers who wrestled as a tag team. In a subsequent, two-on-one "revenge" match, the Yamaguchi twins caved in Oso's shaved skull with a corner stool, a blow that left a two-inch-wide gulley in his forehead.

When the wrestler and heiress both turned to face him, Fade knew the other shoe was about to drop.

"Is your pet homicide dick going to pitch in?" Oso said.

She shrugged seductively. "You have to ask him yourself."

DaddyDaddyLet'sFindMyDaddy was what Fade was expecting. But no…it was worse.

"Next time you cross over to the other side," Oso said, "I want you to find my mee-maw and warn her about something."

Fade looked at Lindsey in disbelief. "You told him about *that*?"

Lindsey arched a brow. "That you can travel back to Hollywood? Yes, of course I did. He's an old friend, and you're the only one who can help him."

"I've got to get word to my mee-maw. My grandmother. Muckie," Oso went on.

Fade blinked. "Muckie Lazaro?"

Oso nodded. "That's her. You know her?"

"I've read her rap sheet."

"Then you see the problem," Oso said. "She's gotta clean up her act, or when she dies she's going to end up in this shit hole. Or the Worse Place."

Unpleasant and disturbing as Deadtown was, it was just a waiting room.

For the bus home.

To the Worse Place.

"I don't know," Fade said, "she's a tough customer and—"

"Muckie only seems tough," Oso cut in. "Because of, you know, all the murders. But deep down, she's really sweet. We had so many good times. She goes by *Muckie* because of me. She used to call me her little monkey. But I couldn't say the word *monkey*." He sighed. "She showed me how to do an armbreaker. And a back body drop. She ran the gym, taught me everything about the world of professional wrestling."

"The world that got you killed," Fade said.

"Yeah, but that wasn't her fault." Oso kicked at the glowing embers of his campfire. "We used to play Parcheesi…."

Fade shook his head. "This won't work."

"It will, Johnny. It will." Lindsey coiled herself around him like a python and pursed her lips together.

In life, Fade and Lindsey had used each other ruthlessly. For sex, for revenge, for power. That it had gotten them both murdered hadn't changed the dynamic one bit. Truth be told, they had only had one romantic encounter, a motel room-trashing sex marathon that left him panting for more. Fade's feverish memories of that one-night stand—along with other deep ruts in his brain—had survived death, at least temporarily. And though sex between ghosts was pleasureless, a sad fact they had discovered together, that didn't stop him from wanting her with every last speck of ectoplasm. Like all doomed spirits in Deadtown, what drove him in life held him fast in death. An endless loop of guilt and desire.

"Rachel can pass the message to Muckie," Lindsey assured him.

She was referring to Rachel Alcina, the only person who could summon Fade to Tinseltown, to the living world. The only person on the other side who could see and hear him.

"And how is that going to convince Muckie of anything?" Fade countered. "A complete stranger giving her advice from her dead grandson?"

"If you tell Mee-maw something that we kept secret between us," Oso said, "then she'll know it's on the up and up, and she'll have to listen."

"Like what, for instance?" Fade said.

"Like she keeps five one-hundred-dollar bills pinned inside her underpants. For emergencies. She calls it her 'safety deposit box.'"

"Ooh, that will work," Lindsey said. She beamed at Osie, then gazed with expectation at Fade. "And you will do it."

She pythoned Fade tighter, and everything began to spin. He'd never loved her. Never trusted her. Alive or dead, the gorgeous, spoiled-rotten rich girl was fifty miles of bad road. But—and this was the strangest part—he could still *taste* her. Like a bottle of raspberry soda, shaken, top popped off, the memory fizzed and frothed inside his head.

"Okay, okay," Fade said, freeing himself from her embrace. "But only one try. If it doesn't work, no do-overs."

Oso reignited his cinder, then offered Lindsey the bag of marshmallows. She plucked one out as if it were a rare jewel and slid it onto the stick Oso held out to her. His task assigned, Fade's presence was no longer relevant.

"I need a drink," he said. "I'm heading back to the Teardrop."

No one was listening.

He descended the staircase and passed through the hotel's deserted lobby. Melted-to-nubbin candles flickered in the floor-standing candelabras, making shadows dance across a forest of ornate, smoke-stained Mission Revival columns. Outside, a steady drizzle falling from the low-hanging overcast hit him in the face. In Deadtown it was always gray, always raining, and always 1:43 a.m. Fade tipped down the brim of his fedora and jaywalked across the empty, gleaming wet lanes of Wilshire Boulevard.

He had good reason for wanting to keep a lid on his ability to ping-pong between the planes of life and death. Every ghost in purgatory had living relatives or lovers or enemies they wanted to get messages to. Once word got out, they'd all be lining up and he'd never hear the end of it.

He didn't give two hoots about finding Daddy's missing ghost, but he was determined to rescue his former partner from the Worse Place. No way Marcus Sherman deserved to be sent there. He was the straightest, smartest homicide cop Fade had ever met. He had to be: he was the only black detective in Los Angeles in 1933.

The curbs along both sides of the street were lined with cars resting on rusting wheel rims. Parked and left to rot. The one- and two-story buildings that still stood had no window glass, no roofs. And nobody was home.

Down the block on Olympic, a neon sign sputtered on and off: a pale blue martini glass with a winking, toothpicked green olive. In Tinseltown, the Teardrop had been a cop bar, and on this side of the veil it still was—only the habitués were all dead, and all bent. Booze, like everything else, had no taste or kick, but they kept the doubles coming.

As Fade reached for the fake leather-upholstered front door, he watched the substance of his outstretched hand dematerialize. Even as that registered, a pull at the base of his skull jerked his head backwards. The pressure increased until it drew his eyes to slits and his lips from his front teeth. Then ectoplasm gave way with a wet sploosh and the released bits of memory, all that remained of Detective John Fade, were sucked through a pinhole into a black void. Though there were no landmarks, it felt as if he was falling head over heels.

In the midst of the endless nothing, a tiny something appeared.

The speck of light rushed up at him, expanding in all directions until it blotted out the emptiness, then swallowed him. When he hit the membrane that walled off the living world, it broke his fall. Through the bubble-studded, translucent film he could make out a blur of light and color on the other side. The barrier held for only an instant.

When it split, he crossed into the tiny séance room of Madame Grimaldi, Medium to the Stars. He had been summoned here many times before. The ceiling and walls of the converted bungalow bedroom were draped in pale red gauze shot with streaks of purple and gold; the air reeked of incense. He couldn't tell if he was remembering a symphony of past sensations—sight, sound, smell—and didn't care. It was a feast for the starving.

Sprawled on the floor beside her overturned séance table, the turbanned Madame Grimaldi jerked like a galvanized frog. The room's other occupant—a slender dark-haired beauty in fox stole, veiled black hat, black gloves, and slinky red dress—had tears in her big brown eyes.

"Oh, Johnny, I'm in big trouble!" Rachel exclaimed.

"Who did you kill now?"

"No one, but I'm ready to kill myself. They put me in a movie that will ruin me forever!"

"So? You can just walk away. It's a free country."

"Are you being funny with me? The movie's backed by *the mob*, Johnny. They say if I don't do what they say, they will make my death look like an accident, and cash in on the insurance policy they made me sign with a gun to my head."

That changed the picture.

"Is the movie really that bad?" he asked.

"It's a big stinker, Johnny. They're gonna call it *Blood on the Ropes*."

As Rachel rapid-fire detailed the plot, Fade recognized the source material as Oso the Maneater's true story, only stood on its head and decked out with heart-wrenching tropes and a gushy happy ending. In other words, a standard Tinseltown treatment.

"My part is the killer wrestler's kid sister who's taking care of their wheelchair mother," Rachel said. "Johnny, she is so frumpy, always in slouchy yarn hat, baggy clothes, and clunky shoes like from Russia. No sparkle! No pizzazz! Johnny, it is *not* me! Madame Grimaldi says I will never live it down if this movie comes out. You will see for yourself. I have to watch dailies tonight and you have to come with me. You will not believe how horrible it is!"

"If I'm still here." He never knew how long he would remain in Tinseltown. He had been pulled back to Deadtown in the middle of Rachel's many predicaments before. That might be to his advantage; it was clear to him Rachel's movie and Osos's request had more than a little in common. He didn't know how long he could keep that information to himself.

"Oh, my God, Johnny! What am I gonna do?"

"I'll figure something out," Fade said. "In the meantime, there's something *you* can help *me* with."

She looked dubious. "In the middle of my emergency? Really, Johnny? What is it?"

"We gotta make a bad grandma change her ways so she doesn't wind up in Deadtown like her grandson. Make her see the light."

"How are we going to do that?"

"You're gonna sell it, Rachel."

The view of the San Fernando Valley from the backseat of Rachel's limo brought a smile to Fade's insubstantial lips. Bright sunlight. Blue sky. Palm trees. Green lawns. People on the sidewalks pushing baby strollers, walking happy dogs. Everyone, everything in motion. He started to say something to Rachel but caught himself. Her chauffeur had lowered the privacy window. Any conversation between them would come across as one-sided, and Pepe would think she'd gone loco, talking to herself.

The limo pulled up in front of a brick two-story building between a tire repair shop and an empty lot. The weathered billboard sign above the double doors said: Lazaro's Arena and Gym.

Rachel pushed through the doors, her high heels clicking on the pavement. Pepe was right behind her, formidable in his black uniform, cap, tall boots, and sunglasses. Fade brought up the rear, Mr. Invisible.

Around the wide room, sweaty, cauliflower-earred palookas punched speed and heavy bags. In the elevated center ring, surrounded by rows of folding chairs, a pair of large guys in shorts grappled in slow motion, shuffling their ankle-high, lace-up shoes.

"If you two girls want to kiss and hug," a hoarse voice barked from ringside, "do it on your goddamned day off! This fight is supposed to be a grudge match. That means you stumble bums hate each other!"

"Who is that person yelling?" Rachel whispered.

"That's Grannie," Fade said. "Muckie Lazaro."

Muckie Lazaro jumped up from her seat, cigar butt clenched in the corner of her mouth. She looked like a fireplug draped in a pinstriped suit jacket, unbuttoned shirt collar flattened over the lapels. She wore baggy cream-colored trousers and black and white saddle shoes, long gray hair pulled back from a blocky forehead into a screaming-tight bun. The hand-tooled, black leather holster on her hip held a chrome .32 Colt automatic.

Shaking a fist at the frozen combatants, she shouted, "Fight, you dimwits! Show me some goddamned action or go back to blowing up balloons at the zoo!"

"Time to work your magic, Rachel," Fade said.

The actress rolled her eyes. "Come with me, Pepe," she said, and they headed down to ringside.

Incorporeal, Fade glided through the intervening rows of seats and beat them there.

Rachel stepped up behind the irate grandma. "Excuse me, Señora Muckie?"

The woman whirled around. When she saw Rachel's face, her fury turned to astonishment. "You're that actress!" Muckie exclaimed. "*Moonlight in Mexico*! And the Western where you're a nun singing and dancing for poor little orphans!"

"Yes, that's me."

"You're the one starring in the new movie about my grandson!"

Rachel's eyes narrowed, but ever the trouper, she didn't miss a beat. "Can we speak in private for a minute?"

"Sure thing. My office is this way."

Rachel followed her and Fade followed Rachel. Pepe waited outside the door, brawny arms crossed, eyes hidden behind dark glasses. The cluttered, dusty space was decorated with memorabilia: curling posters from boxing and wrestling matches she'd staged; framed photos of Muckie with battered, bloodied fighters holding up trophies and prize belts. There were no photos of the battered, bloodied losers who'd taken dives and made big money for her and the Zorba mob.

On a table in a corner was a shrine to her late grandson. Above the cluster of votive candles and paper flowers were photographs of Muckie and Oso over the years, and of him in posed publicity shots. There had been speculation about her involvement in the contract hit on Gaetano Yamaguchi, but never any proof. The two-on-one revenge match that followed had been her promotion, its fatal turn definitely not in the script. The most recent photo was of a stone-faced Muckie in black suit and fedora standing beside an enormous, flower-wreathed coffin.

The promoter plopped down on a wooden swivel chair behind her desk and lit her cigar stub with a match. "What's this about, doll?"

Rachel got right down to business. "I bring you a message, Señora Muckie. It's from your Oso."

With a pained expression on her face, Muckie slowly leaned across the shambles of her desktop. Biting off each word like a piece of tough steak, she said, "My dear boy's no longer with us."

"That's the point," Rachel said. "I mean, where he is now is the point. I have this connection to the afterlife. And your Oso told me to tell you, whatever you're into, get out of all of it fast, straighten up or you're going to end up alongside him."

"Really." She puffed on her cigar. "And just *where* might that be?"

"He's in a place where dead people go who've done really bad things. It's the last stop before the Worse Place." Rachel leaned forward earnestly, making her pitch. "*Infierno*, señora. Oso wants to protect you from that. He loves you so much."

Muckie looked utterly baffled for a second, then a grin spread over her face. "Doll, I don't know what kind of skunk you're smoking, but it's messing with your *cabeza*. You should be buying all your loco weed from me. I got harder stuff, too. I can supply all your movie pals whatever they want, give you a nice cut on every sale, cash or product. And I deliver, no extra charge."

"Tell her you want in," Fade said. "Give her your address. Tell her to come tonight."

Rachel hesitated, but did as he asked.

Walking back to the limo, she hissed, "The stinky mob movie is about her dead grandson, the one who gave you the message? You could've told me!"

"Tinseltown gobbles up real stories all the time. It's easier than making them up," Fade said. "The rest is just coincidence, trust me. It doesn't change anything."

"She doesn't believe the message is real," Rachel said, "and now she thinks I want to buy drugs from her? What have you got me into?!"

"You're not going to buy drugs, Rachel. It's safer if she's not on her home turf when we drop the boom."

"Safer, but not *safe*?"

Fade thought of Lindsey and Oso blithely roasting marshmallows in Hell. Now *that* was safe.

If not entirely comfortable.

Three hit movies in a row had made Rachel Alcina the toast of Tinseltown. Accordingly, she had moved into new digs: a spectacular Spanish Colonial Revival mansion high in the hills overlooking Hollywood. With lush, gardenia-perfumed gardens. Splashing fountains. Champagne in frost-beaded silver ice buckets. Sheaves of cut roses in vases. Sparkling, ornately framed mirrors. White-liveried servants galore.

Tonight, however, there was only one servant in evidence: Pepe, in his chauffeur uniform.

He led a trio of visitors onto the quarry-tiled veranda bordering the gardens, then positioned himself behind his mistress's armchair. Muckie had brought two broken-nosed thugs with her; one of them lugged an overstuffed doctor's satchel. Big fans slowly turned overhead, spreading the sweet scent of night-blooming flowers.

"Good evening, señora," Rachel said without rising. She gestured at the armchair across the low table from her. "Please, have a seat."

Muckie plopped down, and her muscle stationed themselves behind her, brawny arms folded.

Pepe leaned over to whisper something to Rachel and his short jacket fell open. Fade saw the butt of the broom-handle Mauser machine-pistol nestled under his armpit. From the expressions on their faces, the thugs had seen it, too.

"Now, honey, what can I do you for?" Muckie said, hoisting her bag of wares onto the table.

"I want you to please listen to me," Rachel said. "Your Oso passed on a secret from the other side that he says only you and he know. He says it will make you believe the message really comes from him."

Muckie rolled her eyes. "Cripes, not this again…"

When Rachel discreetly played their hole card, bad granny leaped to her feet as if her safety deposit box was on fire.

"Get out of here!" she yelled at her goons. "Wait for me at the car!"

Only after Pepe showed them out and returned did she continue. With brimming tears, Muckie said, "How did you find that out? You can't… He's dead…"

"It's straight from him," Rachel assured her. She laid a hand on Muckie's forearm. "Trust me. I am here on a mission of mercy."

Muckie was silent for a while. Then she said, "Go on."

"He says he wants to spare you from his fate. He's suffering terribly for the bad things he did. He says you have to break your mob ties, confess to all your crimes, and go straight. Or…" Rachel made a dramatic slicing motion across her throat.

Muckie huffed. "If I confessed to the Los Angeles D.A., I'd be dead in ten minutes, guaranteed. Not much time to turn my life around."

"You can go to the Feds. They'll give you witness protection."

"Only if I rat out everyone in the Zorba mob. No dice, honey. Rats go to Hell, too."

Actually, based on Fade's experience, they didn't. Nor did dogs, cats, or water buffalo. No matter how Rachel pleaded, Muckie Lazaro refused to budge.

"Missus Muckie, I am sorry that I cannot convince you," Rachel said. "Your Oso is so worried. Very worried. Very, very, *mucho*—"

"Can you get a message back to him?" Muckie asked.

Fade nodded to Rachel.

"*Sí.* What do you want me to tell him?"

"That they're making a movie of his story," Muckie said, eyes shining with pride. "His wrestling legend is going down in history. He'll be a hero to young and old forever and ever."

Rachel's mouth dropped open. "*What?*"

Fade stopped her with a raised hand. "Invite her to watch the dailies with you," he said.

"Would you like to see some of the movie tonight?"

Muckie smiled and nodded, wiping her eyes with the back of her hand.

Rachel passed on the details and arranged to pick her up in the limo.

The motion picture lot looked like a lit-up Army base. Most of the buildings were windowless and all were painted beige and stencil-numbered. Instead of soldiers marching around, there were cancan dancers, knights in armor, cowboys on horseback.

Pepe parked and remained beside the car as Fade trailed Rachel and Muckie into a Quonset hut. Fade had been a Hollywood cop and he had never seen a screening in a ramshackle building like this. No carpet on the concrete floor. Unpadded chairs. Walls painted flat black. Clearly, *Blood on the Ropes* was not a big-budget production. It was most definitely a comedown for a huge star like Rachel.

The "financiers" were already there, sitting in the second row from the front. Fade recognized them at once: Leon Detloff and Mario Mariano, Numbers Three and Four in the Zorba mob chain of command. Rachel had pushed Number Two, Alvin Grossbinder, out a five-story window; Fade had framed Number One, Spiros Zorba, and got him sent to the gas chamber. In the row behind Detloff and Mariano sat a quartet of mob muscle, and on either side of them, a man in a beret and silk cravat, and assorted anxious-looking people.

"What are *they* doing here?" Muckie said, pointing at two guys in matching double-breasted suits and ties, black hair slicked straight back.

The Yamaguchi twins.

"They're in the movie," Rachel said. "They play themselves." She added in a whisper, "But they are terrible at it."

As Rachel and Muckie took seats directly in front of Detloff and Mariano, the man in the beret rose to his feet, clipboard in hand, and said, "This afternoon we're going to screen footage from scenes sixteen, eighteen, and twenty-five."

"I want to die," Rachel muttered.

A loud rumbling noise came from outside the Quonset hut. Motorcycle. After an even louder roar, it cut off.

"Who is playing my boy?" Muckie asked.

Door swung open and in walked a very tall, very tanned man in a gaudy Hawaiian shirt and shorts. "Cheers, all!" he bellowed,

British accent very evident. "Made it by the proverbial skin of my teeth. Had the bloody motorbike up to seventy on Melrose."

"He is," Rachel told Muckie. "Reginald Fitzwilliam, Reggie for short. A famous London stage actor."

The room lights dimmed and grainy black-and-white film began to roll.

Rachel and Reggie sat in a grim dressing room. "Oso" towered over his terrified little sister, wearing what looked like a gorilla costume without the head mask. A bald skull cap. Phony beard.

"This is before the fight with Gaetano Yamaguchi," Rachel whispered. "It's my biggest scene so far."

"You're conspiring with Gaetano Yamaguchi!" Reggie yelled at her in his British accent. "You're his moll! I know you're having an affair! And you are going to steal all my money!"

Dowdy Rachel, crying, hands clasped in prayer, dropped to her knees.

"Gaetano is only trying to help us," she sobbed. "We have to have money to help *mama*. She is so sick in her wheelchair."

There was scattered laughter from the audience, and Rachel groaned.

Then the scene faded to black as Reggie/Oso raised a hand to give her a mighty smack.

"I got that last line wrong," Rachel muttered. "Not that it matters…."

Fade looked over at Muckie, who sat eyes wide, in shocked silence.

The next scene showed a gorilla-suited Oso, with obvious glee, strangling Gaetano by wrapping his neck in the ring ropes.

Muckie clenched her cigar butt and shifted in her chair.

"Who did you say wrote the script?" Fade asked Rachel.

"I didn't," Rachel whispered. "Xavier LaPierre's name is on it. But it isn't good like the ones he stole from V.V."

Virgil Vorhees was a dead client of talent agent LaPierre, who had made a career in Hollywood by putting his own name on V.V.'s unsold scripts.

"Maybe LaPierre wrote it himself this time, or got some hack to pound it out. Why isn't he here?" Fade asked. "Where is he?"

"I don't know."

Rachel had been chosen for the film because of her star turns in the two *Moonlight* movies and *Stampede at Red Rock*. LaPierre had no doubt been commissioned to write the wrestling script because the mob thought he had created the trio of box-office hits. A job he couldn't refuse. No wonder he hadn't shown up for the screening. He was probably in Buenos Aires by now.

The projector clacked away as the next scene began to roll. Now the Yamaguchi twins were tag-teaming Oso in the revenge match. One twin pinned Oso's arms behind his back while the other jumped onto the top rope to deliver a blow with a stool.

"Ouch!" one of the twins catcalled from the third row.

The mobsters guffawed. So did the actors and the man in the beret. Fade figured him to be the director.

"They're destroying my Oso's memory!" Muckie snarled around her cigar butt. She started to get up.

Rachel pulled her back down into her chair. "No, no, *please*, you must not interrupt."

In the last scene, Rachel broke the news of Oso's death to her wheelchair-bound mother. They hugged each other, weeping… *with joy*. They were free of the monster.

When the film ended, the screen went white.

As the room lights came up, Muckie was on her feet, turning, her hand dipping inside her coat. Apparently oblivious to the fact that their film was horrible, everyone was smiling and congratulating each other.

Everyone but Rachel, Fade, and Oso's mee-maw.

"You lousy crooks know that's all a lie," Muckie shouted at the mobster entourage. "My Oso never had a mean bone in his body. You bastards contracted the hit on Gaetano! You threatened to ice me if Oso didn't play ball and take him out."

"*Dios mio!*" Rachel exclaimed as the shiny Colt appeared in grandma's hand.

The grins vanished a split second before the pop gun popped. Nine pops with no answering fire. A point-blank shooting gallery. Dead ducks slumping in their chairs while horrified survivors sat paralyzed.

Dropping the empty pistol, Muckie ran for the exit.

"Rachel, get out of here," Fade said.

As they rushed out the door, Rachel collided with Pepe, who had drawn his own gun.

"Where did the lady go?" Rachel asked him.

Before he could reply, on the far side of the limo an engine started up. With a roar, Muckie sped off on Reggie's motorcycle. Skidding wildly, bent over the handlebars, she disappeared around a corner.

"Time for us to go, too," Fade said. "Before the cops show up."

Rachel, Pepe, and Fade climbed into the limo. As Pepe exited the studio lot, privacy window up, Fade assured Rachel that the bad press from the massacre—and the deaths of the financial backers—would kill the movie's release. "You have nothing to worry about on that score. But you're going to need a lawyer, pronto."

"Me?"

"You brought Muckie here."

A couple of blocks later, he began to dissolve. Deadtown was calling in its markers. Rachel's arms swept through empty space as she tried to grab him. "No, Johnny! Stay! I need you…"

Stay was the one thing he couldn't do.

✝

With Lindsey in the lead and a flaming candelabra in his hand, Fade trudged back up the stairs of the Los Altos to break the sad news to Oso. His astral intervention had only made things worse for Muckie, if such a thing was even possible. Did six additional murders earn her a first-class ticket on the bus home?

When they reached the third-floor hallway, braying laughter erupted from the open door of Room 323. Amid the smoke and leaping firelight, somebody was having a good time.

Not for long, he thought as they entered through the haze.

Oso sat on the sofa amid heaped cardboard and rags, toasting a pair of marshmallows over the campfire. His mee-maw was snuggled up beside him. Their teeth blackened by ash, they were happy as clams.

"What the hell happened?" Fade asked Muckie. "You were making a clean getaway."

"Never made it off the lot," Muckie admitted sheepishly. "Ran the goddamned motorcycle smack into a telephone pole. Spread myself real thin, real quick. Not so bad here, though. We got each other."

Oso put a hairy arm around his grannie's shoulders. "And Parcheesi, too."

Lindsey threaded a fresh marshmallow on a pointed stick and offered it to Fade.

"Come on, Johnny, live a little."

MYSTERY MEAT

A DAN SHAMBLE,
ZOMBIE P.I. ADVENTURE

BY KEVIN J. ANDERSON

The giant fly was frantic as she buzzed into the offices of Chambeaux & Deyer Investigations. Her long translucent wings vibrated like stained-glass windows made of Saran wrap. She clutched her top two sets of articulated arms in dismay.

"My maggots are missing!" she wailed, then accepted a tissue from Sheyenne, our receptionist (and my ghost girlfriend), so she could dab away tears from her multifaceted eyes.

I shambled into the front office when I heard the loud buzzing sound, and I could immediately see that this human-sized insect needed our help. As a zombie detective, I'm ready to solve even the oddest cases featuring unnaturals.

The mother fly buzzed back and forth, bouncing off the window in desperation, then coming back to where Sheyenne and I could soothe her. "Take a breath, ma'am, so we can figure out how to assist you." I extended my pallid hand, then pulled it back, not really wanting to be grasped by those clenching claws.

"My babies!" With great effort, the large fly forced her wings to settle down. Her proboscis uncurled, then curled like a New Year's Eve party favor as she took a deep breath. "The whole brood! They're all I've got. I need to engage your services, Mr. Chambeaux. You're the best there is in the Unnatural Quarter."

After all the years since the Big Uneasy, I guess my reputation preceded me. "So, it's a missing persons case, then?" I said.

"Missing maggots," Mama Fly corrected. I almost made a wisecrack about needing to call out the SWAT team, but that was in poor taste.

The big insect's name was Mama Fly, because apparently flies are so common and have such small brains that any one name will do the trick. At least it was easier to spell than some of our Lovecraftian clients, like Maug-Shugguleth.

Robin Deyer, my passionate human lawyer partner, emerged from her office ready to offer advice. As usual, this case was going to be a team effort.

After we calmed her down, Mama Fly managed to offer explanations. "I need a private investigator, and I need a fly spotter." She still looked as if she might hurl herself against the already-flyspecked window, so I eased myself back toward it and opened the glass, just in case.

Sheyenne prepared a New Client intake form to jot down details, while I was eager to gauge the severity of the threat.

"Tell us what happened to your maggots," Robin said. "How many of them? And what did they look like?"

Here in the Quarter, we were used to monsters, demons, mutations, ghosts, and mythical beasties of all kinds. More than a dozen years ago, a cosmic event called the Big Uneasy had shifted the world, rewritten the natural laws of science, magic, and superstition, and brought all the myths and legends to life. After the initial uproar, they came together to live in the Unnatural Quarter. I'd been a down-and-out human P.I. who set up his shingle here, because monsters got divorces too, had property disputes...went missing.

With a ghost or goblin on every street corner, you wouldn't think I'd let my guard down, but someone shot me in a dark alley. Fortunately, I came back as a zombie and got back to work. There were new cases every week to keep me, Robin, and Sheyenne busy.

Still, I'd never had to search for missing maggots before.

"My babies wriggled off to the playground, just like always," said Mama Fly. Her proboscis uncurled and curled again. "And they never came home! I've talked to other flies in the neighborhood, and they're buzzing with gossip. At least two other maggots disappeared at the same time."

"And when did they disappear?" I asked.

"This morning—hours ago! But a mother knows when something is wrong. We need to search the entire Quarter. Find them! You have to hurry— It's urgent."

Robin and Sheyenne determinedly took notes.

"I understand your worry, Mama Fly," I said, "but there's no immediate reason to suspect they're in danger. We have time."

"No, we don't!" The fly's wings fluttered again. "Our lifecycle is only a few weeks, and they need to pupate! Oh, my babies!"

Now we understood her extraordinary urgency.

After we took down the pertinent information, Mama Fly buzzed off.

II

In the Unnatural Quarter, alas, disappearing creatures—even insect ones—was not an uncommon occurrence. I put out word on the street to my meager network of informants. At the UQ Police Department, I met with Officer Toby McGoohan, my best human friend, and gave him a heads-up. I even filled out a missing larvae report.

As a zombie detective, I am good at aimlessly shambling, and I would begin pounding the pavement soon, but Robin and I needed to strategize. Because it was lunchtime, we met at the Ghoul's Diner, our usual unpalatable eating place. My little vampire half-daughter also joined us; Alvina is the only one who actually likes the miserable food served by Albert Gould, the proprietor— but the kid usually orders a prepackaged box of Unlucky Charms, because she likes the way the cereal made the milk turn blood red.

The diner was filled with the usual (actually, unusual) lunch crowd: vampires slurping blood soup or taking IVs to go, two slender she-wolves eating salads, a lanky necromancer who came in every day to order the "dead things" special. My taste buds haven't worked since my death, so I'm pretty much immune to whatever flavors show up in the mess served by Albert. It's the companionship I like, and eating at the diner with friends, partners, or clients was just part of the ritual.

We found an empty booth. I took one side, bending my stiff knees and tucking myself into the corner. Alvina scooted in next to me, bubbly and squirmy as always, while Robin capped the other end.

"Those poor little maggots," Alvina said. "So cute and cuddly! I hope we find them."

"We'll do our best, kid." I nudged her with my elbow. She nudged back. It was a sophisticated game we played. She's a few years older than her ten-year-old appearance, but now that she'd been turned into a vampire, she would never grow older. Even so, Alvina wore "cute" as a badge of honor, and she was good at it.

Robin set her briefcase on the sticky Formica tabletop, but before we could discuss Mama Fly and her offspring, Esther, the obnoxious harpy waitress, sashayed over and glared at us. "I suppose you want coffee instead of just the water!"

"You haven't brought us water yet," I said.

"Quit complaining," Esther snapped. "You get your coffee, but refills aren't free today." I usually couldn't stomach more than one cup anyway. Esther shrieked toward the kitchen where Albert was slaving away, dripping slime and rotting tissue into everything he cooked. "Three lunch specials!"

"Lunch special," Albert replied in a slow, slurred voice. The gaunt ghoul seemed to thrive on the drudgery, though his sullen face seemed capable of no expression other than sullen disappointment.

"No, I want a box of Unlucky Charms," Alvina said.

Robin straightened, not fazed by our shrill waitress. "I'd like my usual peanut-butter-and-jelly sandwich. With a pickle."

"Make your own damn peanut-butter-and-jelly sandwich," Esther said. "We don't serve that here. This is a fine restaurant."

"I order it every time I eat here," Robin said, still maddeningly calm. "A peanut-butter-and-jelly, please, and a pickle."

Esther fluffed her feathers, which were razor-edged and gleamed like metal dipped in an oil slick. "If I give in to one of your stupid customer demands, then you'll always want something special, and you probably won't tip!"

"I won't tip unless I get my peanut-butter-and-jelly sandwich." Robin had faced the most combative litigants in court; she had no trouble facing off against a waitress.

"Unlucky Charms, please," Alvina repeated.

I did my best to mollify Esther. "I'm okay with the special, Esther. Bring it on."

Esther stalked off. "It better be a damn good tip!"

Robin took out her papers, and we reviewed notes of where maggots were frequently seen, places where flies frequented. We studied a small map of the Quarter to determine where to start our efforts.

Eventually, Esther came back with Alvina's box of cereal and a pitcher of milk, as well as Robin's PB&J. She placed a blue plate in front of me with a large round slice of meat marbled with paler swirls, garnished with just a dab of gravy. It looked juicy, almost tasty.

"What is this, Esther?" I could even smell it…and it actually smelled good.

"Lunch special—just what you ordered." She turned about.

I poked at the meat with a fork. "What *is* the lunch special?"

"Mystery meat."

From behind the counter, Albert looked up and groaned. "Lunch special. Mystery meat."

I might have been intrigued, but the ghoul's lunch specials were often questionable, and some questions are better left unasked. This meal seemed less offensive than usual, however—the flesh not so gray and without the usual colors and signs of decay. Or the smell of rot.

Curious, I used my knife to cut off a piece, tender and meaty all the way through, and the smells were even savory. I popped a bite into my mouth and chewed. I blinked in surprise. "This is actually palatable."

"New source," Albert said. "Mystery meat."

I took another bite, tasting it more, even savoring the meat. "In fact, this is delicious."

"I thought you couldn't taste anything," Robin said.

"Usually not, but this…"

Alvina stole a bite and agreed that it was yummy—high praise indeed for someone who prefers breakfast cereal with artificial colors and flavors.

"Mystery Meat. Good protein." Albert grinned, which was unfortunate, because his snaggly, rotted teeth were enough to make anyone lose their appetite. "Bug based."

I hesitated. "*Bug* based? You mean I'm eating…insect steak?"

Distracted in the kitchen, Albert used his forearm to whisk a handful of skittering cockroaches from the kitchen counter directly into the stewpot. "You always eat insects here."

I knew that, even though I hadn't wanted to see.

Robin had an opinion. "Insects are a viable protein source, Dan. Considering food shortages, climate change, and agricultural disasters, traditional sources of meat like massive cattle herds are costly, not to mention destructive to the environment. In recent years, we've seen many advances in delicious meat substitutes, plant-based, soy-based, even textured algae products."

Remembering her vast knowledge from Wikipedia, Alvina said, "Lots of cultures eat bugs—crickets, grasshoppers, earthworms, beetle grubs, termites."

"You're making my mouth water, kid." I looked down at the half-eaten Mystery Meat steak on my plate.

Robin said, "Be open minded, Dan. Unnaturals eat rotting flesh and brains all the time. Don't be queasy about a different, environmentally safe kind of protein."

I grudgingly took another taste, which was not bad at all. I offered a bite to Robin since she was so insistent, but she politely declined. Instead, she bit into her PB&J, followed by half of the dill-pickle spear.

The moment we were finished, Esther sauntered by to snatch our dishes like a shoplifter. When she looked down at my lunch plate, her already pinched face tightened even more. "You cleaned your plate! Now what am *I* supposed to eat?"

She huffed off, and we quickly laid money on the table so as to avoid facing her again with the actual bill.

As we left the Ghoul's Diner, I heard the rumble of a large engine and saw a delivery truck in the back. It was pulling away after having dropped off large crates. The side of the truck said *Gold Boris's Abattoir. Home of Mystery Meat!*

Curious, I watched the truck roar off to make its other deliveries.

III

Though we had already set wheels in motion to find the missing maggots, Mama Fly was impatient and desperate. She buzzed back into the offices carrying a stack of printed flyers. She wore a red polka-dotted scarf tied around the top of her head, just above her multifaceted eyes.

Sitting at her homework table, Alvina started to giggle. "Flyers! I get it." She'd been posting notices about the missing larvae on her Monstagram and SickTok accounts.

Sheyenne chided, "This is serious business, sweetie."

I didn't think it was any better than my SWAT team joke, but at least I'd kept that one to myself."

Mama Fly's wings fluttered. "I don't understand."

"F-L-Y...ers?" Alvina said, waiting.

Mama Fly shook her head. "I'm a fly. I don't know how to spell." She set the stack of papers on Sheyenne's reception desk. "But I had help with these."

Each flyer had a bold headline. "Missing. Have you seen this maggot?" Beneath were photos of featureless pale worms, long thick grubs with slightly pointed heads, no eyes, a small rounded mouth.

"Oh, you have pictures—that'll help," I said. Every one of them looked identical.

Mama Fly said, "I'll leave these here with you." Her wings twitched and fluttered. "I have to get to work processing the town manure pile." The proboscis uncurled and curled in frustration. "The boss wouldn't give me time off."

I took the flyers. "We'll put these all around the Quarter, ma'am, and continue our vigorous search. But I need some more information. You said your grubs were at the playground when they vanished. Could you provide more details about exactly where they were last seen?"

"At the maggot playground," Mama Fly said. Her insectile forelimbs twitched with worry. "Everyone knows Dumpster Row. Where else would maggots go to play?"

As the insect flitted off, I picked up the flyers and looked at Alvina. "Kid, you want to come along? Let's go post these flyers."

IV

I'm always glad to have quality father/half-daughter time, so Alvina and I spent the afternoon walking through the Quarter and taping Missing Maggot flyers to wrought-iron lampposts, on the sides of abandoned buildings, onto crypts in the Greenlawn Cemetery— all the places where they would get the most traffic. Even, with Albert's permission, on the door of the Ghoul's Diner, right next to a new poster that advertised "We now serve Mystery Meat on select menu items."

I remembered how good the food had tasted, though I still found something unsettling about it….

We decided to take a look at where the grubs had disappeared. Maybe other children had seen the poor maggots on the playground. Alvina would be my secret weapon, since she was cute as a button and had good rapport with the offspring of any species.

Following directions, we made our way to an industrial part of the Quarter, where fly-by-night businesses were housed in corrugated metal buildings. There, Dumpster Row was not at all the playground I had expected (though it was true to its name). The open paved area was like an airport long-term parking lot for garbage receptacles, filled with row upon row of dumpsters, as if the receptacles had reproduced like…well, like flies. Green ones, brown ones, orange ones, and others so rusty I couldn't tell what the original color had been.

"Is this where dumpsters go to die?" Alvina asked, shading her eyes to look down the endless rows.

"Let's not be morbid, kid," I said. "Maybe they're all just asleep."

The sun had set, and twilight layered extra shadows and gloom onto the complex. I saw small forms scurrying between the containers, squirming underneath them, ducking between and rushing over them. Likely, packrat demons, scavenger squids, or gremlin treasure hunters who would ransack the dumpsters for collectible trash.

Alvina skipped ahead, banged on one of the dumpsters, then went to the next one. She lifted the groaning lid and peered inside before she dropped back down and let the lid slam. She shook her head. "Nothing interesting. I wonder who would want to play here?"

"Giant maggots, I suppose." I cupped my hands around my mouth and shouted, "Hello? Any maggots out here?"

I heard a faint rustle and stirring, a few muffled bumps on metal walls, but there were thousands of dumpsters here, and I had no way of identifying where the sound had come from. More shadowy figures scuttled around the containers.

Adjacent to dumpster row, a neon sign on the corrugated roof of the nearest industrial structure flickered on, and the sizzling letters spelled out *Gold Boris's Abattoir, Home of Mystery Meat*. A smaller line beneath said *Public Not Welcome*. Boxy delivery trucks pulled up to a loading dock in the back.

With a sinking feeling in my stomach, I remembered that the Mystery Meat substitute was supposedly "bug based." If Mama Fly's larvae liked to play in Dumpster Row, what if Gold Boris— whoever that was—had thugs engaged in maggot snatching, then fed the protein-rich grubs into the abattoir?

The industrial building had no windows whatsoever. One of the delivery trucks rumbled to life, spurting noxious exhaust fumes into the air, then rolled off into the Quarter to make deliveries.

I'd have to look into this further—but I needed more backup than a little vampire girl.

V

After putting up all the flyers and exploring the sinister Dumpster Row, Alvina and I returned to the offices. My vampire half-daughter ran into the kitchen where she was playing a game of Curses With Friends with the sentient mold growing on the wall next to the microwave.

Time was of the essence, considering the life expectancy of a fly (giant or otherwise). I needed to bring in the big guns—two guns actually, Officer Toby McGoohan's police special revolver and his police extra-special revolver loaded with silver bullets.

But it wasn't all about weaponry. I wanted McGoo with me for moral support, as well as law-enforcement support. I got ready to call him.

Sheyenne flitted up and gave me an air kiss, but my attention was suddenly drawn to the office TV, which was playing her favorite afternoon talk show, *Conversations With Dick the Head*, where the decapitated host interviewed local celebrities.

I was more interested, however, in the commercial break. Peppy circus-like music accompanied an announcer extolling the virtues of "Delicious, Nutritious Mystery Meat!" Images showed juicy, savory slabs of the undefined protein mass. The narrator promised the substance was completely organic and that no living creatures were harmed in the production of Mystery Meat.

Inherently suspicious, I muttered, "I wonder if that means they use undead creatures."

Then the voiceover continued, "And no undead creatures were harmed either! It's the perfect protein, a renewable resource. Healthy, tasty Mystery Meat from Gold Boris."

I removed my fedora and hung it on the rack. I scratched around the bullet hole in the center of my forehead as I pondered. Something about the ad struck me as odd. Renewable resource—I couldn't stop thinking about how fast flies breed.

Sheyenne had watched the commercial with me. "Have you ever tasted that, Beaux?"

"Just yesterday at the Ghoul's Diner. It was their lunch special."

"I never thought of you as a possible vegetarian." She had a teasing glow.

"I never thought that myself either. I permanently gave up eating brains, but I'm not sure if I could ever do without a good cheeseburger."

But I wasn't thinking about cheeseburgers, or any food whatsoever. I had lost my appetite, more than usual.

I thought back to all the questions I had surrounding Gold Boris's Abattoir.

VI

"I've studied the reports, Shamble, and quite a few maggots have gone missing over the years," said my best human friend, McGoo. He cocked his patrolman's cap as we met up outside the Chambeaux & Deyer offices. "If you've got suspicions about Gold Boris, then we'll check out that abattoir." He pursed his lips. "Besides, I hear Mystery Meat is pretty good."

"The Ghoul's Diner serves it," I said.

McGoo made a face. "Even if it started off pretty good, that place turns my stomach."

We made our way to the industrial park near Dumpster Row. McGoo whistled out loud as he scanned the giant parking lot filled with garbage containers. "You think that's where dumpsters go to die, Shamble?"

"Alvina already suggested that," I said.

"Our daughter is a smart kid," McGoo said.

"Takes after me," I replied. He just snorted.

Four more delivery trucks were parked behind the big industrial building. There were no windows in the corrugated walls, only a thick metal front door with the sign *Public Not Welcome*.

"We're not the public, Shamble." McGoo used the sleeve of his blue uniform to polish his badge. "Two-week life cycle, you say? I'd call that extenuating circumstances." He pounded on the door. "Police! Open up. We've got some questions."

For good measure, I added, "Zombie detective!" You never know what might impress or intimidate people.

We heard scuttling sounds behind the door, but it remained closed in our faces. McGoo's expression darkened, hiding his freckles. He was ready to yell and threaten, but I took a different approach. I turned the doorknob, and found it unlocked.

We entered a small reception area, a front room with file cabinets, a water cooler, a credenza with an old coffeemaker, a folding chair, and a reception desk with a phone, a typewriter—yes, an actual typewriter—and a rat man in a lab coat stationed at the desk. He looked up at us with beady, close-set eyes, and his ears pricked up. His lips curled back, and his whiskers twitched. "No visitors! No public tours! Gold Boris's Abattoir has trade secrets."

"We're not here for a tour," I said.

McGoo leered into the rat man's face. "We need some answers about Mystery Meat."

"And missing maggots," I said. "There's a very distraught mother fly looking for her grubs."

"Maggots?" the rat sniffled. "Are you suggesting that our Mystery Meat is contaminated with maggots?" His whiskers twitched in horror. "We have never failed a public health inspection!"

"When was your last one?" McGoo demanded.

The rat man squeaked. "We're a relatively new company. Our Mystery Meat product is fresh on the market. We have patents pending, and secret recipes."

"I'm an officer of the law, and I don't cook," McGoo said. "You can't keep secrets from me. We have a lead on some missing children, and we need to know what you know."

"I know a lot of things." The rodent man sniffed. "I'm a lab rat."

"And a receptionist, I see," I added.

The rat's whiskers twitched again. "I get paid extra. Nothing here in Gold Boris's Abattoir concerns you. We have no involvement with any missing children, maggots, grubs, larvae, or otherwise." His pink nose wiggled. "I despise killing living things. So many rats have been slaughtered over the centuries it makes me shudder!"

Appropriately, he shuddered.

"So many rats have been eaten, murdered in traps, hunted down in the sewers. Thus, I'm a devout vegetarian."

I admitted, "I've been hearing a lot about meat alternatives lately."

"Yes, yes!" The rat man's beady eyes glinted. He rubbed his little paws in front of him. "Gold Boris is changing the world for the better."

"We need to see Mr. Boris," McGoo said. "Ask him some questions."

Behind the receptionist desk, the rat man recoiled. "No, no! That won't be possible. Gold Boris sees no one. He's our trade secret!"

"We're good at keeping secrets," I said.

The rat man turned in a panic, looked toward a set of wide metal doors behind him that led into the industrial bay.

"We'll just go have a look for ourselves," McGoo said, and I shambled beside him toward the doors.

The rat scrambled to block our way. "You need a search warrant."

"I also need a million dollars," McGoo said. "But I can live without it."

When the rat man couldn't stop us, we swung open the set of doors to the back bay. McGoo put a hand on one of his service revolvers. (I wasn't sure which one.) An earthy, savory smell wafted in our faces.

Stepping forward, we entered the abattoir's cavernous bay, and we finally met Gold Boris.

VII

I had expected to find caged, kidnapped maggots. Not this.

One summer vacation when I was a kid, we stayed at a lodge on a lake. I would go out fishing with a can of worms, plucking one of the wriggly critters to impale it on a fishhook. I'd drop a line on a bobber and wait for bluegills to come nibbling. More often than not, they would just eat the worm and leave the hook alone. Then I'd have to repeat the process with another squirmy worm, looping and sticking it on the sharp end of the hook.

The enormous worm that filled the abattoir bay was nothing at all like one of those.

Gold Boris was the size of several freight-train cars hooked together. A pinkish worm with tiny eyes set on the top of his blunt, rounded head. Ringed segments rolled down his long serpentine form which encircled the perimeter of the abattoir's main bay. His round mouth was like the door to a wind tunnel, wide open in an invertebrate expression of surprise. Startled, the worm reared back and pulled away from McGoo and me.

Half a dozen rat men in lab coats squeaked as they rushed to take shelter behind the worm's enormous tail. They all wore thick gloves on their paws, and their lab coats were stained with ichor. They carried sharp axes, machetes, and other ominous cutlery. In the back half of the warehouse bay, meat-processing machinery thrummed.

McGoo gawked. "What the hell is that?" He drew his police special revolver, then yanked out his police extra-special revolver, just to make sure, although he was a lousy shot with his left hand. I drew my .38, and we both crouched in a defensive firing stance.

The worm waved its huge head back and forth like a dancing cobra in front of a snake charmer's flute. "I am Boris," he said in a thick Russian accent. "You can call me Gold Boris, my current nickname."

That defused the tension a little.

"Uh, pleased to meet you, Boris," I said, dropping the tension down another notch, although the sharp implements clutched by the rat men still looked ominous.

The rodent receptionist ran in behind us, squeaking. "You can't see. You can't see! Mystery Meat is a trade secret."

"It's still a mystery to me," I said. I realized the furry little butchers had been cutting off chunks of Boris's long tail, slicing it like a vermiform cucumber.

Gold Boris lowered his huge, rounded head. "You were not supposed to see this. Diners should not witness how sausage is made."

"Or Mystery Meat, apparently," McGoo said.

I was still looking around for Mama Fly's missing larvae. "But… We thought you were kidnapping giant maggots and processing them."

"Maggots?" Boris cried. "Ewww! My Mystery Meat is pure, free range, homegrown, and harvested from my freshest, youngest, and tenderest ring segments."

At the tail end of the huge creature near the meat-processing machinery, the terrified rat men backed away and held up their goo-stained cutting implements. As we watched, the severed end of Boris's tail sprouted a pink new ring segment. It popped out of the raw tip, grew swiftly until it was the size of a life preserver, and was followed by another segment that extruded through the tip.

"As you see," Boris said, "one hundred percent renewable, sustainably produced."

"I'm still confused," McGoo said.

"You're always confused, McGoo, but I'll join you as a partner in confusion."

"Isn't it mythologically obvious?" Boris bobbed and dipped his huge head. "I thought my name would give it away! The modification seemed obvious to me, but perhaps I overestimated how conversant the average person is with classic Gnostic legends."

"Your name? Gold Boris?" I asked. "It's still not clear."

"Oro means gold," the worm said, waiting.

"And Boris? Oro Boris…" I still waited. I glanced at McGoo, but no light bulb went on over his head either.

"Ouroboros!" he said, squirming and wriggling.

"Oh, now I remember," I said. "Ouroboros, the worm that eats its own tail."

The huge creature bobbed his head. "The name was too challenging for most people to say—or spell—so I modernized it, catered to the lowest common denominator. Thus…Ouroboros became Gold Boris."

McGoo took off his cap and scratched his red hair, clearly still confused.

Defensive, the giant worm added, "Lots of famous actors do the same thing when their real names aren't catchy enough, or American enough. Martin Sheen is really Ramón Antonio Gerardo Estévez, and Ricky Martin is Enrique Martín Morales." He leaned closer to us. "Or for an even bigger mouthful, how about Anthony Quinn's original name? Manuel Antonio Rodolfo Quinn Oaxaca!"

"Okay, I get the name change," McGoo said, "but that's the only part I get."

More ring segments sprouted out of the severed tail end, and the worm kept growing longer and longer with alarming rapidity.

"So, you're the mythical worm eating its own tail…" I left the sentence dangling like a worm on a hook.

"Like sucking on a thumb! Disgusting habit!" Boris said. "But I finally broke myself of it, pulled the tail out of my mouth, and never touched it again." A shudder rippled through the whole serpentine body. "But once I unrolled myself and stopped devouring my own tail, the tail just kept growing and growing! Something had to be done about it.

"Yes, I was biased, but I thought that the taste of my tail meat was delicious, almost addictive. So I stopped always grabbing a piece of tail, and instead I decided to make the world a better place. I hired assistants with similar mindsets, rat men who wanted to stop the environmentally damaging and inhumane practice of raising large animals for meat, and we set up shop here. Those soy substitutes taste terrible—but not my Mystery Meat! It's real meat, solid protein, humanely harvested, and voluntarily given."

And I'd eaten one of those steaks yesterday. My stomach churned, even though I told myself it wasn't any more gross than eating a hot dog.

At the rear of the abattoir bay, the tail segment kept growing. The rat men by the processing machinery began to grow nervous. "We need to keep harvesting, boss, or we'll fall behind."

"Indeed!" Boris bobbed his huge head. "Get back to it. We have orders to deliver."

"I see why it's a trade secret." McGoo looked at me and shrugged.

I shrugged back. "I'll check with Robin on the legal issues, but I don't think they're doing anything against the law."

"I can give you free samples," Boris said. "Enough to fill your freezer."

"No thanks," we said in unison.

The rodent receptionist squeaked. "You can't reveal this! No one can know the source of Mystery Meat! Otherwise, we'll have competitors springing up out of the ground like nightcrawlers after a rainstorm."

The rat crew began slicing and dicing the fast-growing end of Gold Boris's tail.

"That still doesn't help us find the missing maggots," I said. "What are we going to tell Mama Fly?"

"No maggots here," said the worm. "We run a clean processing plant."

VIII

As we left the abattoir, the flickering neon sign gave McGoo's face a strange and sickly pallor, much like my own. "There's no more mystery to the Mystery Meat, Shamble," he said. "But that doesn't help us find the missing maggots."

We walked away from the abattoir, facing the vast Dumpster Row and its hundreds of dark garbage containers. The complex had no security lights, since the chances of dumpster robbery were low. Staring at the countless rows, I couldn't imagine what frisky young maggots found so enticing about the place.

Unexpectedly, Sheyenne's spectral form swooped in front of us with a faint blue glow. "Anything to report to Mama Fly? She's getting really anxious. What about Gold Boris?"

"Now, that's a long story," I said.

McGoo grinned. "Better yet, it's a long *tail*."

"Don't make me any more queasy than I already am, McGoo."

Across the eerily silent dumpster park, I heard the usual restless skittering, intermittently accompanied by the rhythmic thumping from before. Maybe some young scavenger demon was practicing on a drum kit. The banging increased, and it seemed to have a frantic undertone.

Sheyenne perked up. "That doesn't sound right. Isn't this where Mama Fly's grubs liked to play?"

"Maybe somebody needs help out there among all the dumpsters," I said.

McGoo regarded the endless collection of garbage containers. "How do we know which one? That'll be like finding a needle in a haystack."

"Or a maggot in a dumpster farm."

"We'll have to search row by row," Sheyenne said in a determined voice, and she flitted ahead.

I looked at McGoo. "How long could it take? There's only a thousand or so of them."

We split up, and I shambled down one row while McGoo headed along another. Unburdened by a physical form, my poltergeist girlfriend was able to cover more territory.

The urgent pounding echoed off the other containers, confusing the sound. I reached the end of one row and doubled back down the next one, but I didn't seem to be getting any closer. McGoo pounded on a dumpster, waiting for a response like some trashy game of Marco Polo.

Sheyenne circled overhead, listening closely. The thumping grew louder, more desperate. I was sure we were on to something.

I went to the next row. Maybe I was getting closer. Sheyenne drifted next to me. "I think it's…"

The thumping increased.

I yelled, "I think it's over here, McGoo!"

Trying to locate the source of the sound, Sheyenne flitted ahead and called out, "This one! Here's the dumpster we've been looking for."

McGoo and I reached it at the same time. The heavy lid had fallen shut and the latch bar clicked into place, but something inside was pounding—trapped. Hearing our voices, the banging increased.

Sheyenne hovered above the container while McGoo and I worked together to wrench open the metal bar that locked the heavy lid shut. We finally got it free and heaved up the lid.

As soon as we raised it, maggots boiled out. It was like turning over a ripe rotting corpse, except in this case the maggots were the size of thick pool noodles. They swayed, eyeless and frantic, their tiny mouths puckering and unpuckering in expressions of excitement, gratitude, and relief.

"We're saved, we're saved!" the maggots squeaked as they sprang out of the dumpster.

Sheyenne tried to be reassuring. "There, there, you're safe. We'll get you back to your Mama Fly."

"What were you doing in there?" I asked.

"Just playing like always," said one of the maggots. "We built a fort in our favorite dumpster, but then the lid fell shut, and we were locked inside. We couldn't move the latch."

"Dumpsters aren't designed with emergency exits," McGoo said. "Not even for unfortunate young maggots."

One grub wailed, "We didn't think we'd ever be rescued!"

"We've been trapped in there for days," said another larva.

A third said, "Mama Fly told us we had to get home early before it's time to pupate."

"We're gonna get a whupping!"

The grubs waved back and forth, bowing their heads. I think they were crying, but it was hard to tell, since maggots have no facial features. I couldn't identify them from the pictures on the MISSING posters, but I was pretty sure these were the ones we were looking for.

"Come on, squirm after us." I gestured as I set off with McGoo and Sheyenne. "We'll get you home."

IX

Mama Fly was buzzing with joy when she returned to our offices a few days later. She was glad to have the case solved, of course, and she was also eager to write us a check for our fee. It's not often a client is so quick to pay their bills, but Mama Fly insisted that she wanted to settle up.

She entered the office, still wearing the polka-dotted head scarf. In her top sets of limbs, she cradled four capsule-shaped bundles, each wrapped in a baby blanket. "As you can see, my babies safely entered their pupae, thanks to you."

Alvina came bouncing out, smiling. "They look so cute. Can I hold them?"

At first Mama Fly flinched, but then handed over the fuzzy cocoon and blanket. The little vampire girl rocked the pupa back and forth and sang an off-key lullaby; Mama Fly rocked the other pupae in time.

Robin was satisfied, as she always was upon successfully closing a case file. "I'm sure they'll grow up to be strong, young houseflies," she said.

Mama Fly seemed to be in a hurry. "I just had my retirement party today at the manure pile." Before long she took the other cocoon back and turned about, thanking us again before she left.

I smiled along with Alvina, Sheyenne, and Robin. I waved as Mama Fly took her leave. "See ya around."

She swiveled her head and regarded us with her large compound eyes. "Not likely." Her proboscis extended and retracted. "Two-week lifecycle, remember?"

She flitted off. I was glad to know that the rest of her brief lifespan would be a happy one.

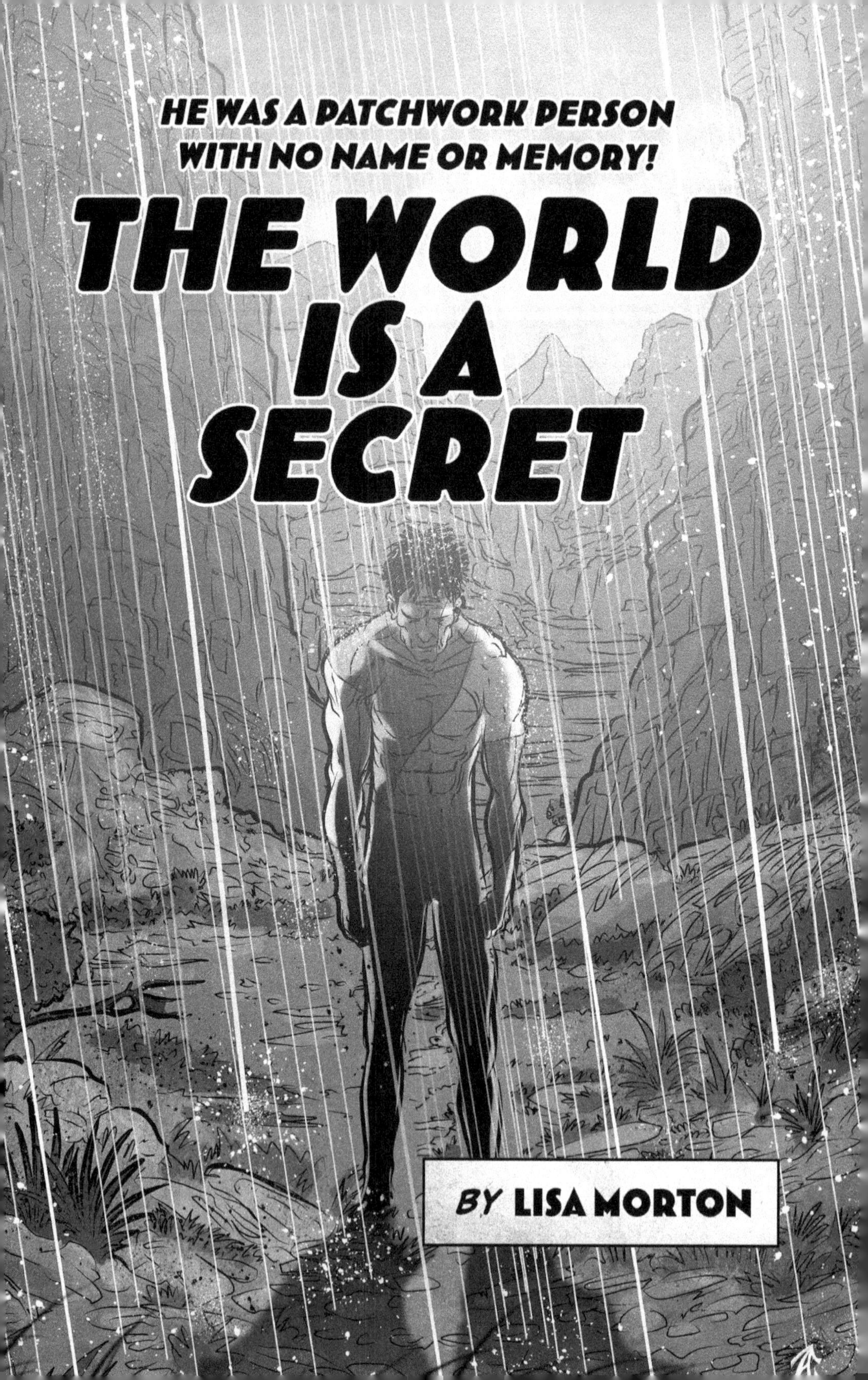
HE WAS A PATCHWORK PERSON
WITH NO NAME OR MEMORY!
THE WORLD IS A SECRET
BY LISA MORTON

LOS ANGELES, JANUARY 1972.

It was about 3:30 a.m. when I came staggering up out of the garbage-filled canyon on a rainy Los Angeles night.

I don't remember this; it's just what I was told afterward. I was spotted by some passing motorist as I clambered over the edge of Mulholland Drive, covered in dried blood and pieces of trash, stark naked. I fell onto the pavement; the driver called the police when they got home. I was found thirty minutes later, barely alive when they rushed me to a hospital.

My memory starts there, when I came to three days later. A nurse saw me open my eyes and she ran from the room, squealing. Two minutes later, I had my first meeting with handsome Dr. Singh, who filled me in on where I was and how I'd gotten there.

Then the questions started. What was my name? What did I remember? How had I wound up sans clothing in the bottom of Benedict Canyon?

I had no answers. I remembered nothing.

Twenty minutes later, the doctor was joined by a detective named Luanne Jeffries. Detective Jeffries was a veteran cop who was like something out of a gender-flipped Chandler novel: probably younger than she appeared, but her brow had been creased in worry for so long that it looked like it belonged to an eighty year old. She wore a dark blue pants suit, a rumpled white shirt, and functional flat shoes. Her hair was going gray and had been cut in a short Afro; she was trim in a way that made me guess she was a runner. She peered at me as if she'd just paid a quarter to enter a circus tent.

No, I repeated; I didn't know my name. I couldn't remember who I was or what had happened to me.

"So," Jeffries said, "you can't tell me why your fingerprints match a guy who was dead in the county morgue a month ago?"

"No," I answered, staring at my hands. They were big, meaty, strong. I turned them from side to side, hoping the action might spark off some shred of recall, but nothing came.

When I looked back, the detective and the doctor exchanged a whisper before they both turned to stare at me wordlessly. After a few seconds, I asked, "What?"

Jeffries asked, "I suppose you can't explain your legs, either?"

I glanced down, saw my lower half was currently covered by a hospital gown and a starched sheet. There were tubes running under the sheet, as well as the IV in my left arm.

Doctor Singh stepped forward and grasped the top edge of the sheet. "Maybe you just need to see for yourself."

He pulled the sheet back, and whatever I'd been expecting—terrible mutilation, even a missing part—I hadn't been prepared for *this*.

My legs didn't match. As in, not even close. One was thick, brown, defined—the leg of an athlete. The other was slender, pink, and at least three inches shorter than its counterpart. There were scars around the top of each leg where they joined my differently hued torso.

I was too stunned to speak. I reached down to touch each leg, but I couldn't feel the sensation. I ran my hands up from there—

I stopped in alarm, not because I had a catheter, but rather what the catheter was inserted into. I couldn't feel my penis.

Something was incredibly wrong with that, even more wrong than my mismatched legs, but I knew I'd have to deal with that later because right now my visitors turned away in embarrassment as I ran my fingers between my legs. I pulled the hospital gown down and the sheet back up, explaining, "I don't have any sensation in my…down there." I realized then that, at least there, *none* of me felt anything, although the good side of that (if there was one) was that I had no pain.

"Oh," said Singh. "Frankly, we don't know *what's* going on with you. We were hoping you could tell us."

I ground my teeth, thought hard, but my head was just blank. Basic skills—movement, language—were in place, but *I* wasn't. "What was that you were saying about fingerprints?"

Jeffries paused to pull a little notepad out of a jacket pocket. She flipped through a few pages until she found what she was looking for. "When you came in without ID, you agreed to let us run your fingerprints. Do you remember that?"

I shook my head. "No."

"We were hoping to find out who you were. Your prints matched one Manuel Sosa, a minor-league prizefighter from Boyle Heights who was shot to death last month in a gang rumble. Where it gets even stranger is that when we pulled Sosa's mug shot and stats...well, the guy was six-foot-two with a face that looked like it was carved from hamburger meat."

"Not me?"

Doctor Singh went to a side table, pulled open a drawer, came back to give me a handheld plastic mirror. I looked into it, hoping a face—that most intrinsic part of us, that defines so much of who we are—would jog something. I was mildly surprised to see I was young, with the features and complexion of a Pacific Islander, fairly good-looking despite a few bruises I probably got from climbing through two hundred feet of scrub to get out of that canyon. My head looked as if it had been shaved, the dark hair just starting to grow back.

Moving the mirror down, I got another shock: halfway down my neck, I had a series of livid pink scars, and the skin of my torso was a distinctly different color, the lighter tan of my thick boxers' hands.

"I don't understand," I muttered, staring at myself in the cheap pink-rimmed mirror.

"We should form a club," Jeffries responded.

+

The next few days saw me working with nurses, doctors, and physical therapists to get back on my feet; I focused on regaining strength while they eyed me sidewise with no small amount of discomfort. Because one leg was significantly shorter than the other, a special boot was made for me; soon, I was making Quasimodo jokes with the nurses but walking well enough.

At night, I had dreams with flashes of…pushing aside stinking garbage, a coyote's eyes glowing from a cactus patch, stumbling past a small fleet of rusting wrecked cars, grasping at roots and branches to pull myself up a rocky slope covered in sagebrush until there was level asphalt beneath me… In other words, I still remembered nothing before waking up in that canyon.

I also found other parts of my body that didn't work well. I had no hearing in my left ear; I couldn't move my left thumb; and no matter how many times or where I was poked with needles (frequently), there was no pain.

When my doctors thought I was up to it, the parade of physicians, psychiatrists, cops, and social workers began. There were professors from local universities who wanted to study me. There were psychologists who wanted to help me remember. There were people from the city with programs they claimed would assist in my recovery. Thankfully, the hospital staff kept me out of the papers so I didn't have to deal with press or lookie-loos. Because by now it had become apparent that I was a…well, let's use "anomaly" instead of "freak."

Doctor Singh knew I'd been through a variety of surgeries before I'd arrived in his hospital, but he couldn't explain why nothing matched but mostly worked. When I asked, he wouldn't even speculate. "It's too crazy," he'd say. But we both knew the truth:

I was a patchwork person, created from parts in a way that was impossibly advanced from modern medical science.

A monster, in other words.

My savior was a doctor named Armand Balakian, who headed the Southern California Biomedical Research Institute at UCW. He was a tall, slender man in his fifties with wavy gray hair and a kind face; he could arrange financing and a place to live in return for allowing his group to study me. I wouldn't be forced to do anything I didn't agree to, and if they learned anything from me, it could be used to help others.

A few days later, I left the hospital and moved into a one-bedroom apartment in West L.A., near the university. I was given an identity: I chose the name Thomas Quinn, although I wasn't sure why.

I was sure of one thing, though: I was going to find out who had done this to me, and what I was, and *why*. We all ask those questions at some point, but they obsessed me. Why was I monstrous? Why did parts of me not work? Who was I really? Was I more or less than the sum of my parts? Why had I apparently been abandoned by my creator, thrown out like particularly odious trash?

Dr. Balakian and his team began their tests. I was poked and prodded and X-rayed and scanned. I gave samples. I answered questions. I took tests. I turned out to have a surprisingly high IQ and I could write essays about literary classics. I just couldn't remember why.

Detective Jeffries proved a surprisingly sympathetic ally. I think she felt like an outsider—a visit to the station where she worked proved that LAPD wasn't exactly overrun with non-white women—so she was willing to help. She wasn't quite sure how to approach my case since I hadn't committed a crime and it was unclear what exactly had been done *to* me. "Officially, I've got a half-dozen other homicide cases I have to work on, but…unofficially…"

We already knew Manuel Sosa had provided my fingerprints; the next thing Jeffries turned up was my face. She asked me to come see her one day; I took a taxi to the station, curious. On the way to downtown, the taxi's radio station played "Riders on the Storm" by The Doors, and I realized I could sing along to it. How was it possible that I knew the lyrics to a song but not my own name? Our minds are strange and confounding miracles.

I arrived at the station, found Detective Jeffries at her desk, and stared in shock when she set an arrest record in front of me.

It belonged to a man named Philip Juan Bautista, a Filipino hustler who'd been in the U.S. illegally and had been stabbed by a client during an altercation over money.

The face in the mug shot was mine.

"So I'm…" I stopped to read the name again. "Philip Juan Bautista?"

Jeffries answered, "Or at least you've got his head."

Something felt wrong. It took me a few seconds of scanning the pages Jeffries had set in front of me before I figured it out. "Bautista was Filipino, right?"

"Right," the detective answered.

I pointed out something in the case file. "It says here he'd only been in Los Angeles about a month."

"Okay," she said, not yet following.

"Did he speak English?"

She got it. "Oh Christ…" She glanced up, saw a man working at the next desk over, his jacket off, tie loosened, cigarette clamped between his lips, laboriously typing with two fingers.

"Al," she called.

He didn't turn. "Yeah, Lu?"

"You handled that case of the Filipino gigolo, right? About two months ago, kid was nineteen and stabbed to death?"

"Yeah—" He spun in his chair, saw me, and froze, his mouth half-open. "What the fuck is this, a twin brother?"

"Seems so," Jeffries said, then asked, "Al, did that kid speak English?"

The other detective shrugged. "His clients said he knew how to talk sex in English, but beyond that he only spoke Tagalog. Why?"

"I'll tell you later," Jeffries said, before turning to look at me, eyebrows raised.

"I don't know a word of Tagalog," I said.

"Soooooo…" Jeffries was apparently unable to finish.

"Somebody else's brain is stuck inside Philip Juan Bautista's pretty head."

Jeffries slumped back in her chair. "Jesus Christ." After a few seconds, she looked at me. "And you still don't remember anything?"

"Not really, although I turned out to be surprisingly good at the literature section of an SAT test. I also love to read."

She sighed before saying, in a low voice, "Okay, let me dig a little more. I'll get back to you."

"Thank you." I got up to leave.

Behind me, I heard Detective Al call out, "Nobody ever said anything to me about Bautista having an identical twin."

The tests continued at the university. Dr. Balakian was a compassionate patron, always asking about my well-being, both inside and out of his clinic. He made sure I had his private office phone, told me to call anytime.

One day a new lab assistant appeared, a young man named Adam. He was absurdly perfect looking—hair, face, body, the entire package. He seemed oddly naïve, rarely speaking and even then in a soft voice, and not entirely educated in the ways of medicine, but he was an eager learner and charismatic. I asked Dr. Balakian about him one day, and the doctor chuckled slightly. "He's a relative— my nephew." Adam did have Balakian's soft brown hair and light olive-hued skin, but something about Adam stuck in my thoughts, something I couldn't identify, something neither uncomfortable nor worrisome, but…strange.

It was the least of my mysteries to be solved.

Two nights later, there was a knock at my apartment door, which I opened to reveal Detective Jeffries. "Sorry, I probably should have called first, but"—she gestured with a plastic bag dangling from one wrist—"well, you need to see this but not at the station."

I invited her in. She quickly scanned my sparsely furnished apartment (a long-honed professional skill, no doubt), pulled a manila folder out of the plastic bag, said, "You should probably sit down first."

I did. So did she, placing the folder before me on my scarred coffee table. "Working from the assumption that your—uh, *parts* were all acquired from the county morgue about two months ago, I did some digging through their records to see if anyone might have come in about the same time who had a higher-than-average IQ and a literary background."

My heart sped up. "And you got a match?"

She nodded, then looked me in the eye and said, "But it might not be who you think…"

She flipped open the folder and I looked down at an autopsy report. It was for an English professor who had died in a car accident two months ago.

It was a woman. Her name was Dr. Quinn Schechter.

It was me.

Thomas Quinn/Quinn Schechter.

"Are you okay?"

I felt as if every neuron in my brain—Quinn's brain—fired at once, creating an explosion of awareness. It wasn't that memories were unblocked and flooded me, but rather a sense of *myself* I'd been missing was restored in that single second. I knew why I'd never felt at home in this body, even beyond its obvious flaws and failings. "I'm...sorry; it's a lot to take in."

Jeffries started to reach out a reassuring hand, but pulled it back. "I've got to go," she said, rising. "That's a copy you can keep, but...well, *I* didn't give that to you. And I can't work on this anymore. My captain is riding my ass about letting the other cases pile up; my position in the department is already precarious enough..."

"I understand." I stood, walking her to the door. "I'm so grateful for what you've done. I really can't thank you enough."

At the door, she wished me good luck and left.

It was up to me to solve my own mysteries.

I read the autopsy report carefully, feeling each new line of information lock into my consciousness like a key that fit perfectly into a lock. Quinn Schechter had been thirty-five years of age. She had a spouse named Thomas Schechter (Thomas—of course). There was an address in West L.A., maybe ten minutes from where I was now.

Thomas Schechter. Her husband.

My husband.

It was 8 p.m., not late. I called a cab.

At 8:15, I stood before a small house on a quiet side street. It had a magnolia tree in the front yard, standing sentinel over a green lawn, and a row of dying roses that made me sad.

My roses. Dying now that I was no longer there to tend them.

The house itself was a classic California bungalow, painted light tan with dark blue trim. Two bedrooms. Probably built about twenty-five years ago, during the postwar housing boom.

I didn't remember it. The withered roses provoked a sense of melancholy, but nothing else.

I took a deep breath and walked up the concrete walk to the front door, painted a matching navy hue. I rang the doorbell.

After a few seconds, a man answered.

My vision went supernova—then shrank back, still denying me recognition. I *felt* the man who answered the door, but I didn't *know* him.

"Yes?"

I had no idea what to say. He was mid-thirties, short brown hair, glasses... I didn't know what he did for a living, but I could imagine him being that cute college professor that new students fantasized about. "Mr. Schechter?"

"Yes?" he said, eyeing me warily. I had to remind myself that he saw a young Filipino man with large, heavily knuckled paws.

I wanted to tell him I was Quinn, his wife; I wanted to tell him I was still here, trapped in this body...but I knew I couldn't. After a few silent seconds, I came up with what I hoped was a plausible fabrication: "My name is Thomas Quinn, and I'm a private investigator who has been hired to look into your wife's death."

"Hired by whom?"

Time froze. I stared at him, this man who had been/was my husband. My brain didn't remember him, but I felt connected to him on some deeper level; if my body had been capable of responding, it would have. But it was a body I was trapped in, one at odds with its own controller...and probably with Tom Schechter, who gazed at me now with uncomprehending eyes.

"Someone she worked with," I blurted out.

Tom snorted and looked away, angry. "That's a laugh. Someone she worked with is probably who got her killed."

"*Killed?* Not just a random car accident?"

He shook his head emphatically. "No. No. Look, I told the police this already, but...the night before she died, Quinn came home from work upset about something. She wouldn't tell me exactly what it was, but...well, she didn't get angry easily, and she was *really* upset that night. All she told me was that somebody at school said something really bad. She said she'd explain it all later, but—she was dead the next day, so there was no *later*."

Instinct wanted me to pull him into my arms, but of course I couldn't, not now. "She didn't give you any idea what was going on?"

He shook his head, biting his lip. "No."

"Are you suggesting that the car accident was a homicide?"

Tom looked away, jaw muscles knotting. "Quinn was a careful driver. That night of the accident...well, there was no reason for the car to spin out like that. She'd driven that section of Sunset a thousand times. Hell, it wasn't even raining that night."

An image—or rather a series of images—ran through my head: a car accident, a car spinning out between the mansions that lined Sunset; a corpse arriving at the L.A. County Morgue; an autopsy, then a secret visitor who took the brain via a few perfectly placed payoffs...

"Uhhh...are you okay?" Tom was looking at me with concern...and I wondered if there was some recognition there, something he felt on a deep, even cellular, level.

But, despite that connection I could think of only as "spiritual"...no memories were revealed, no dam of pent-up recollection was cracked. I wanted to be able to tell him about a special shared moment—a laugh, a kiss, even an argument—but nothing was there.

"Sorry," I said, "it's just that...I knew Quinn. Not well, but... I'm sorry she's gone."

Tom didn't respond, just looked at me strangely. I excused myself and fled. The taxi was still there, waiting.

I was glad the driver didn't ask why I was crying in the back seat.

Next stop: the morgue.

Whoever made me had gotten my parts from the county morgue, so they either worked there or were paying off somebody who worked there to let them know about new arrivals. I started with a trip to the downtown public library, where I researched the morgue's recent history. Thomas Noguchi, the Chief Medical Examiner-Coroner for L.A., had been the subject of a lot of controversy and wasn't thought of highly by many peers, so he seemed unlikely to be a secret mad genius capable of restoring life to the dead. After some more reading, I ruled out the possibility of anyone working at the morgue being my maker.

That left someone there who was selling information.

I couldn't go back to Jeffries—at least not yet—so I'd have to figure this out on my own. I knew I couldn't just walk into a county morgue, so I thought about it for a few days.

I'd seen Dr. Balakian give a few press interviews, and I thought I could pass for a reporter. Bautista's face was charming enough to possibly open some doors; I even practiced with it in a mirror, trying to master the ingratiating smile.

I had some fake business cards printed: they read only "Thomas Quinn—Journalist" and my home phone. I had one nice shirt and jacket.

When I was ready, I took a cab downtown. I didn't have the cab wait this time; if this went well, I'd be there a while.

The cab left me in front of a red and tan brick building with a façade that came from another time. I strode up the flight of steps (moving cautiously, since the boot made me clumsy), pushed through the glass doors, and found myself in a reception area with marble walls, tiled floors, dark wooden stairs leading up, and red leather couches. A door to the side led into a small front office;

I entered, found a middle-aged woman sitting behind a counter, typing.

She peered up at me through tortoiseshell glasses perched beneath a bad perm. "May I help you?"

"I hope so." Trying to look as experienced as possible, I whipped out one of the business cards I'd stashed in my jacket pocket. "My name is Thomas Quinn, and I'm a journalist working on a story for *Pacific West* magazine."

She glanced at the card, plainly unimpressed, before setting it aside to focus on whatever she was typing up. "Never heard of it. Sorry, but we can't talk about ongoing cases."

"Oh, I'm not writing about a case. I'm working on a human interest piece about the people who work in a county morgue."

I saw a flicker of interest in her eyes. "Really? Well, that's new."

With what I hoped was my most winning smile, I said, "That's what I'm hoping for. I would imagine it must take a pretty special type of person to work here."

She chuckled and then murmured, "You don't know the half of it."

"I'd like to."

She gave me a long hard look before saying, "You should talk to Jeremy."

"Jeremy?"

"Works the late shift. He's not a doctor, just an intern, but he loves to talk."

"Great. How do I talk to him?"

She glanced at her wristwatch. "He'll be coming on in two hours. Can you come back then?"

I thanked her, told her I'd be back, found a nearby diner, and settled in with a tuna sandwich and coffee.

Two hours later, the sun was just setting. When I entered, I saw a kid who couldn't have been more than twenty-two or -three, long face still covered in acne, with a haircut that looked like he'd done it himself, chatting with the woman in the front office. As she saw me, she pointed and the kid strode up with a big grin.

"Hey," I said, extending a hand, "you must be Jeremy."

The kid took the hand, shook it too hard, like he didn't understand how handshakes worked; then he stopped and looked at me strangely. "Have we met?"

Oh, damn—it hadn't occurred to me that he might be smart enough to remember my face. "No," I said, gambling he wasn't, "I don't think so."

He peered for a second longer before shaking his head. "Weird. So Stella says you're doing a magazine story..."

"I am. Is there someplace we can talk?"

"Sure."

The kid led the way up the stairs. At the top a door opened onto a long hallway—and the smell hit me first. Jeremy must've seen my reaction because he laughed. "Hey, it's only February; try being here in July. You can never get rid of that smell, no matter how many showers you take. But you get used to it."

I couldn't imagine *ever* getting used to that. Jeremy led the way to a door that opened onto a small conference room, with a long table surrounded by chairs; the windows on one wall looked out over L.A. as the sun set behind it. Jeremy threw himself down into a chair like he owned the place, and I noticed that he wore a big, shiny gold chain over his dull green scrubs.

"So," he said, "ask me some questions."

I sat, pulled out a notepad and pen, and realized that I hadn't completely thought this through. What was I going to ask? "Have you taken money from a mad doctor who wants body parts?" probably wasn't my best starting point.

"Okay," I ventured, "how long have you worked at the morgue, Jeremy?"

"Six months."

"Like it?"

"Sure. Especially right now."

I looked up at him. "Why is that?"

"I just got back from the best vacation of my life. Went to Hawaii. It was so *cosmic.*"

Hawaii? How could this kid afford a trip like that? Was it possible I'd gotten lucky right off the bat? I was certainly owed some good fortune, I thought. "Go by yourself?"

"Yeah, although I wasn't by myself for most of the time I was over there, if you know what I mean."

I nodded knowingly, although I wanted to gag. "Sounds expensive."

"Oh, it was, but my Uncle Bill just died and left me a nice inheritance."

"Uh-huh." I pretended to make some notes, and then pointed at the chain. "The inheritance buy you that nice jewelry, too?"

He looked down at the chain, then back up proudly. "Oh, yeah. Pretty cool, huh?"

"Sure is." It was time to escalate. "Uncle Bob must've been well off."

"He was."

Jeremy hadn't caught it. He couldn't even keep his lies straight. *It's this stupid kid, who should've spent some of that money on a decent haircut.* I had him.

I closed the notepad, set down the pen, and walked over to check the door. It didn't have a lock inside. I'd have to risk it.

"What's going on?" he asked.

I perched on the edge of the table beside him, tried to make myself seem as big as possible. "Jeremy, I know where you really got that money."

"Oh." I saw a flash of panic in his eyes before he recovered and said, "Did you know Uncle Bob?"

"You said his name was Uncle Bill."

"No, I didn't."

I leaned down close, sticking Philip Juan Bautista's face right into his. "Remember this face?"

"I thought you said we hadn't..." He remembered, went pale. "Oh *shit*."

I pulled down my collar so he could see the scars surrounding the base of my neck. "See these? The man you've been selling parts to has been putting them to some really strange use."

Jeremy looked like his eyes were going to pop out of his head. "Oh, c'mon, that...can't..."

Holding my hands up, I said, "See these? *You* sold him these hands. They belonged to a boxer, Jeremy. A *boxer*."

He tried to jump up and run for it. Those same hands grabbed him by the collar and threw him back into the chair. "You're going to tell me his name, or I'm going to turn you over to my friends at the LAPD and let them get it out of you."

"I can't!" He held up his hands, as if warding off a blow I wasn't even sure I could deliver. I was a teacher, not a fighter. But all I had to do was convince this kid that I could throw a piledriver punch.

Balling up my fist, I asked, "Why not?"

"Because I don't know it! I don't know his name!"

I lowered my hands, trying to keep him talking. "What *do* you know?"

"I've got a phone number—the one he gave me to call him whenever he came in. He always wore a hat, glasses, a surgical mask, so I'm not even sure what he looked like."

I pushed my notepad and pen across the table to him. "Write down the number."

He did, pushed the pad back.

My heart—whosever it was—nearly stopped when I saw the number. I knew it well. Jeremy must have seen something in my expression because he said, "Look, I'm really sorry. I didn't know what he was doing. I thought…"

"Never mind." I stuffed my pad and pen back in a pocket as I said, "Look, I'll make a deal with you: you don't call him now to warn him, I won't tell him how I got his number, and we'll just forget this whole thing ever happened."

He nodded frantically. "Deal. Yeah. Thanks, man."

That last word rang in my ears as I left.

Twenty minutes later, I stood in Doctor Balakian's office. When he entered, I said, "Hello…father."

He peered at me, feigning perplexity. "What's that, Thomas?"

"You should probably call me Professor Schechter."

His eyes widened in surprise as he nodded. "So your memories returned."

"No, they haven't; I figured things out without them. Whatever you did to that part of my brain worked. Just tell me: did you usually call me Professor Schechter or Quinn?"

Balakian looked genuinely hurt for a moment before saying, eyes averted, "I really did care for you, Quinn. I told you that the night before the accident—but I swear I had nothing to do with that. In fact, I wanted to save you after."

Anger rushed through me; at least he hadn't turned off *that*. "So you stuck me together with these pieces that don't quite fit or work, and then tossed me into a canyon? You've got a strange definition of *saving* someone."

"I thought I'd failed—that I hadn't restored life to you. It shouldn't have been possible for you to come back. Quinn, I'm so sorry. Believe me, I was heartbroken. Let me make it up to you; we'll continue to work, find a new body for you, make you the first perfect human being—"

Another voice spoke behind me: "You said *I* was perfect."

I turned to see Adam, Balakian's beautiful "nephew"…and I knew.

Balakian tried to smile but couldn't. "Adam. Yes, of course, you are perfect…"

Adam held up his left arm, pulling the sleeve back, revealing that his wrist had turned an awful purplish-blue hue, which was clearly spreading up his arm. "Then what is *this*?"

Balakian stumbled forward, holding up his hands. "We'll fix that, Adam—"

"He won't." I turned directly to the unfortunate creature—my brother, I suppose. "He won't fix it, Adam, because he can't. He's brilliant, but not brilliant enough."

Rage fired in Adam's eyes. He uttered an incoherent cry and leapt forward at Balakian. As his hands closed around his maker's throat, I turned and left the room.

That was a month ago.

Detective Jeffries got Balakian's homicide. I told her what happened. Adam disappeared after slaying his creator. My guess is that he ran until he fell apart somewhere. I hope he was as pain-free as I am.

As for me…I'm not dissolving—at least not yet. The parts Balakian didn't bother to fix—the ability to feel pain, the thing between my legs, the memories—still don't work and never will, but I've accepted that and I'm moving on. Balakian's institute has helped me enroll in UCW, majoring in English. I may not have Quinn Schechter's memories, but I think I have her love of literature. I doubt I will ever feel truly at home in this body; I hope things will change in the future.

I've thought about going back to see Thomas again, imagining that we might be friends…but I know it will never happen.

I'm not really Quinn, after all. There's some of her in me, but I'm me—Thomas Quinn. I'm not a monster; I'm a human being, with a life to live.

It's time for me to start making my own memories.

DEAD TO ME

A MONK ADDISON ADVENTURE

BY JONATHAN MABERRY

I died twice.

Didn't take.

2

I was halfway through the crossword puzzle, doing it in pencil because I'm not an officious dick. God only knows how many cups of coffee—my eyes were jumpy, and I think I was hearing colors. They had some goofy-ass Christmas radio station playing. I was trying to shut out any reference to Mommy kissing Santa, for fuck's sake. And I was in no mood to rock around anyone's Christmas tree.

Last two weeks were ass-kickers. Three bail skips in three different towns across two counties. One was a biker—one of the Cyke-lones who spend so much of their free time being world-class dicks, and all their work time running fentanyl from Miami to Philly along I-95. Local cop nabbed him for running a red light and doing sixty-five in a thirty-five residential zone. If he'd kept his mouth shut and just took the ticket, he'd still be a free man. Instead, he mouthed off to the cop, who was a woman. When she pushed back, he shoved her. All 275 pounds of him. Downside of that story was she wasn't taking shit that day and showed him how a Taser works. He skipped his court date, and when I found him, he wanted to try me, too.

I'm 240, none of it fat. One of my exes told me I look like a cranky silverback. She isn't wrong. So no, I wouldn't mess with me either. He did, and now he's in Northeastern Hospital waiting for his release so he can start physical therapy.

Second guy was less violent, but thought he was smart. Crooks are seldom smart, and those who skip out on a court bond are demonstrably stupid. He started crying as soon as he opened his front door and saw me.

The third guy was a wife beater, and when he went missing, I knew where to find him. Sitting in his wife's car, hoping to continue the conversation that local PD had interrupted. The wife's bruises were nearly healed, but she was doing therapy three times a week and looked like she hadn't slept all year.

Only thing is, it wasn't her who opened her car door. Nice, remote parking lot. No witnesses, which was his pick. Worked for me, too. I think it's fucking hilarious that he's in the room next to biker guy. Maybe they'll have wheelchair races.

So, I was beat and not looking for work or fishing for trouble.

The chief of police there in Pine Deep, Pennsylvania, slid into my booth. He wasn't smiling, which is not a good thing because he's one of those happy guys who laughs at everything. Wasn't laughing now, though.

"No," I said.

"Hello to you, too, Monk."

"Look, Crow," I said, "I am off the clock. I am so off the clock that I wouldn't trace a bail skip if he was sitting at the next table."

We were in the back corner of the Scarecrow Diner.

Crow placed a folder on the table and slid it across to me.

"No," I said.

"Just take a look."

"Not a chance."

"Monk, this is a bad one. Just take a look."

"No," I insisted.

He reached across and flipped it open. The top picture was the kind you never want to see. Ever. And I have seen some shit.

Seeing that photo meant he wasn't here about a bail skip. This was him asking me to do my *other* job. The one I do well but don't like doing. No, scratch that. It's the job I absolutely hate. He took a small glass vial from his pocket and stood it next to the folder. There was a dark reddish sludge in it—flakes of dried blood floating in holy water.

"No," I said.

But we both knew I meant yes.

3

"What's her name?" asked Patty.

She's a little Vietnamese woman who weighs about as much as my shadow. Her eyes are about a thousand frigging years older than the face they're in. Hard grief lines cut around her mouth and between her brows. She had a little girl's face tattooed on the back of her left hand. She drilled that ink after some bad men in 'Nam took her child away and ruined her in every terrible way you can imagine. Left her dead in the dirt like trash. I found them and did what I do, but it didn't—couldn't—bring her back.

We bonded over the whole long, sad, awful time. Sometimes we go to bed together, mostly we don't. We drink, we get high, we cry a bit. There's no definition for what Patty Cakes and I have. Friendship doesn't say it right, and family isn't it, either. Crow calls it being Children of the Storm Lands. People who are connected by the intensity of what they've suffered and who somehow manage to keep hold of their empathy. He's weirdly sentimental and philosophical for a small-town police chief, but he's not wrong.

I was in the middle chair in Patty's tattoo parlor, watching as she mixed the blood with black ink.

"Kristin Howell," I said. "Eleven going on never grow up."

"It was bad?"

"Worse than bad."

She turned and gave me a long, flat stare that was as hard, as uncompromising—and as fragile—as ice.

"You'll find him," she said.

"Yes, I will."

The reference photo I gave her wasn't the one Crow first showed me. This one was of her smiling. Taken last Christmas. When she thought monsters were something in the movies.

"Take your shirt off," she said as she finished her alchemy with the ink.

To this day I still don't understand how it works. Neither does Patty. We've figured it all out over the years. The process sounds simple—blood from a crime scene where someone died mixed with ink Patty has imported from back home in Tuyên Quang. She does the faces in black and white. Her style is photo-real. She leaves one section, maybe a line, unfinished until she's satisfied with the face. Then she does that last bit.

Then it hits me.

Hard.

Like a cruise missile directly to the brainpan. As soon as the art is done, I feel it and see it and *am* it. I relive the last few minutes of the victim's death. I see what they saw and hear what they heard. I feel the things done to them. And when they die, I *feel* that, too. Every last goddamn moment of it, all the way to the point where something like a black veil drops over my eyes. The vision ends with the last beat of the vic's heart.

No, it's not a superpower. Not sure it's a curse, either. It is what it is, and I live with it.

The worst part for Patty is when the vision kicks in. Apparently, it's not much fun to watch. Plus, there's all the screaming, if I don't bite down on a leather strap.

The worst part for me is the fact that the dead are usually the ones who contact me to do this sort of thing. Tell you all about that next time we have a bottle of really good bourbon on the table. Short version is that the dead—those who contact me, which is about half or a little more of these kinds of clients—take a big damn risk, because if I do catch the bad guy and cash him out, they don't just go into the light. Their faces are tattooed on my skin. So as long as I'm alive, they're stuck with me. No one else can see them except the other ghosts. And me.

Some of them are quiet.

Some are screamers.

Nights for me are long.

What makes it all worth it is taking someone off the board who won't go on to kill again and again and again.

Oh, yeah, and about the two times I died…one was in Afghanistan. I was on a night op, and we walked into some fancy shit—Russian-made fragmentation mine. The two guys in front of me got all of it, and we buried them in bags. I got hit in the throat and nearly bled out. Went flatline in the evac chopper and some young medic brought me back.

That was before the tattoos.

Second time I was careless and walked into a different kind of ambush. Thought I was chasing a regular off-the-rack bail skip and instead got in the middle of a Thai gang war. Took two 9mm in the chest. Circled the drain and tried to ride it all the way down. When I woke up eleven days later, some of the tattoos had faded out and about a third of the ghosts with them. I don't understand it. Not then, not now.

For the record, not looking for a hat trick. Two's fine, thank you. Three would be playing truth or dare with the Grim Reaper. Hard pass.

"How'd it happen?" asked Patty as she bent over her gear and made a thoughtful selection as to which needle to use.

"That's just it," I said. "Crow doesn't know. They found her body in a vacant lot on the west side of town, two doors down from the yarn shop. Nobody saw nothing. No stores in the area with surveillance cameras. No passersby, nobody walking their dog. Couple of teenage kids found her while they were cutting school. They lost their shit, seeing something like that. Crow said one of the EMTs spewed chunks, too. There's dead and there's dead, and this is the other kind."

She nodded. She grew up in Vietnam. And even though she missed the big celebration of bloody pointlessness that we called a Police Action, she still saw her share. The regime there loves tourists but seems to hate its own people.

Plus, she saw her little daughter.

"What do the police know?"

"Forensics got jack and shit," I said. "No hairs or fibers, no footprints—ground was frozen solid. No semen. Just the girl, her blood, and the worst day everyone who knew her will ever have."

Patty came around and stood right in front of me, the needle in her hand. She wore a mask with most people but not with me. I saw her eyes, the set of her mouth, the scream of a mother's grief implied in the way she looked at me.

"You'll find him," she said. Not a question. A command.

"Yes," I said again. "I will."

She nodded once and then began to sink the ink.

4

The first thing that made me realize something was wrong was the fact it didn't hurt.

I mean, sure the needle stings, but there wasn't any of that *other* pain. I didn't need the strap.

You'd think that would be some kind of relief. But it wasn't.

Any change in the process took me immediately into unknown territory, and I am not a fan of that zip code. I don't *like* doing this kind of thing in the first place, but I've gotten used to the process. In the few times there have been variations, it hasn't been something good. No hugs and puppies.

The second thing that made me realize this was off the rails was a weird, deep, twisted feeling that I *liked* it.

That scared the piss out of me.

And I don't scare easy.

5

The room went away. Patty Cakes, her studio, the ink and equipment, the artwork on the walls, the Tom Waits music on the box, and everything else.

Gone.

I felt myself change. That part, at least, was familiar. It meant I was stepping into someone else's body, connecting to their nerve endings, aligning with all five of their senses.

It's as strange as it sounds, and since the people whose lives I briefly inhabit are in the process of being brutalized, hunted, tortured, and murdered. It's also pretty fucking awful.

This had a different quality entirely.

There was a kind of joy.

A sense of freedom.

A wild surge of personal power.

Things that you cannot even remotely imagine are the feelings of someone being destroyed by a psychopath.

I looked down at my hands and felt both surprised and disappointed that they were not covered with blood.

I wanted them to be.

I needed them to be.

I could actually *feel* the warmth of blood spilling over my fingers and knuckles and the palms of my hand. My left hand. I could smell the blood…a very distinctive scent, like freshly sheared copper.

That smell usually turns my stomach because of its association with so many dreadful things I've seen. It's the most powerful mnemonic for pain and suffering, misery and degradation. It calls to mind vile treatment of the innocent.

And yet…in that moment, as those experiences became *my* experiences, there was an entirely different set of emotions flooding like a burst soil pipe through my mind, filling my senses.

This was beautiful.

This was powerful.

This made me feel like a god.

I tried to get up from the chair and blundered into something. Warm, yielding. Frightened. I made a grab for it, stabbed at it.

Stabbed.

That's what I tried to do. Yes. Stab.

Cut.

Slice.

Open.

Reveal.

God help me.

There were sounds. Two voices raised in screams of different intensity, the timbre carrying different meanings. One was younger, weaker, more acutely terrified; and that one was filled with that special kind of revelation that bursts upon the mind when the very worst thing that could ever happen *was* happening. With no way to stop it. There was a helplessness and a kind of acceptance.

Half of me hated that. I wanted to recoil from even the thought of it. Turn, stagger away to a safe distance, to remove myself from the experience.

The other voice was older. Wiser, but in sad ways. I could feel that depth of awareness, of understanding. I felt the resignation that such things happened because the world was wired way. That voice spoke from a cynical and yet objective understanding that despite the Christmas decorations and fairy lights twinkling all along the streets, there was no Santa Claus, and maybe no Jesus, either. That bad things happen because God doesn't really give a cold shit. Read the Old Testament, you'll see.

I saw.

I know she was right. But in that moment, I didn't know *who* she was.

I did know the younger voice. I had watched her every day. She walked past the cellar window of my house. Her and a whole pack like her. Taunting me. Daring me.

Asking for it.

Asking for what I was giving her now.

For...

What.

I...?

Wait.

I fell onto hands and knees. There was something wrong. The ground beneath my feet wasn't cold concrete. There was no snow or ice left. How? That made no sense. I'd stepped out of my van not two minutes ago. It was seventeen degrees. Last night's snow hadn't melted.

What I felt was... Tile?

I looked around, but what I felt did not match what I saw. The floor—and it was floor, not pavement—was cool but not cold. There was warmth around me. And music playing. Some guy with a growly voice. No idea who it was, but I thought I *should* know.

What I saw was the girl.

The one I wanted.

Eleven. I wanted to stop her, save her, protect her from—

From what? Not from me. No...from growing up. From becoming one of those *older* girls. The ones who flaunt everything that I can't have. The ones who make me feel stupid and impotent. The ones who laugh at me. Or, worse, don't even look at me.

I wanted this girl to die pure. Untainted by *needs*, to stop her from learning how to hate and ignore and...

Stop!

Fucking stop.

Just fucking stop.

I pushed myself up off the floor and turned toward my car. I could see it, but it looked strange. Like I was seeing it through the smudged lens of a broken camera. I hurried over to it but stopped immediately. Where was my knife? Shit—did I leave it in the...

The girl?

Did I leave the damn knife in the girl? That was stupid. They'd know. The only thing I touched with my bare hands was the knife. I needed to feel her. Skin. Hair. Teeth.

Blood.

God, how I needed to feel it. Warm. Hot and salty, too, when I tasted it. Feeling how quickly it cooled on my skin. Delightful. Made me have other thoughts. Hungry thoughts.

But this wasn't about that.

Not really. Not entirely.

It was all about setting her free before she became one of *them*.

I looked at her, lying there in the snow. Old, withered weeds, frozen at angles like people leaning in to watch and to share. She was there. Opened up so God could see her. Opened wide so the angels could find her innocent heart and take it to Heaven.

Like the others.

How many now? Eight, was it? Nine?

That made her number ten. Sweet and pure, and she'll be that way forever.

Where was the knife, though?

I'd taken it to church with me two days ago. Dipped the blade in the font of holy water. Prayed over it. God spoke to me from the patterns in the oak paneling in my bedroom. Telling me great secrets. Telling me what to do. What I *had* to do. Calling me to my good work for the Lord.

God, you see, doesn't want girls like that to grow up and become vile and hateful and...

The knife. Focus. Where's the knife?

Is it under her?

I bend and turn her, and there it is. I have to work fast because the Devil has people, too. They pretend to be nice and decent and all that bullshit. But they're not. They're evil. They're dead inside. There are no hearts in them for the angels to find. I know. I've opened them to look. Before.

Before I found God's work.

The knife is stuck. Damn. Damn. Damn. Stuck hard.

Shit, I cut myself with it.

Then I stop, watching my blood drip down, chilling as it falls. Joining hers. Caressing her skin. My blood.

Her blood.

Our blood.

God must have wanted this to happen. A sacrament. I'll have to remember that.

For next time.

And the time after. And all the times after that.

The ritual changes, evolves. And I must be dutiful to my purpose. I look at the blood. It's there. It's part of this. Part of her.

They'll never know, though, will they? Blood mixed with blood. Only a little of mine mixed in with all of hers. They'll never know.

No one will ever know.

I put my gloves on. That makes the cut hurt, but it makes the blood warmer.

No one will ever know that it's my blood.

No one. Ever.

I mean, how could they?

I get in my car and drive home. Inside the garage. In my house. Up in the bathroom. I don't wash off yet. Not yet. I need to do the dirty thing first. I always have to. Better to do it when I'm alone and no one's looking.

Then bed.

Then sleep.

Then dreams.

6

She slapped me awake.

Patty.

Not being nice about it.

Slapping my face one way and backhanding it the other.

It hurt, and I growled at her, pawed at her, trying to block. She slapped my hands away and hit me again. And again.

"Wake up," she snarled, then yelled it louder in Vietnamese. "*Thức dậy!*"

I covered my face with crossed arms. "Stop it, Pats, for Christ's sake. Stop."

She did.

My brain came back into my own head. I was on the floor of her tattoo parlor. She was straddling me, clamping my floating ribs and belly with her weirdly strong skinny thighs. As I slowly—carefully—uncovered my face, I saw her face was red with stress and anger and a hell of a lot of fear. Other emotions, too. Private ones.

"Are you *you*?" she demanded.

I had to give that some real thought. *Was* I me?

"Yes?" I said, and I heard the rising inflection, making it a question.

Patty balled a hand into a knotty little fist and punched me in the chest. She is remarkably strong, and it hurt.

"Are you *you*?" she roared.

"Yes, yes, for fuck's sake, it's me."

"*Mẹ đồ ngu.*"

Motherfucker.

Then she got off me and stood up, panting, sweating, fists still balled. There were tears in her eyes. "*Mẹ đồ ngu,*" she said again.

I pulled myself up and leaned my back against the wall. I was as out of breath as if I'd climbed a mountain carrying a bag of rocks.

"What happened?" demanded Patty. "Why'd you go nuts like that?"

"Like what?" I asked.

Her eyes narrowed and she gave me a long, cold, appraising stare. "Tell me about her."

She pointed at the tattoo of the eleven-year-old girl.

It took me a very long time to make sure my head was my own. Though, I could still remember it all. Could still feel it all. I have been inside the heads of murder victims, victims of torture, of rape, of nearly every kind of violent madness. This was different. This was a different kind of violation. The stink of it was on me. My hands tingled with someone else's touch. It was disgusting. It was terrible beyond any words I know. Even my blood felt polluted.

"It…it wasn't her," I said, tripping over it.

"What do you mean? It was her blood, her face." She jabbed me on the forehead of the face she'd just inked. "I didn't do it wrong."

I felt a shame that ran deeper than anything I've ever felt, and I have done some very bad things. I used to be a black-ops shooter for Uncle Sam and then a military contractor in one of those don't-ask-don't-tell kind of private companies that did wet work for multinational corporations. I have a lot of red in my personal ledger. This I know and I accept the penance and punishment that goes with it. My ghosts. The work they want me to do. It's what I deserve.

But this…

No. This was different. This was a shame—a self-disgust that was like leprosy of the soul.

It took a lot of time, but I told Patty all of it. Everything I felt, saw, heard, knew, wanted, and did. I watched how it changed her face. Paling her skin, bruising her mouth, setting fires in her dark eyes. She took a step back from me, because what she was hearing was the kind of thing men had done to her daughter all those years ago.

And what that *felt* like was in my head. I had felt everything that *he* had felt, and there was a dark joy lingering at the edge of my mind.

Patty had taken only one step back. She hadn't fled. She didn't do that, and even with all she's done for me over the years, the fact that she did not abandon me in that moment made me love her more than I've ever loved anyone. Not talking romance, and I think you get that. This was love on a level where human beings are supposed to relate but usually don't. It was empathy in the way empathy should be—a superpower. And, on top of everything else, that was what defined Patty Cakes.

She did not help me up. That was fine. I wouldn't want to touch me, either.

I stood there, swaying, unable to look at my own face in the mirror.

"Where's my jacket?" I mumbled. She picked the leather off the floor and handed it to me. When I took it, I made sure not to touch her. Not yet.

Patty walked over and unlocked the door, but paused, her hand on the knob as she looked up at me.

"The blood," she said, "do you think they know? Crow? The cops?"

"That it's his and not hers?"

She nodded.

"No. Crow wouldn't do that to me. I don't think they know there was more than one person's blood."

"You said he only bled a little, but that was the blood Crow gave you. Are you *sure* he didn't know?"

I just shook my head.

"Do you know who he is?"

I had to think about it. I don't usually share specific thoughts. With dead people I just relive their deaths in a kind of five-dimensional Sensurround. But that's because they're dead. This man was alive, and somehow that changed things.

"No," I said.

Her eyes went wide. "Then you can't find him? You'll have to tell Crow. He has to get you *her* blood."

I put on my jacket and zipped it halfway. Then pulled my biker gloves from the pocket. My left hand still hurt where he had cut himself. He was a lefty. He'd still have a cut.

"I don't know his name," I said. "But he took me home with him. I know where he lives."

Her eyes changed. They stopped being shocked and sad, and instead took on a reptilian coldness. There was no trace of mercy in them at all.

"Then find him," she said.

7

Pine Deep wasn't a big town. Covered a lot of acreage, but most of it was farmland. The center of town was just a few blocks wide. It didn't take me long at all. I went to the crime scene, started there, and I let the cocksucker guide me all the way to his front door.

He was even smiling when he answered.

Tall guy. Soft, though. Weak blue eyes, fleshy lips, rosacea on his cheeks giving them a healthier pink glow than the rest of his worm-white skin. I saw his hand. He was wearing a uniform shirt from a company that installs residential security video equipment. I saw that, and understood. I saw the bandage, too.

I smiled at him.

And his smile went away.

I pushed him inside.

He tried to scream.

Tried to run.

Even tried to fight.

Fuck that, though.

I dragged him by the hair down into his basement. There were pictures on all the walls. Photos lifted from digital cameras. Bedroom and bathroom stuff. Awful. Children. Little girls.

He tried to explain. God and angels and purity. Shit like that.

I broke his jaw first so I didn't have to listen to it.

I knew it. I was there.

The house stood alone on three-quarters of an acre. No one right next door. No one to hear.

I didn't use a knife. Didn't need a goddamn knife.

He made a lot of noise.

I let him.

It was a very long night.

But later, when I finally got home and showered for over an hour, I slept. The ghosts all around me were quiet. For once, they let me sleep.

When I dreamed, they were my own dreams again.

Thank God.

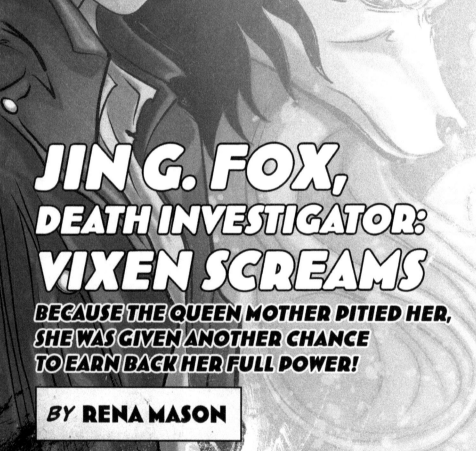

JIN G. FOX,
DEATH INVESTIGATOR:
VIXEN SCREAMS

BECAUSE THE QUEEN MOTHER PITIED HER, SHE WAS GIVEN ANOTHER CHANCE TO EARN BACK HER FULL POWER!

BY **RENA MASON**

APRIL 14, 1906.

Jin stood at the edge of a pier in a trench coat and pair of red heels. Boatmen shouted instructions to a crane operator pulling something up from the water. A high wave crashed against the breakwater and sloshed the fur between her toes. She stepped back and sniffed at the air: briny ocean with a hint of decay. An odor easily determined with a fox's nose.

When she'd received the orders, Jin had had her paws up on the desk, painting her claws red in her cozy office in San Francisco's Chinatown. The Queen Mother of the West had sent Jin straightaway across the bay to the cold and damp of Oakland to investigate one of their own who'd gone missing and was obviously someone important to the Queen Mother or to her plan for a "new" Chinatown. Even though Jin thought it a silly idea, which she kept to herself. Chinatown had been around for only a little more than fifty years. No need for a new one.

But since Jin ranked so much lower after her death, she knew better than to inquire. Of course, if Jin had not been killed by a handsome, young scythe-wielding farmer full of rage and vengeance as soon as she'd gotten her fourth tail, she'd be anywhere but California and interacting solely with the living and draining their spirit energy rather than gleaning what she could from the dead and soon-to-be dead. But because the Queen Mother pitied her, Jin was given another chance to earn back her full power *and* a peach of immortality by working for the goddess, doing her bidding.

Several bystanders gasped in chorus as the crane hoisted what appeared to be a lifeless mermaid from the bay. Long, wet black hair shrouded a face. Tattered white fabric hung off flaccid, pasty shoulders. Seaweed clung to the torso, overflowing leafy strands streaming liquid back into the bay. A thick iron chain weighted its waist, pulling it downward as if the ocean struggled in a tug of war to win the return of one of its creatures. Then it all sloughed off in a clump and hit the water with a splash. The body swayed naked from the crane and then reeled back, eliciting screams from an increasing crowd.

Not a mermaid then, but a dead Chinese woman—a kindred sister—swung from metal claws as her exposed breasts moved like a pendulum for all to see. Blanched legs dangled, a patch of black hair between them. Humiliation and a surge of anger gushed through Jin. She screamed at the roaring ocean below. Her back arched, her four tails shot straight up, and she puffed out.

"Get her down, right now!" She pointed to the crane operator. "And cover her up."

The men worked fast as Jin barked out orders.

It calmed her somewhat to think her shouting had some effect on Westerners even though their beliefs kept them from seeing or hearing her. Of all the things Jin missed about being a live fox spirit, being seen and heard—at least by those who knew of her existence—was at the top of her list. Having full control of her powers came in second. Jin had only infallible capabilities now when the Queen Mother watched directly over her shoulder. Jin didn't care for the overbearing scrutiny, but it had gotten her out of most certain death a time or two since her initial demise. Regularly, though, Jin dealt with unreliable powers, moving in and out of fox form, sometimes only partway, shifting man to woman, woman to man, and often at the most inconvenient times. She supposed it came with the territory of being dead and favored, but still, if she could only go back in time to when she'd seduced that farmer… But never mind that now; she needed to keep the past in the past and focus on pleasing the Queen Mother to give her another chance at life.

The deceased Chinese woman had no spirit energy around her corpse, no spectral glow. She'd either gone to the Heavens, in which case the Queen Mother wouldn't have sent Jin to an Oakland pier, or the woman had been dead a while and walked aimlessly, or the woman had just recently left. Jin scanned the crowd for her ghost. Fresh ones always radiated brighter. Among the onlookers, a Westerner in a crisp white suit, who stood out like a moonflower under a full moon, watched the spectacle as he leaned against a fancy motorcar. Then he turned his gaze and focused it on Jin. *Can the white devil see me? How?* Likely just her imagination playing tricks. Jin glanced at her feet and noticed the fur had disappeared. She had shapely women's ankles again. Might be a sign, but for what she didn't know.

Curious, she made her way around and through the spectators toward the man, but he got into the back of the car, and it sped off.

"It's these damned high heels slowing me down. They might as well be lotus shoes. Same foot-binding torture, different era is all. But still, they're quite lovely," she said, admiring her shoes before clacking away.

Back in San Francisco's Chinatown, Jin meandered to her office—a single white door and matching frame hidden in an alleyway between two buildings on Pacific near Stockton where "Eastern" and "Western" inhabitants of the city blurred lines. Centered on the door, her name—*JIN G. FOX*—and *Death Investigator* etched underneath in bold black characters, sharp and bleak. Only the dead or dying seeking out her services could see the door, but even the living rushed right past with some sense of knowing in their stride. Word traveled fast in both realms, it seemed, so it didn't surprise her the alley remained desolate.

Jin reached for the door. Someone grabbed her from behind. She sunk her teeth into an arm around the top of her chest.

"Ouch!" a man shouted. He yanked her hair and tightened his grip until she released him. Then he dragged her screaming and kicking to the street and shoved her into the backseat of a sputtering motorcar. Up close it looked just like a carriage on wheels.

The white devil in the white suit leered at her. "Was that you making those unnatural howling sounds?"

Unnatural to you, Jin thought. She huffed, adjusted her coat's stiff collar, and smoothed her hair as the driver got behind the wheel and motored away.

"How can you see me?" she said.

"The bitch bit me," the driver said.

"Really?" the man in white said. "She's quite the vixen it seems."

The driver turned his neck just enough to scowl at her.

"Answer me," she said.

"Sorry about Sam," the man in white said. "He can be a little rough, but he's all soft on the inside. Aren't ya, Sam?"

"Yeah, boss," the driver said.

"Excuse my manners, miss? I'm Carl Worthington, but please, call me Mr. Worthington." He raised Jin's hand and kissed it.

Disgusting practice. Jin slipped her hand from his and tucked it under her leg.

"Now, who are you?" he said. "And what do you know about the woman dredged up from Oakland Bay?"

"How can you see me?" she asked. No Westerner had ever spoken or admitted they'd laid eyes on her before. Jin wondered if it was part of Queen Mother's plan for the new Chinatown. If so, Jin didn't like it. Not one bit.

"Trust me, I can see you just fine, china doll. Now you answer my questions."

So, a true ghost man, Jin thought. And her first. She wondered how he and his driver would die and what it had to do with her. They had to be connected or involved. "I have inquiries of my own, Mr. Worthington," she said. "Where are you taking me?"

"Thought we'd be more cozy back at my place. Have a drink or two and loosen up." He placed his hand on her knee and gave it a squeeze.

Jin yipped in surprise and then squealed. "Aiya!"

He laughed and put his arm around her. "Cute sounds you make. That's more like it."

"It's Jin," she said. A scent on his breath and around his mouth had her sniffing his chin.

"Sorry," he said. I had some moo goo gai pan for dinner and my breath probably—"

Chicken! Her favorite. She licked his lips and then put her mouth onto his and sucked the flavor of tasty fowl from his tongue. After Jin finished, Mr. Worthington swiped saliva from his jaw.

"You're really something," he said. "You better step on it, Sam."

Mr. Worthington lived in a nice home in a very wealthy neighborhood. The driver pulled into the carriage house and snuffed out the lamps. Mr. Worthington placed his white jacket over Jin's head and rushed her inside. She giggled at his and Sam's attempts to be clandestine and that they didn't know the only reason they saw her was because they'd soon meet their ends.

A large mirror in the foyer reflected a woman shrouded in white for a funeral. Appropriate, she thought as she followed the white devil into an adjacent room.

"Come, sit down here," he said. "Warm yourself by the fire."

Jin approached him as he patted the spot next to him on a green velvet sofa. Draped across the back was a blanket made of fur. She stopped and emitted a low growl.

"You like it, huh? A friend in Upstate New York sent it to me. It's fox."

He yanked her toward him and forced her hand onto the blanket. "Feel it," he said.

Tears welled in her eyes as she stroked, but she forced them back. Jin refused to let the white devil see her cry. Then he put a glass half-full of amber liquid into her other palm and slid his fingers up her arm.

"You women have skin like silk."

"That tickles," she said. Her eyes still fixed on the blanket, she downed the alcohol in one gulp and then glowered down at him with her back to the fire, fantasizing about his fate.

This man is filthier than a bear! Jin giggled and snorted at the thought of freeing her tails and warming them. She set the empty snifter on a side table.

"You know what else tickles?" Mr. Worthington pulled her down beside him and pressed his face into her skin and passionately kissed her neck.

"Wow wow wow." Jin shoved him onto his back and then she pounced and straddled him. Her hair fell around his face like a curtain, and she stared into his eyes, dominating him. She'd never seduced a Westerner before, but Mr. Worthington didn't need much in the way of her wiles or witty words, and she needed information. Besides, he'd soon be dead and go wherever the dead go according to his beliefs. She'd never see him again.

Afterward, she lay alongside him, nuzzling and purring into his arm.

"Now that…" He pulled smoke from a cigarette into his mouth. "That was something," he said through exhaling. "I've never been bitten and nibbled on like that before. I think I liked it."

Of course you liked it, you stinky coyote. Jin laughed and gently scratched the hair on his chest the way she liked her fur scratched when she was in fox form.

"And I know you enjoyed it," he said as he reached over to refill her brandy glass. "Because I've never heard any woman, Chinese or not, scream and howl the way you did."

"Speaking of screaming Chinese women, did you know that woman those men pulled from the water?" Her voice went from soft and squeaky to deep and baritone. *Oh, no! Please, please, please don't transform into a man now.*

Jin coughed and took a sip of brandy. She slowed her breathing and concentrated to stay in female form. It was difficult without a human skull cap, but how could she behead a ghost or an almost-ghost without causing a scene?

"She's married to this Chinaman we're doing business with, Ming Li. You know him?"

As if we all know each other. Jin tugged the hair around his nipple.

"Ow," he said. "Take it easy. You're not ready for another round, are you? I need a little break before I can do all that again. Not all of us are as industrious, or as filthy, for that matter."

"Be nice!" She clawed him.

He raised his hand to strike her, but she cowered and gave him her best pity eyes. Jin prayed she might witness his soon-to-be death.

"Please," she said. "Just tell me the truth." She stroked his chest where she'd left red marks. "Did you kill her?" Jin didn't know how else to phrase it. Sometimes simplicity worked best.

"No. Not us. We don't know who did, but we know it wasn't an accident. Ming's reported her missing, and told his business partner, Lew Hong. It got us thinking that maybe he's hiding something. Trying to scheme in with another interested party, perhaps even the Tong gangs, and we especially don't want them anywhere near what we're trying to do, or his principled partner."

"Which is?"

"Ha! I'm no fool. I don't care how much you bite me or how much I like it."

"Why exactly am I here then, Mr. Worthington?"

"Sam and I thought maybe you knew her. But then we followed you toward the brothels and realized our mistake. She was apparently a very loyal and good wife. Not someone like you. So I decided that while I was in the area, I might as well finish my evening off with more Chinese."

She opened her jaws to bite him.

"But, I'll admit. You're different. In a bad way that's good, for me anyhow. What do you say about working for us on the side and finding out who offed the Chinaman's wife?"

Hmm, working both angles might be a good idea until I get solid information.

"Only because you asked me nicely," she said.

"Now that's more like it." He pulled her on top of him and she licked his face for any remnant chicken taste she might've missed.

APRIL 15, 1906.

Jin hung back and moved in a thick dark fog, allowing it to conceal her as she tracked her next lead. As much as she enjoyed the sex, she hated Mr. Worthington, and wished him guilty of murdering the Chinese woman so the Queen Mother could end his life and call off Jin's search for the woman's killer. But now, at least Jin knew who the woman was, a Mrs. Li, which on any other day would be like looking for a Mrs. Chin in Chinatown, but the fact that her husband's name was Ming Li and a prominent businessmen made Jin's search for him far too easy.

She followed Ming Li onto a ferry from San Francisco to Oakland. When she appeared before him, and he physically saw her, Jin wasn't surprised in the least. If he did business with Westerners and the Tong gangs, he was bound to be one of the soon-to-be dead. Jin did her best to conjure her powers, seduce, and then scare him. She even lied and offered to marry him and bear him sons. Undeterred, proud, and stubborn, he dismissed her, and Jin left without learning anything new. A rude man he most definitely was, but that didn't mean he'd killed his wife.

Jin tailed him in Oakland. Mr. Li walked to an ironworks, gave the foreman some orders, and then read a lot of paperwork, which bored her to tears. She thought it likely he didn't know they'd pulled his wife from Oakland Bay. Jin resisted her urge to tell him in case he *was* guilty. She hadn't ruled him out completely. The same went for Mr. Carl Worthington. Perhaps he thought he could out clever Jin by asking her to spy for him in order to deceive her. Or maybe Mr. Li's business partner, Lew Hong, had found out about Ming's underhanded activities and decided to handle the matter himself, starting with Mr. Li's wife.

Alone on the docks, Jin sat until it got dark, first looking for any sign of the dead woman's ghost and then staring out at the black sea, replaying the moment the young farmer had killed her. There was no moonlight over the water to help calm her racing thoughts about her own death or who'd murdered Mrs. Li, the clouds too thick to emit even the slightest glow. Something else, though, made its way through the night air, barely there but catching on protuberances like loose cobwebs in the wind. They came at her, and she absorbed their energy the way she did when she was a living fox spirit. This strange power from the air bolted through her and tingled the hair on her head. Jin felt stronger than she had since she'd died.

An attractive young man with a pushcart full of chains rounded a corner to her right, spilling the heavy metal in a clangor. Jin wished to help him, but he appeared solid and vigorous enough in his efforts. As she watched him, the thought of draining some of his spirit energy and what it might feel like teased her. The scattered chains reminded her of her duty to seek out who killed Mrs. Li.

Another young man who looked much like the clumsy, tough one rushed down the docks.

"Bohai," he shouted from one end. "Looks like you need some help, brother."

Together, they lifted the last piece of spilled metal, a small anchor, back into the pushcart.

"It's good to see you, Han." Bohai patted his brother on the shoulder. "Thanks."

With trepidation in his voice, Han said, "I have grave news."

Bohai shook his head. "No. Don't—"

"Sit down. What I'm about to tell you will make you weak."

Bohai's eyes went wide. "What is it? Tell me, please."

Jin heard the desperation in his voice and felt sorry for Bohai. Unable to see her, the brothers sat on her bench, Han's body halfway into hers.

Han rubbed his arm. "It's cold right here. Move over." He slid out of Jin's body and sat closer to his brother.

"Go on, now. Tell me," Bohai said.

"After asking around, one of my Tong brothers told me that your boss's boss's boss's wife is missing. He said to go to a local establishment known to entertain factory workers. And so I did, not thinking much would come of it at first. I ordered drinks, sat back, and watched all the men come and go. Waited. Then on the third night, I overhead a conversation two men behind me were having. One of the men, a disgruntled foreman, works at the same ironworks you deliver for. He talked about his wretched boss and how everyone knows his boss beats his wife because she's given him no children. Then the foreman said he tried to tell his other boss, Mr. Hong, that Mr. Li was up to something, but Mr. Hong wouldn't hear him out.

"So I turn around, pretend I'm you, and complain about the deliveries, and say that Mr. Li had been rude to me as well. The men asked me to join them, and I bought them drinks, and then inquired about Mr. Li's wife. They told me her name, what she looks like, what she wears, and I told them I'd keep my eyes and ears open around the docks.

"I have no doubt the woman they'd described matches the one you'd told me you had relations with. It's Xi," Han said.

"No." Bohai put his face in his hands. "I won't believe it."

"I think she might have been with you to get pregnant. Do you think you did that?"

"Did what? Put a child in her? How am I supposed to know this?"

"There's something else," Han said.

"What?"

"Stories from boatmen to dock workers about a dead Chinese woman they pulled out of Oakland Bay."

Bohai raised his head and gazed out across the water to Oakland. "Why are you telling me this?"

"You have to go and see the body before it's too late. They'll get rid of it soon."

"I can't."

"Just go. I'll ask Feng to take you over there. He's either out having a drink or at home. Go wait by his boat. I'll be back soon with him."

Bohai nodded and Han left. Quiet tears trickled from the corners of Bohai's eyes.

Jin sensed that even though he had hardly known Xi, he had loved her, and Jin wished she could tell him that the Queen Mother loved Xi, too. So much so that the goddess put her best and only—although that mattered little—death investigator in Chinatown on the job to find out who'd murdered her.

Then Bohai whispered out to the ocean. "You in the Heavens, give her and my unborn child peace. And for me, only vengeance."

Jin trembled at the words and shifted into fox form. She moved closer and stared into his eyes, waiting for any sign he saw a fox with an open mouth full of sharp teeth in front of him. Certain he did not, she embraced him and wrapped her four tails around him in an offer of comfort and to exchange some of his negative energy for her positive. As he stared blankly through her and out over the bay, he shivered in her arms and tails, and whispered, "Please. I beg you."

Jin scampered off in a rush of emotions.

APRIL 16, 1906.

Back at the office, she had her hind legs up on the desk, brushing the fur on her legs to help think more clearly. Perhaps it was as she'd suspected, and Mr. Li's business partner, Lew Hong, wanted the iron factory all to himself and was willing to do anything to make that happen. The thought revived the energy she'd taken from the strange air at the docks and then given to Bohai. She threw on her trench coat and closed the door behind her. As soon as she got near crowds, she noticed people looking directly at her, gasping, and then turning away. *How could it be that all these people see me now?* Was it possible so many would die? Jin needed a visit from the Queen Mother to ask, but that could be days or months away. She needed to solve the crime.

On her way to the ironworks, Jin noticed a small gathering of panicked people in the doorway of a modest home, so she stopped to investigate. Men and women loitered among the rooms and halls with worried looks on their faces. A few of them physically saw Jin and scurried away. Jin moved past and through others, to the center of all the commotion. A pregnant woman lay on a bed mat in the farthest room, expressions of pain twisting her face.

A man ran in. "Yu!" he shouted.

"Lew," an older man said, "you must take her to the Western hospital. Something isn't right."

Jin waited for anyone in the room to notice her, but even the suffering pregnant woman did not see her, so Jin knew Yu would live. How fortunate she stumbled into the home of Lew Hong, the other ironworks owner she'd set off to find. The old man made plans and shouted out his instructions to others. Lew kneeled by his wife and kissed her. When he stood, bright red blood had pooled toward his mass and stained his knee.

Jin gasped.

Lew Hong ran out the door, and Jin followed after him. She listened to him talk to himself and pray under his breath. He did not seem like a dishonest or untrustworthy man to her. All this man wanted was to save his wife and child. Another dead end, Jin thought. Then again, she knew not to eliminate him as a suspect completely. Greed can turn men into monsters. Besides, now she was caught up in the turmoil and wanted to know how everything would turn out with Yu Hong and her unborn child. Queen Mother's plan for a new Chinatown wouldn't work and grow without children.

Mr. Hong went to the Western hospital and met his wife there, but the doctor told them to go to another hospital many hours away. Lew didn't have a way to get his wife there and told the doctor this, but the Western doctor simply shrugged and then left.

White devil! Jin chased after the doctor and screamed at his back until he re-entered the hospital.

The translator stayed behind and whispered to Mr. Hong. He said he had a friend in the Tong gangs who knew a Westerner that worked with them, one who owned a motorcar.

Jin knew a Westerner with a motorcar, too! She had to try Mr. Worthington in case the translator's gang connections didn't come through. Jin, back in the form of a woman, walked into a wind that carried her to his fancy house.

+

APRIL 17, 1906.

Sam the driver opened the door, and as she stepped in, three men rushed right past her. The men brandished pistols and fired at Sam. Bullets struck him in the head, and as he lurched back, one exploded his nose away and blew off the back of his head. Offal splattered the floor before the rest of Sam's head landed on top of it with a moist thump.

Jin darted this way and that, screaming and howling in distress, even gekkering at the men to get out of her territory. Unable to tell whether or not they saw her, she ran for the stairs while the men continued ransacking the rooms below. Upstairs, Mr. Worthington stumbled and tripped around his bed while yanking his pants on. A trembling, nude Western woman had blankets pulled up to her chin, fear in her eyes. She screamed when Jin entered Mr. Worthington's bedroom. Had the circumstances been different, and the two weren't about to die… Jin took a moment to consider the amusing possibilities.

Carl looked up at her and said, "Bad timing, china doll."

"Sam's dead," Jin said. "Who are those men?"

"Could be this one's husband and his friends for all I know." He turned to the woman in his bed and then back to Jin. "Unless it was you. You tell anyone about working for me?"

"No," Jin said. This must be why Sam, Mr. Worthington, and now this woman could see her—the secret underhanded dealings among Ming Li, Mr. Worthington, and Sam so tightly connected to the dead pregnant Xi.

Jin's ears pricked at the sound of footsteps coming toward them. She couldn't be killed by bullets from men unable to see her, but what if they could, like Mr. Worthington and Sam, because they're involved as well? She had no way to know if the pistol-wielding killers knew Xi, or even possibly murdered her. Jin moved aside and slipped into a closet. She peeked out through slats as the men barged into the room, firing repeatedly at Carl and the woman in his bed.

After the men looted and vandalized Worthington's once-fancy home, they left. Jin came out and went to Carl, crouching down beside him. She'd gotten her wish and witnessed his and Sam's deaths. Carl gasped.

"You're still alive!" she said.

Blood sprayed and then burbled from his mouth. Jin peered down into his eyes.

"What do you see, Mr. Worthington?" she said. "Tell me, please."

His dying gaze moved past her. His eyes widened. Jin saw fear there, smelled it. She turned, sniffed at the air, saw nothing.

"Shh...Shadows," Carl said.

A deep and bitter cold passed through Jin, and then Carl died. The frigid air left, too. It must have taken his spirit energy. She'd heard Westerners call it a soul.

"Interesting," she said.

"You should not be here." Queen Mother's voice reverberated above her.

"Did you know Westerners can see me now?"

"It's rare," said the Queen Mother. "But sometimes, when it's—"

"Many more people can see me now, too, it seems. And there's something else. An energy building all around the city that I can't explain but can feel and feed from."

"I believe something is coming. Something very important is going to happen soon."

"What?"

"Be patient, and stay on the task I've given you. It may answer your questions."

"Yes, Queen Mother."

The goddess's voice vanished, along with the vital energy that surrounded her and made Jin more powerful and corporeal in her presence.

Jin glanced at Worthington and then over to the woman in his bed one last time and wondered if perhaps the woman's husband and his pals were guilty of the murders. Jealousy is ugly and bitter, driving many men to do terrible things. She stood and then left the room. Jin needed to find Bohai.

After scouring the docks and sniffing through the workmen in her fox form all night, Jin headed for the ironworks still in search of Bohai.

APRIL 18, 1906.

Jin hoped that in the early hour, she'd locate Bohai at the factory retrieving his deliveries for the day. She moved through unlocked doors, but saw no one at first. As Jin moved farther into the building, she heard shouting. Jin ran toward the fuss and stopped near the foreman who argued with Ming Li. Ming stood halfway across the room, opposite a tall piece of machinery. The foreman held papers and called Ming a traitor.

When the worker saw Jin, his mouth opened, he stuttered and then said, "Huli Jing!"

Jin grabbed the papers and read them.

Ming Li sold the San Francisco factory to Mr. Worthington, agreeing to move all operations to Oakland!

"This would crush business in Chinatown," Jin said. She held up the papers and shouted to Ming, "Why would you do this?"

"Chinatown is finished here," Ming said. "I made a big money deal with the Westerners who want us in Oakland. Now give me those papers!"

"You bastard! Only someone as terrible as you could kill their own wife," Jin said.

"You are wrong about me, fox spirit! It was a bastard that was inside Xi. So they both deserved to die!" He ran toward her waving and yelling, slobbering from his mouth like a rabid coyote—maniacal.

Ming came at Jin so fast that her mind faltered to fight back. He barreled into her, and she flew backward, stopping on impact against an iron furnace.

As she struggled to rise, she watched Ming rush the foreman and tackle him. The men wrestled on the ground. Ming punched the worker twice in the chest and then grabbed the papers. As the foreman rose and regained his balance, Ming pushed him. The foreman stumbled back, into the tip of an anchor that pierced his chest in a spray of blood and glossy pink gore.

"Traitor," he said before dying. Jin watched his spirit energy gather in a fog that took the foreman's human form, it nodded at her and then ascended to the building's ceiling. The ground shook and the ceiling broke apart, allowing the foreman's spirit to continue upward.

While she shielded herself from the falling rubble, Ming ran at her again. The sky above became a dark vortex that rumbled with fierce power.

"Stop!" Queen Mother said. "You will not harm my Huli Jing, you foul man. Jin, go now and protect Lew Hong and his wife and unborn child. Mr. Hong is good. Together, we will rebuild a new Chinatown."

Jin rubbed the back of her head. "Yes, Queen Mother. But—"

"You must hurry. Léigōng heard the cry for vengeance in the Heavens and not just from Bohai but from many of our people."

"The god of thunder is coming here?" That explained the energy in the air. Jin pictured him with his mace and hammer. "Alone?"

"Yes," Queen Mother said.

Without his wife, Dianmu, to light up his target, he would smash the entire city.

"Go, now," Queen Mother said. "He travels in jaded winds and will arrive any moment."

As Jin departed, the earth shook behind her.

Mrs. Hong was in surgery when Jin caught up. She sat next to Mr. Hong in the waiting room and did her best to assure him his wife and infant would be all right as the ground quaked gently underfoot. Jin prayed they'd made it far enough away to avoid Léigōng's mace and hammer.

A young boy clung to the other side of Mr. Hong. The toddler must have been their first son. It gave Jin relief neither father nor son saw her.

Jin went into the operating room and stood next to Mrs. Hong. The woman screamed at the sight of her, became hysterical.

Oh, no! She saw me. Jin panicked as the hospital workers quieted Mrs. Hong. Then Jin took the pregnant woman's hand and squeezed. Jin took in the energy all around her and then shined it back with a burst of intense light.

Jin woke on the floor of the empty operating room. Her mind filled with clouds, she left the room in search of Lew Hong. He and his son were gone. Fear pulsed through her. Queen Mother had told her to watch over and protect them. She couldn't fail the goddess now. Jin stormed down halls and pushed open doors, one after the other. She rushed into the last room about to scream.

Inside, Lew Hong sat at his wife's bedside with their toddler son on his lap. Mrs. Hong held their newborn son in her arms. Jin hopped up and down and screamed with happiness and delight. Mrs. Hong no longer saw Jin.

Jin knew Mrs. Hong would've died if Jin hadn't saved her. Nothing else explained the woman seeing Jin earlier but not now. Jin hadn't been able to change the course of someone's fate since she'd died. She'd not felt pain before, either. It had to have come from Léigōng's energy in the air. It made her alive again. So many strange firsts had happened. Jin didn't know how to make sense of them. She worried if they meant good or bad. She hopped onto a chair in the corner of the room and picked at her tails, contemplating all the unusual things and their meanings.

Next thing she knew, Mr. Hong stood in front of the hospital room window, looking out. Jin got up to see and gasped at the sight. A thick black veil hung over San Francisco far off in the distance. The ground continued trembling softly underfoot.

Jin knew San Francisco had crumbled. But she also knew her office door still existed between piles of destruction. In her mind, she saw a line of people around what used to be the corner, the dead who required her services. So many of the same unlucky people who saw her on the streets in the days before Léigōng came and destroyed the city.

Even though she'd lost a couple connections, she'd made at least one she'd use. Bohai's brother, Han, the Tong gang member. It remained just a matter of time before the handsome young man saw her. Then she'd seduce him for information and maybe he'd like to hear her screams, too.

THE GHOST THIEVES

A SAUL WHEN ADVENTURE

BY JOHN JENNINGS

I t's Halloween in New Orleans and my face is shoved in a bag. Even with my face tucked away in this satchel, I can hear Janice grumbling about our last case. She knows full well that werewolves are always tricky clients. At any rate, her time is up and now Micah has to carry the burden until next Halloween.

Which burden, you ask? Well. Me.

I'm the burden. Saul When: Halloween Detective. You see, I saved Janice's life. I saved Micah's life. I've saved more people on this planet than I can count and they owe me. They all owe me their service when I need them. I don't have a body in this world, and in order for me to work on this plane of existence, I need one. My work? Well, that is complicated. When I was a human kicking around on this mud ball, I was a detective. I don't remember my name. I think that's why I'm so obsessed with them. Names, that is. That's another story, but I do remember that I was a damn good detective. I also remember that I didn't really believe in all of this *hocus pocus* and tomfoolery, but now I'm up to my neck in it. I was killed by some kind of evil warlock while on a case, and because of the spell he used, my soul ended up in the Hallowverse. What's that? It's exactly what it sounds like—a dimension where the Pumpkin Lord and all his underlings live and work in service of the night when the veil between here and the OtherWorld are at its most thin.

So, there I was, stuck in the Halloween Dimension. No Heaven. No Hell. Just Halloween 24/7! The Pumpkin Lord took pity on me and gave me a job. You see, there's plenty of trouble that needs to be handled here on Earth. Random spirits that need saving. Devils and goblins who are in need of aid. Any kind of supernatural and phantasmagoric so-and-so that needs a case solved or needs the Pumpkin Lord's attention; I'm there to help. Me and my avatar.

So, for the last year, that has been Janice McBride. She is a lovely redheaded thirty-two-year-old parole officer and single mother of two. One night, about five years ago, she was almost cleaved in two by a rampaging creature that you would not want to meet. I saved her life. She owes me that life. So, my spirit lives in a goblin mask. She wears that mask and while she's helping me work my case, she becomes…me and can wield all my power. She's dropping my face off to the next avatar—Micah Tandem.

Micah is a graphic design grad student, and I'm sure he's so excited to see me again. This is his third year on the *team*. I can't wait to tell him what our case is tonight.

Janice knocks on Micah's door. She has a heavy hand.

"I'm coming!" says Micah. I can hear him growling through the door.

I hear the door open, and Janice steps across the threshold.

"Hey, Micah."

Janice has a nice voice, and it sprouts from a lovely body to boot. I think I'm going to miss being in it. It's, well, comforting. Anyway, Micah and Janice make small talk for a few ticks, but only a few. Time is tight.

"Janice, how've you been keeping?" Micah is trying to stall. Even in my satchel, I can hear the anxiety in his tone.

"I've been good. Kids are growing like weeds and business is booming. Lots of crime and lots of former inmates to deal with. Even with our friend's affairs to handle, I can't much complain. You?"

Micah begins with a sigh. "Well, I'm still seeing Toneisha. She's great. Super super smart, you know? I do have a massive design final coming up and a graphic design history course that's kicking my ass. This professor is a hard case, and I'm not sure if I can really do well. I have to keep at least a B-average to stay in the program, and I worked really hard to get in, and—"

Janice interrupts. "All great, kid. I need you to take it. I gotta get home to my kids. It's…heavy. I need you to take it. Now, please."

"Okay." Micah sighs again. I hear him step toward Janice. Then I feel the satchel, all ancient and leather, shift from her to him.

"You know what the case is?" asks Micah.

Janice is almost running for the door when she says, "Don't know. Don't care. Just hope it's not werewolves."

I hear Janice turn around for a second.

"Micah, you take care. Don't take his mess when you don't have to. Okay?"

Then she's gone with a thud of the door.

"She gets so touchy, right?" I blurt out from my bag. "I mean. She's seen much worse than ancient werewolf gods!"

Micah doesn't say a word.

"Micah? You gonna get me out so we can get to work, or not? Time's a wasting. We have to work at night. You know that."

Micah unhitches the silver clasps on my satchel and takes me out. Well, this me, at least. There's lots of my masks all over the world. You have to franchise in order to cover more ground. Anyway, he holds me up so we're face to face. Micah is a good-looking kid. He's about six-foot-three. Dark brown skin. Dark eyes and shoulder-length locks. It's always cool being in his body as well. I feel like an action hero. Don't remember much about my first body, but I'm sure it wasn't as nice.

"Hey, kid," I say, "let's do the thing."

Micah looks me in the eyeholes. He puts on the mask and says the words: "EGO SUM NOX LARVA."

The mask glows and undulates, and slowly I start to creep into Micah's body. He groans and trembles as he takes a backseat in his own mind. Bones crack and shatter. Teeth gnash and clatter. His locks straighten and recede. Brown skin becomes green. In fire and smoke and brimstone, I'm transferred into his form.

"I'll never get used to that," he says from inside our skull.

"It's no walk in the park for me either, kid!"

I'm lying, of course. I feel free when I get a body.

I'm much too large to be inside of a damn mask. It's not like we will be doing this every night, though. Only when we have a client who needs us.

I go over to the mirror to make sure the transfer is good. My face is in place perfectly. That is very important. Wouldn't want any mishaps to occur. My face and my mask are one. Black midnight hair spikes out the top of my jade skull. A whip of white follicles dance up the front of my hair. I look at my hands. Black driving gloves decorated with skeleton bones. Yep. My eyes glow yellow like a jack-o'-lantern. My ears point to the skies and my nose points at my target.

I check out my purple-crushed velvet jacket. Red vertical lines run down the front. Very nice. A black T-shirt with matching purple pants and black leather boots finish the look. However, the best thing? The best thing is my scary scarf—a mystical piece of cloth that drapes around my neck. It's orange with giant black stripes running its length. It's saved the day many a case.

"Okay, kid, looks like we're all intact."

"What kind of evil insanity are we headed into this time, Saul?"

"Nineteen-Nineteen Tiny Tree Lane," I say.

"Is that where the client lives?" asks Micah.

"No," I say, "that *is* the client."

I take out a long rope of red licorice from my satchel and loop it around us in a ring on the floor. The candy rope lights up and…poof! We're on our way!

||

Treat magic. I never get tired of it. Yep. Magical candy from a magical place on a magical night.

I'm on seven other cases around the world tonight. Eight faces on the trail. However, I've never had one quite like this.

"Hello, Nineteen-Nineteen Tiny Tree Lane. We're at your service tonight."

The two-story Craftsman-style house looks like it used to be quite nice.

There's a for-sale sign that looks worn and weathered. The neighborhood is nice enough except for this house. Well, let's just say it's going to be a while before they move this home. It has character, but that character might not be for the faint of heart. That heart is probably buried in the floorboards, let me tell you.

The night is alive with monsters, demons, and witches. I can feel them both real and imagined. A really great pirate costume walks past us. Five kids dressed as mice run down the street. A grown man dressed as a mummy runs after the kids. I love Halloween.

The door is locked but not for long. Some quick treat magic with a candy cane pops the lock.

We step into the house and flick on a light. I can feel Micah bristle inside our head. "Okay, this is a creepy ass house."

"I knowwww!" I exclaim. "It's amazing! I can smell the horror!"

Right as I state my glee, the caretaker comes in. "What are you doing in here? This is private property, sir! You need to leave!"

We turn around. I stare down at a tiny mouse of a woman. Soft brown hair pulled back in a neat bun. She looks at us sternly through her powerfully prescripted round eyeglasses.

She's in pajamas, decorated with gold five-pointed stars. A dark blue background makes them seem even brighter. Even in the dim room, I can see the little fake fur on her tattered pink housecoat.

I feel our face become a smile, and I ask, "And who are you?"

She seems surprised that someone would even care to ask. "Well, I'm…I'm Chelsea Catterling. I live across the street. And I saw the light come on! How'd you get in here?"

I answer casually, "Well, I walked in the front door, of course. So, are you just a concerned neighbor or…?"

"I-I take care of this place."

"Do you now? Ms… What was it again?" I inquire.

"Catterling…your face…" She notices that my mask and face are one. It does tend to freak people out.

"Such a nice name. I'll have that one!"

I take out my pad and scribble down her name and the date. Ever since I lost my own and became Saul When, I've grown a bit obsessed with curious names. It's a bit of an addiction.

Did I mention that? I probably did. Still *Catterling*. What could be the origin?

"That's with two T's, yes?" I ask.

"Yes," she answers, "Ummm…who are you again?"

"Oh. Forgive me. My name is When. Saul When." I stick out my hand to shake hers. She shakes my hand out of reflex.

I then ask, "Do you know anything about the missing ghosts?"

She takes her hand back quickly. "Wh-What?"

"Don't freak her out, Saul. You need to be more subtle! I keep telling you," Micah says in our head.

"Okay, okay," I say back to him.

"Well, Ms. Catterling with two T's. This house is…or was… haunted. You do know that, right?"

"I don't know any such thing. There's no such thing as ghosts and…" She turns red and gets really determined to be tough. "I-I'm going to call the police, mister!"

"Go right ahead, but it won't get your ghosts back. Nope. Not at all."

"Wait. What?" Micah asks.

"That's right, Ms. Catterling. Someone stole this house's ghosts, and they did it right under your nose. Some caretaker you are!" I cross my arms pretending to be disappointed in her.

"There are no such things!" She shakes with rage. It amuses me because I know what comes next.

"Okay, smarty pants! Why did the house call me then?" I ask. "Why did it report a ghost-napping?"

She laughs with a very tiny chuckle that then explodes into a full-blown snorting laugh. It surprises me actually.

"Oh, you really had me going! Wow! You are good! Great trick! Just great."

I look at her in the most serious face I can muster. "Oh, Miss Catterling with two T's. I'm afraid that I am very serious. I track down missing tricklings and I handle cases that deal with supernatural creatures. It's my job that I do for the Pumpkin Lord, King of Halloween and ruler of the Hallowverse."

I take out my spirit gum from the satchel. "You are badly taking care of a very, very haunted house. Like, a lot of horrible things happened here. However, all the phantoms have been... taken away and Nineteen-Nineteen Tiny Tree Lane is *not* happy about it."

Micah reminds me not to overwhelm the caretaker.

"This gum will help you see the truth," I say.

"You are insane, mister. Can...can you please leave so I can go back to my *Friday the 13th* marathon? I was watching the one with the telekinetic girl."

I pop the gum in my mouth and start chewing rapidly. Gotta work up the energy for the spirit gum to take effect.

I exclaim through the chewing and smacking: "Oh, I like that one! It was a nice break from all the slash-hackery that Jason usually does!"

Just so you know, spirit gum allows you to talk to inanimate objects. Everything has a soul, you see. Everything has a little ghost in it. It's both fascinating and terrifying, right?

I blow a bubble, a huge bubble. I watch the caretaker's eyes grow almost as big as the bubble, which glows green and becomes a perfect orb. Inside of it, a green spark pulsates.

Then the house speaks.

"Huh…huh…hello? Hey. Wow! I can hear myself speak! This…This is weird!"

The light in the bubble resonates with 1919 Tiny Tree Lane's low but bubbly voice.

"Aieeeghhhhhhh!!" Ms. Catterling screams. It's a pretty great scream actually for someone so tiny.

"How…how are you doing this?" she asks tearfully.

I love that she's still here. I can sense her wonder and amazement taking over her overt fear of the unknown. She's growing on me, this one.

"Treat magic, my dear!" I retort gleefully. "Magical treats from the Kingdom of Halloween! You have no idea what's in here! Tasty delights for any fights. Now let's talk to Nineteen-Nineteen. Is it okay to call you that?"

"My name is Quinton. Please call me that," the house says. I am disappointed in that name, but I made a note of it anyway.

"Okay, Quinton. Tell us what happened. Leave out no details."

The light in the bubble pauses and then begins undulating again with the house's tale.

"Well, it happened three nights ago. I was talking with the five ghosts that live here—Milton, Trisha, Billie, Tandie, and Mark Schelling. They were a family that was murdered in their sleep by an axe-wielding maniac. A mother and father with two girls and a boy. It was totally horrible, but they loved this house. So they stayed, and we were all happy here. Together." The house takes another pause, like it's holding back tears.

Then it continues.

"The Schellings were playing charades like they always do. They were laughing and playing badly as usual. Then they came! They were all dressed in white from head to toe. They were the ones who looked like ghosts! They had on masks, all four of them. They just barged into me unannounced! So rude! I knew they were going to be trouble. There was nothing I could do, though. They had these...contraptions and they...they could see my ghost family! Clear as day! They turned on those things and...*schhhlooop*...sucked them right up! Then they left with my ghost family and took my poor heart along with them! That's when I put in a call to the Pumpkin Lord. I knew he could help. Thank you for coming! Can you find them for me? Bring them back?"

My heart broke from Quinton's story. "I promise," I say. I am not sure how, but I am going to find those spirits or else.

I remember those murders. The killer is actually possessed with the spirit of the legendary Axe Man. He still pops up now and again. Poor souls.

"Okay, we have to get moving," I say. "Thank you, Quinton." I make a motion to pop the bubble.

"Wait. Wait! I have something to tell Ms. Catterling," Quinton says.

"Make it quick," I order.

"Ms. Catterling, I just wanted you know that you're a very good caretaker. I love that you put fresh flowers in the windows. I prefer Gerbera daisies, by the way. I also love how much you clean me and make me feel brand new although I am so very old and rickety. Thanks for the Stevie Wonder songs you hum when you're working. I really like his music a lot. The Schellings do, too. Thanks for making sure my gutters are clean and keeping fresh paint on the walls. There is a tiny leak happening on the east wall in the attic. It's tiny now, but it's going to be worse soon. Okay, that's it. Thank you."

Ms. Catterling looks at the glowing orb lovingly. "You are so welcome, Quinton. It's an honor to take care of you." Then she looks at me for permission. I nod and she pops the bubble.

The house falls silent.

The caretaker looks at me sternly. "Okay, Mr. When. What's next?"

I look at her in utter confusion. "What do you mean, what's next?" I ask, almost laughing in her face.

She peers up at me with very little fear left in her and says, "Now that I know there's a family missing on my watch, I have to go help them. So, what's next?"

"Are you sure?" I ask. "We have no idea what we're up against here. I've never heard of anything like this before. It could…hell, it could make you into a ghost yourself."

Micah tells me not to let her go. He's always too cautious.

"I'm sure," she says.

I take out my seer sucker and give it a slurp. I wave it about my head seven times and take another slurp from it. It's grape. I like grape. I roll the taste around in my mouth and swallow. I pop the sucker in my cheek and say, "Tastes like we're going to school. Let's go get some education."

I use a big licorice ring for Ms. Catterling and myself, and in a puff we leave Quinton, headed for Pumpkin Lord only knows.

III

We end up in a dark place that smells of mold, heat, and rust. A boiler room, I suspect.

"Where are we, man?" Micah asks in our head.

"Boiler room on the campus of Randolph State University."

Ms. Catterling, in disbelief, says, "RSU? But…but that's clear on the other side of the city! How could some nasty candy do this?"

"Licorice is an acquired taste, to be sure, but *nasty*? I think not!" I am offended. "The licorice lashes have many properties, one of which is teleportation in this realm. Now, let's figure out where these ghosts are! I am sure they are terrified!" The irony of my statement is not lost on me.

It turns out we are in the basement of the metaphysics department. The school is named for famed African American mystic and root doctor Paschal Beverly Randolph. He was a one-of-a-kind sorcerous talent and gone far too soon. While here in the Big Easy, he taught freed slaves how to read and ran a lot of wild experiments on human sensuality and magic. RSU has a reputation for carrying on some of his ideas in a state-funded formalized manner. Sometimes, highly clandestine. It totally tracks that they would be involved. However, I think whoever is behind this ghost-napping is getting some non-human help and that chills me to Micah's bones.

This building seems just as haunted as Quinton. I hate municipal spaces. Always have.

We make our way down the shiny pristine halls of the school. Then a tiny little ghost appears out of nowhere and gives us all a collective coronary!

"Help usss!"

"Ahhrghh!" I can't hold the scream in. "Who…who are you, little girl?"

The little phantom hangs in mid-air. A blue light emanates from her. Her eyes stare out into something just beyond. Multiple gashes and cuts punctuate her torso and extremities. Still, she is a beautiful little girl. Her blonde hair, though matted with blood, still has the shine of youth in it—twisted into little curls.

"My name is Tandie. Tandie Schelling."

Ms. Catterling's eyes began to well up. "Oh, Tandie. You poor, poor thing. Where's your family? Are they still here?"

"Yes. They are upstairs in…the bad room."

I don't even want to know what a ghost would call a *bad room*, but it's my job to know.

"Tandie, what goes on in the bad room?" Everyone waits with an overwhelming sense of dread.

The little ghost's eyes light up with terror. "The bug men tear at us. Make us hurt!"

This piques my interest. "Bug men? Green shiny bugs with human heads, yes? Six shiny black eyes? Is that what you mean?"

"Yes! Yes! Bug men!" The ghost seems relieved to be understood. Overjoyed even.

Night Bugs! Nasty things! They were tricklings from the three thousand, which meant that they were under my jurisdiction!

Let me explain.

About a hundred and fifty years ago, Crummin the Red is on earth during Halloween doing his work. Crummin is a minor lord of the Hallowverse who is charged with dispensing tricks. Traditionally, these tricks are kept in a mystical sack. Well, Crummin is also pretty addicted to apple-bobbing. That fateful night he comes across an apple-bobbing contest and just cannot resist giving it a go. He puts his sack down and off he goes! Four and a half hours later, he can't find his sack. He looks all over creation for it. He finally finds it in the hands of a trick-or-treater. They need an extra sack for their spoils, and since it is laying there, they take it and open it. Crummin begins to sob in terror. Why? Because three thousand tricks of all kinds are in the bag and now they are free to roam the world. So, one of the first things the Pumpkin Lord assigns to yours truly is to track down the tricks. I have tracked down five hundred and sixty-seven of them.

Lo and behold, it seems I have found a few more.

Night Bugs eat spectral energy. So, they literally can consume a ghost. However, a soul is immortal. So, they love that they will have an endless energy supply. I suspect that's why these mortal fools in this department are in league with them.

"Tandie, I know you're scared, but I need you to take us to the bad room." I look as kindly as I can with my goblin face.

She looks scared but resolved. "Oh, okay, mister. Please, save my family."

We follow the little spirit up three levels and are faced with a big angry door.

It's marked up will all sorts of warnings. It is definitely the place. I don't like going into places blind, so I take out another seer sucker. I stick the sucker in my mouth and get it good and juiced up. I take the sucker and a draw a big circle on the door. This, of course, allows us to see right into the room like a magic window. What we see is horrific. The Schellings are held, frozen, in a large orb of energy that is being generated by some kind of massive machine. The four culprits in white watch from behind a protective shield. Inside the orb of energy, ten Night Bugs swarm around the ghosts and feed on them like wild beasts. The excess energy that is coming from the ghosts is being siphoned off into these odd cylinders. The Schellings scream in pain. Little Tandie's spectral sockets pour out tears of blood. That's when we are caught. One of the Night Bugs must have sensed us behind the door and look right at us.

"Oh, damn!" I exclaim. "No sense hiding anymore. Let's get this over with!"

I kick the door open, and we rush into the room of ghostly carnage. The men in white spin around in shock.

One of them, a woman, yells, "What? Who are you? How'd you get in here?" That's when I pull out the jawbreakers! I let about seven of them fly from my hands, and they go around wrecking the machinery and pummeling the folks in white! The jawbreakers bounce and ricochet at lightning speed, and they pretty much destroy the machine. Of course, this sets the Night Bugs free.

I suppose the folks in white have called security because five massive fellows rush in to try and apprehend us. That is a huge mistake. It turns out that Ms. Catterling seems to have had some very serious self-defense classes! She makes one blonde burly guy wish he wasn't born. In a couple of quick moves, he's on the ground with a broken nose and probably a shattered kneecap.

In pure rage, she screams, "You can't do this! You can't treat people's souls like this, you animals!"

Little Tandie takes out two more. She turns into a monstrous manifestation and rips them to shreds.

I take out the rest with my Scary Scarf! I wrap it around my mouth and then the scarf augments my voice into a fearful screech that brings them to their knees in terror. They just pass out from horror. They never knew what hit them!

The folks in white cower in the corner as the Night Bugs descend upon us.

"Whennnnnn!! You will payyyy for thissssss!"

They buzz and hiss at me for spoiling their eternal meal plan. The jawbreakers pummel them into submission in short order, and I pull out mystical candy bars that create a makeshift cage. They change their tunes right quick. They know what's next.

"Nooo! Pleaaazzzz! Let us gooooo! Let us goooo, Whennnn!" The Night Bugs cry and wail and quiver like they weren't just feasting on innocent phantoms a few seconds ago. Some nerve, these tricklings!

The four science folks try and run out. I gum up their escape with some taffy, though. They have to answer for their crimes as well.

"Where do you think you're going?" asks the caretaker. She's quickly becoming one of my favorite humans. She goes over to the ghost-nappers and snatches off their hoods and goggles. One of them is a middle-aged white woman with long auburn hair and flecks of white at the temples. To her left is a middle-aged Black man with light eyes. His hair is receding and it looks like he dyes it. The last two are much younger. A young Korean man and a young white woman with red hair and hazel eyes tremble in fear as Ms. Catterling glares at them. They try to escape, but the taffy holds them fast.

"Please, let us go! We were trying to save the world!" the white woman pleads. "The energy we've collected is clean, and it never runs out!"

"There's nothing clean about any of this!" I scream. I turn my attention back to the Night Bugs. "Ms. Catterling with two T's… you need to get behind me."

"Nnooo! Whennnn! Noooo!" The Night Bugs shake their giant chocolate candy bar cage to no avail.

I take off my mask and reveal what's under it. The Maw of Forever—a direct portal to the Hallowverse. It sends tricklings back to their maker for judgement. I suck the Night Bugs, kicking, bussing, and screaming, into the chasm in my face, and, like that, they are gone along with the cylinders of *clean* energy. I place my mask back on and make a note that the escaped three thousand tricklings are now down by ten.

Tandie and her family embrace each other, and if they hadn't been dismembered and bleeding like cattle, it would have been a beautiful sight. Their hugs and kisses make slick, sticky sounds, and I have to turn away.

Milton Schelling turns to me and says, with teary eyes, "Thank you! Thank you so much for coming to our aid, sir! We owe you our afterlives!"

"You owe me nothing. I work for a higher power. A higher pumpkin," I laughingly decree. Then our attention turns to the four kidnappers. "So, ghost-stealers. What should we do with you, then?" I can almost smell their blood go cold.

"You can let us go," says the redhead, desperately trying to look innocent. The Korean man nods quickly in agreement, his eyes glowing with dread.

"Give them to us," Billie Schelling hisses. Her face is already shifting into a more malevolent state.

I look at Ms. Catterling and we both nod and then leave the room for a while. We listen on as the bad room becomes worse and worse. Then the screaming stops.

The Schellings come out with even more blood on them. We ask no questions as I prepare a portal back to Quinton.

In mere seconds, we arrive in their living room.

"Ms. Catterling, Mr. When," says Mrs. Schelling, "we can't thank you enough. You're both heroes to us. Bless you!" Blood streams from her lacerated face where her eyes used to be.

"You are so welcome, ma'am," I say, as I try to ignore the shiny black ooze that trickles out her mouth. "Anytime," I add.

Ms. Catterling looks proudly at her new ghost friends, the Schellings, and waves at them lovingly as they fade away into the walls of Quinton.

"So, Ms. Catterling, this was better than that movie, right?" I joke.

"Oh, most definitely! I'll never forget this! Thank you for opening my eyes to the wonders of the night, Mr. When. How can I ever repay you?"

"Well, there is one thing," I say slyly.

Micah protests the whole time I talk to Ms. Catterling about some future arrangements.

She listens gleefully way past her *Friday the 13th* marathon.

I leave a few hours before dawn with another case solved and spectral justice served.

I grin a toothy semi-malicious grin as I walk down Tiny Tree Lane, thinking of RSU's Metaphysics Department and its newly haunted top floor.

A DEAD JACK, ZOMBIE DETECTIVE MYSTERY

BY JAMES AQUILONE

THE CASE OF THE RAVENOUS WEREWOLF

"**I** need you to murder me to death," the kook said, his voice serious as the grave. He uttered the words as if someone forced them out of his mouth.

I really needed to watch who I let in the office.

I sat at my desk. The madman, who must have been at least half a foot taller than me, stood wringing his hands.

"Can you sit down, Paul Bunyan? You're making me nervous." I downed a shot of Devil Boy, a blend of whiskey and formaldehyde, and felt a too brief warmth in my bones.

The kook sat and wrung his hands like he wanted to rub the skin off.

"You must have walked into the wrong office," I said. "The letters on the front door say *detective*, not *assassin*."

"Yes, Dead Jack, the ghoul detective. I'm aware of your work."

"*Zombie* detective!" Oswald piped in for no reason. "There's a *difference*."

Oswald, my hero. The little guy never knew when to keep quiet, but that's what you get with a homunculus assistant. He had other strengths, though, like the ability to contort his rubbery body into any shape possible, and some impossible.

"You think because I'm a zombie, I'll do anything? Is that it? Usually, when I kill someone, they don't request it beforehand. Usually they're trying to murder *me*. Or I'm out of fairy dust and hungry. I didn't catch your name, tall boy."

"It's Ravenwood. Mel Ravenwood." Mel Ravenwood shook like one of those hula girls you see on the dashboard of a hot rod. "I need you to murder me because tomorrow is the full Moon—"

"Oh, you're a werewolf. Why didn't you say so?"

"Once a month, I transform into a wild beast with an insatiable appetite and stalk the fields of The Red Garden. If you do not murder me, I will devour scores of innocent fairies."

"Is that a threat, jitters?"

"It is the reality of the truth."

"How do I know you're not lying?"

Again, big-mouth Oswald cut in. "I've read about these killing in *The Daily Specter*. They've been happening for a while on the border between Fairy Land and Wolf End. It's a big deal because there's been a truce between the fairies and the werewolves."

"You're not the only werewolf in Pandemonium's Five Cities," I said. "Try chaining yourself up. It does wonders for folks like you."

"I'm too powerful. I always break free."

"Have you tried killing yourself? It would save you some money."

"A werewolf cannot kill himself."

"You guys don't die easily, huh? So how is a dumb zombie like me supposed to do it?"

"Tomorrow night, in The Red Garden, when the Moon is high in the blood-red sky, you must stab me while I'm in my bestial form." Ravenwood stood, reached behind himself, and pulled out a long dagger from his waistband. "It's silver."

"I'm no killer."

"Either you kill me or I kill dozens."

"I don't go around murdering people for no reason. Can I eat you after?"

"Jack!" Oswald stood with his hands on his hips.

"I have huge stashes of fairy dust," Ravenswood said. "One of the benefits of killing fairies. I never use the stuff myself. I'm terribly allergic. But I understand you take dust as payment."

"Where would you like me to stab you?"

2

It had to be in heart with the silver blade, which I now had in my possession.

"Are you really going to kill this guy?" Oswald said irritatingly as I drove the Studebaker to the ferry at the southern tip of ShadowShade the next night. He sounded disappointed in me. What was new?

"You heard him. He's going to slaughter innocent fairies. We can't have that. We need fairies so they can make more dust."

"I know, but I don't like this."

As I drove onto the ferry, I looked up at the full Moon. I had never noticed the damn thing before this night. I felt the blade in my jacket pocket. Could I kill a man—a werewolf actually—in cold blood? Then I thought of the poor little fairies. I had chowed down on my share of the wee folk since being banished to this twilight dimension along with all of the Other World's supernatural creatures and monsters at the end of World War II. But I feasted because the craving for flesh overtook me. Dust curbs my appetite now…when I can get my hands on it.

It was a short drive from the dock to the middle of The Red Garden, where Fairy Land meets Werewolf End. A lot of blood had been spilled there between the two factions, thus the name Red Garden.

The Moon hung low enough to touch. As I opened the Studebaker's door, a loud baying filled the night air. If I had hair on the back of my neck, it would have been standing up.

Of course, Oswald asked the obvious question. "Did you hear that?"

"My grandmother in the Other World could hear that, dunzy."

I got out of the car and looked around. The werewolf sounded close, but I didn't see him.

We crept into the wild grass, a cold wind blowing into our faces.

I smelled him before I saw him. Stunk like the circus on a Saturday night.

Mel—or what I figured was Mel—came stomping toward us. He must have grown by three hundred pounds and a foot in height. He was covered in hair and muscles. A pair of fairy legs kicked from his slavering mouth.

"Hey, Mel, is that you?" I shouted.

He sucked up the fairy legs like spaghetti and kept coming. His eyes blazed and he let out a roar.

"Do I just kill him?" I asked Oswald.

He didn't get a chance to answer. Mel swatted Oswald, and the little guy went flying.

Then Mel turned to me, huffing and puffing, saliva dripping from his mouth in fat chunks.

"I thought I was supposed to kill *you*," I said. "What are you doing?"

The werewolf took a step forward.

"Now, Mel…" I held the silver dagger in front of me.

Mel howled—I felt it reverberate in my chest—and then he lunged. I jumped back but not quick enough. Mel landed on the dagger, which slid into his chest like warm butter.

I jumped out of the way and he crashed to the ground, on top of the blade. Mel screamed. It began as a werewolf howl but ended as a human whimper. A moment later, his body went up in flames like a steak flambé and turned to a heap of ash. Atop the ashes sat a gold chain with a key attached. Back at the office, he said my payment would be in a locker at the Midtown Bus Depot in ShadowShade and that he'd be wearing the key. I scooped up the key and the blade and headed back to ShadowShade.

3

Just as Mel promised, the locker was filled with dust. I thought he'd stiff me on the payment, but he was an honest werewolf. It was a shame he had to go out like that.

At the office, Oswald annoyingly said, "You should conserve the dust. Maybe it will last you for the year."

But I was feeling sad about killing that generous werewolf, so I took a heap of dust right then and there. The trauma of killing Mel must have been more powerful than I realized, because I kept taking the dust. It had been a while since I had quality stuff like this.

But like all good things, the dust ran out. I awoke sometime in the future in a pool of my own drool beside the bathroom sink.

I shambled into the office, bleary eyed, and saw Oswald reading the paper. His head shot up when I entered. "Are you going to apologize?"

"For what?"

"Where do I begin? Do you remember reciting the Gettysburg Address naked last night? Forget it. We have bigger problems. Have you seen this story?" He was waving a copy of *The Daily Specter* in front of my face.

"The only thing I've been seeing the past few weeks is Rita Hayworth doing the can-can in her birthday suit. Don't ruin it and tell me it was a hallucination."

"There have been killings in The Red Garden."

"There are *always* killings in The Red Garden. What's the news?"

"Do you know what day it is?"

"Is this Twenty Questions? Just spit it out."

"It's the full Moon again. You've been on a month-long bender, you know? There have been werewolf killings at the border over the last three days. I think it's Mel."

Boy, that was a long time to be out. I hoped I had a good time.

"Mel? The guy who turned to dust after I killed him?"

"As I said before, there was a truce. No one else was killing fairies. Who else could it be?"

"Just about any other werewolf. Plus, our guy killed only one day a month. You said this werewolf killed over the last *three days*."

"Yeah, that doesn't make sense. But I've been looking at the dagger you used and I noticed strange markings on the handle. I think it's magical. None of the books I have match up with it, though. We need to talk to Wally."

"You worry too much. We don't need to talk to anyone. I killed the werewolf. I got paid. The case is closed."

"I thought you cared about the innocent fairies getting devoured."

"Come on, you know I was just saying that for the dust."

"And you got your dust. Now we're going to investigate and see how much you screwed up."

I was in no mood for arguing. It felt like two ogres were sumo wrestling inside my skull. When Oswald got like this, it was best to just go along. And as luck would have it, I found a small baggie of dust in the bottom drawer of my desk. I could use a little hair of the fairy that bit me.

4

For once, Wally the Wizard wasn't in prison. The korrigan had more knowledge than anyone I knew in the Five Cities, though he mostly used his smarts to rip people off. His counterfeit Philosopher's Stones could fool Merlin himself.

"Jack, to what do I owe the pleasure?"

Wally was tending his garden. He had a little bungalow by the water in the Little Valhalla section of ShadowShade.

"It's nothing. I'm humoring Oswald or he'll whine about this nonsense forever."

"Wally, this is a matter of life and death," Oswald exaggerated. He took out the dagger. "What can you tell us about this?" He handed it to the wizard. "Jack killed a werewolf with this silver dagger in The Red Garden last month."

Wally studied its handle, turned the blade over, ran a finger over the edge. "This isn't silver," he said, and took out a small pocketknife from his pocket. He scraped the flat side of the blade, peeling off the chrome coating. Underneath, the blade was black. "As I thought, obsidian."

"If it's not silver," I asked, "how did I kill a werewolf with it?"

"You stabbed a werewolf with this blade?"

"He asked us to. Really, he insisted."

"He gave Jack a lot of dust," Oswald whined.

Wally shook his head and held up the blade handle. "See these markings? This is a Phoenix Blade. It's used in resurrection rituals. If you stabbed a werewolf with this blade during a full Moon, you didn't kill him. You brought him back as a permanent wolf, more powerful than he had been before."

What a disappointment Mel turned out to be. "That kook tricked us!"

"Jack, we have to do something about this," Oswald said.

"How are we supposed to kill this guy?

"If you had an actual silver blade, you could do it," Wally said.

5

So we headed back to The Red Garden, this time equipped with an actual silver dagger.

I parked the Studebaker in roughly the same place as before. The field was empty. There was no baying. We sat and waited.

"Now it's okay to kill this kook?" I asked.

"I don't see any other way," Oswald said. "Mel is a much bigger danger. Before, he killed only one day a month. Now he can—and will—slaughter the fairies every day. All because of us. We have an obligation to make things right."

"As long as I have your blessing, Jiminy Cricket. I don't want to do anything you don't approve of."

"Did I stop you from killing him the first time?"

Krrrrrreeeeek! Something scraped against the side of the Studebaker.

I turned to see a brown hairy blur whiz by.

Crash! Something rammed the passenger side, rocking the car. Then another hit and the Studebaker rose a good six inches off the ground.

"It's Mel!" Oswald yelled, unhelpfully.

The werewolf jumped onto the roof and howled.

I leaped out of the car, and Oswald followed.

The werewolf continued to bay.

The beast turned toward Oswald and growled. Os inflated his right fist to the size of a cinderblock. His rubbery arm extended and swung at Mel. The werewolf extended his razor-sharp claws and swiped at Oswald's arm, slicing his hand off at the wrist and sending it deep into the grass.

"Oh, geez!" Oswald exclaimed, and ran off to retrieve his severed fist, leaving me to face the creature alone.

The werewolf jumped off the roof and snarled.

I brandished the blade. "This is *real* silver."

Mel backed up, and then we circled each other like two panthers.

"I knew you were stupid, but not this stupid. You got paid, zombie. You should have left this alone."

"You duped me. You never wanted me to kill you. You wanted me to turn you into a full-time killing machine."

"Who figured that out? The little rubber guy? I know it wasn't you."

"Actually, we figured it out together." I jiggled the blade. "You sure you don't want to impale yourself again?"

The werewolf swatted the blade from my hand, and it disappeared into the night.

Mel advanced, pushing me up against the Studebaker. He stood over me, dripping hot saliva onto my face.

"If I rip off your head, will you die?"

Where the hell was Oswald? He was the one who got me into this situation.

I didn't think I could take the werewolf in a one-on-one situation. I had no weapons, only my little bag of dust. A pinch of the stuff would do me good right about now.

Wait a minute!

A pinch of the stuff *would* do me good right about now. Didn't Mel say he was allergic to the stuff?

The werewolf raised his paw to strike, but I grabbed the baggie from my inner jacket pocket, opened it, and—as much as it pained me—blew dust into Mel's face.

He immediately began to sneeze. His eyes turned red and he stumbled backward.

I moved in and blew more dust into his face, the sweet cotton-candy smell of the powder filling the air. The werewolf roared as he rubbed his wet eyes.

In the distance, tiny orbs of light appeared. The lights twinkled and grew larger as they closed in on us.

I blew another few specks of dust into the wolf's face. He cried in pain and fell to the ground. "Stop! Stop!" he shouted as he rolled in the grass.

The lights were nearly on top of us. That's when I realized it was an army of fairies.

The werewolf was choking now and grabbing at his throat, which had swollen to twice its size.

The lights dissolved and fairies appeared on all sides…pixies, brownies, leprechauns, kobolds… Then Oswald jumped out of the crowd, proud of himself for some reason.

"Where the hell have you been?" I asked.

"Getting reinforcements. And my fist." Oswald's hand had been reattached, though it hung limply from his wrist. "It'll sort itself out," he said.

Mel howled as she clawed at his eyes. "It burns!" he croaked. "The dust burns!"

What a terrible thing to be allergic to fairy dust. But things were about to get more terrible for Mel as the fairies descended on the hairy serial killer.

Payback is a bitch.

As the wee folk ripped the werewolf to shreds with all manner of silver weapons, I whispered to Oswald, "You think they'll give me dust for subduing Mel?"

"You think you deserve it after turning Mel into a permanent werewolf?"

"Why do I even talk to you?"

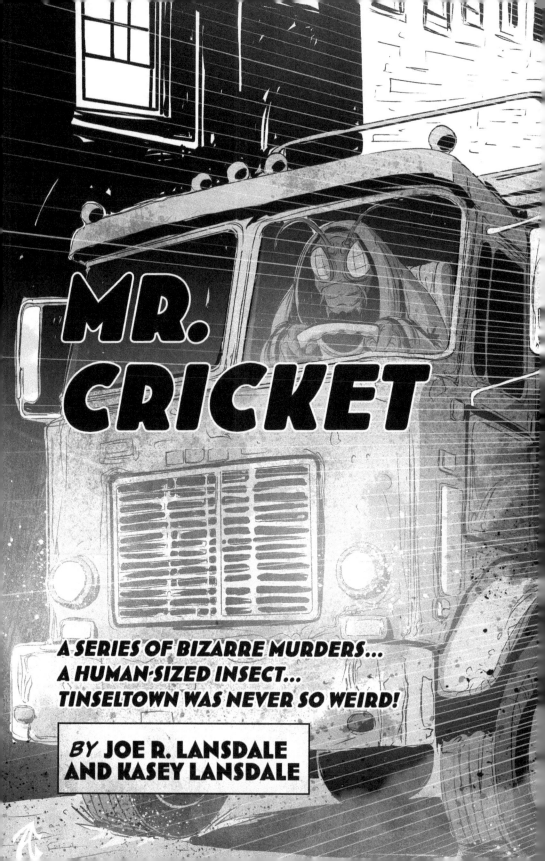

O ne does not stumble on their own gravestone and expect to walk away without questions. But I'll come back to that.

What I remembered best was the crash, the sounds of bending metal and crunching glass. As for the rest of it, I didn't recall much. Beeping noises, crying, a white hospital room, floating above my body, feeling as if I were being tugged away from it, yet somehow bound to it as well.

Being dead is not as straightforward as expected.

But the thing is, I came back. Sort of. This part will need some explanation, but for right now hold your water and let me play some things out.

I arrived in Burbank at my new school during the fall of 2019 after my father was tapped to write for the reboot of a series that had been popular in the '60s. Dad had gone from janitor to professor, to journalist to writer, and then on to scriptwriter. This meant my mother and I had gone from small-town East Texas to bigger-town Texas, to the bright lights slightly north of Hollywood known as Burbank.

It came as little surprise to anyone that I joined the school newspaper as my chosen elective. My weak attempt at fitting in both with my family and my peers.

Unfortunately, I'd accomplished the opposite, become a social pariah. A literal enemy of the people. Hadn't meant to, of course. I'd merely followed the facts. Chased down the leads and let the story take me where it wanted. How was I to know that Sarah J. Riley would end up dead because of it?

While I often wished for death as every dramatic teenager does, I never thought it would happen, at least not until I was old and gray with a heart condition or some such. I was on my way to

Sarah's funeral. Her death had been ruled a suicide, though I was uncertain of that. I had slowed at a light, and to the left, in line with my well-used Ford driver-side door, was an alleyway, and in the alleyway was a garbage truck. Nothing odd about that. Garbage trucks pick up garbage in alleyways, right?

I remember glancing at it, seeing the outline of a driver in a black hoodie, whiskered maybe, crouched over the steering wheel, and the way he was looking at me made me feel a tinge of nervousness. That man and his truck were like a dinosaur observing its prey. Before the light could change, the garbage truck made a whining sound and came out of the alley knocking a couple of cars aside that were passing me in the other lane. But the truck wasn't deterred. It was still coming.

I could see how things were about to play out, so I tried to run the light, not that that would have necessarily worked out well, considering the rapid flow of L.A. traffic. I gassed forward a foot or so, willing to take my chances, when the truck collided with the driver's side of my car.

You can cue up that sound of shattering glass and crunching metal again. And that was my last memory before I heard the beeping sounds and saw myself above my body in the hospital. I knew that accident hadn't been an accident. It was on purpose.

And then it was as if I blinked and was in another place.

A large empty room with chairs and a receptionist window. No one else was in the room but me. I went to the receptionist window and rang the bell there. Nothing. I went back and sat down and tried to sort my thoughts.

That's when a door beside the receptionist's desk opened, and a little man in a too-big brown suit with a black fedora came out smiling. His cheeks were as bright as polished apples.

He said, "I see you. I knew you were here. I'm glad to help you."

This seemed, to say the least, slightly off.

"Where am I?" I asked.

The little man sucked at his teeth and squinted as if trying to focus on something in dim light.

"Kind of depends," he said.

"I am either some place or I'm not. I mean, I'm in a waiting room, so I guess the real question is why am I here?"

"That is indeed the question. You are in between."

"In between what?"

"Some would call it purgatory. A stalling point on your way up or your way down. Neither of those places exists, but Death does have doors, and here you are, waiting for one to open. If it ever does."

I was baffled. I had so many questions I couldn't ask any.

"Some people, no matter what goes on in their life, they die, and go out into the ether and become one with the universe, and *universe* is a cheap term, but it's one you can grab onto. You, you've got some thoughts, honey. You were deep in a mystery, and now you are in another. You can't move on until you solve it. Until then, well, you're kind of neither."

"Who are you?"

"I'm who you've made me. I'm thinking maybe you watch a lot of old crime movies on the Turner Classic Channel. Of course, with these cheeks, I'm not in black and white, like the old noir movies."

This was true. I did watch a lot of old movies. My dad liked them. He liked Elvis too and this guy had the essence.

"I am your assistant," he said. "Or rather, I am your subconscious. You are in one of those hung between spaces by your own will. You can't let go. Not yet. But you can sort of go back for a little while."

"Sort of go back?"

"Well, yeah. You'll be like you always were, mostly, except you could slip back here easy enough. And man, look around. An empty room, some chairs, a receptionist desk, not even a lousy magazine like those they have at the doctor's office. Always some oddball fishing magazine, or something about horses. Not even that here. You solve what's holding you up, and you can become one with the universe. Which means you'll be nothing with the universe."

"Is that Hell or Heaven?"

"Neither exist, girl. You're either nothing, or you go back to your body and live your life, and then you're nothing. But this middle ground—man, this places sucks—and you haven't even had time to get bored yet."

"If I'm here, how do I solve things?"

"Depends on how bad you want to go back, and if you go back, you're dead, baby, dead. But it won't seem that way to others. But unless you get that worry of what happened out of your mind, you'll be left hanging."

I thought about that. "I have a question. The garbage truck driver. How did the wreck turn out for him?"

"He ran off, kid. One witness said he jumped out of the truck, hit the pavement, dodged between two cars, ran into the alley. Said he resembled nothing more than a big gangly cricket with a little rug on his face. I take that as a colorful description. He somehow disappeared in there. Not a trace. The real truck driver, he had gone for a coffee and his truck was stolen. A tip. Don't leave the key in your ride, even if it is a garbage truck. I know what I know of this because I am you and you heard it while in your coma. Cops came into your hospital room, told your parents. Cops looked for the guy, since it was obvious what happened hadn't been an accident. They found a black hoodie in the alley, but they didn't find him. They figure he followed you in that truck. Got ahead of you somewhere, took a side road, set up and waited.

"I want to go back home. To earth. I'm not nearly as excited about being an investigative reporter as I once was."

"That's up to you, kid. Up to you."

And then I was alone in that dreadful waiting room. I closed my eyes and wished hard I could go back to my body. I wished until I nearly strained my brain. I know my neck hurt. And then I opened my eyes in the hospital room, and thought, *I'm back*.

That didn't turn out to be quite what I thought.

I was in bed, but I felt different. I didn't hurt. Next thing I knew, I was standing beside my bed, fully dressed, looking at myself laying there all black and blue in the face, a neck brace on, tubes going in and out. My parents were beside my bed, crying, my mother holding my hand. But now I was wearing the clothes I had been wearing when that garbage truck hit me. I didn't have any pain. I felt all right. There were two of me, and one of me didn't look so good.

I called to my mom and dad, but there was no sound in that room, no matter how hard I tried to talk to them. And they couldn't see me.

I remembered what I was supposed to do, and I set about doing it.

I took a deep breath of nothing, and walked out of there, rode the elevator down to street level, and went out into the night and stood on the street. I looked up and a woman nodded to acknowledge me, way people do. I was no longer invisible. But I knew what Fedora Man told me was true. I could feel it. I might be visible now, outside of the hospital, but I was dead. I stepped back through those hospital doors, I was invisible again.

I was also tired. Dead tired.

I walked to a fast-food place, stopped inside. Checked to see if I still had money, a debit card in my pocket. I did. I had dollars, too. Even my phone was there along with a few provisions I had put in my coat pocket—a granola bar, a bag of peanuts, a switchblade knife, and a lot of lint. I was touching and feeling, without my hands passing through. I checked to make sure my hands wouldn't pass through other things that were not a part of or on me. Like the outside walls of the eatery.

So far so good. I was me now, or at least an acceptable version. I thought it might seem weird if I came back home and had used my card at a time when I was in bed in the hospital in a coma. To hell with that. I went in, bought food and a drink with the bills, but when I sat down to eat, I couldn't taste the food. I realized I didn't really want it. I wasn't hungry, just ghost-stressed. I looked over to the glass expecting my reflection, but it was Fedora Man staring back at me. He lifted his arm, tapped his wrist with his hand, mouthed, "Time flies."

But what was I to do?

I thought about Sarah, how she had led to all this.

How was I to repair my situation? Not end up back in that waiting room without magazines or social media.

Could I fix it?

I had done this before, expected to go in search of the murderous creature, but he'd found me first. And ran me over with a truck, no less.

Sarah was a quirky senior with a fashion sense that combined decades of choices in pants, skirts, dresses, scarfs, leggings, trainers, and lace-up boots. Her hairstyles were just as variable. She was smart, but impetuous, or so said her mother, a once-famous actress who looked on the rise again due to a TV show that bored me to death but seemed to excite the intellectuals in the acting field. Sarah said that meant there were some Hollywood thespians that might be on a good day as smart as cows. I should note, Sarah has issues with her mother and her mother's friends. "When I'm in a room with them," Sarah said, "my IQ drops ten points and gets a cold, feels suicidal."

I had briefly been around her mother, who always smiled at me like I might be an ant at a picnic. It seemed at any moment she might slip off her shoe and swat me.

Me and Sarah had done a few journalistic pieces together. She was a senior writer, and I was the new girl. I got jobs writing about high school fashion and what the cheerleaders thought while performing in front of large groups of high school football fans.

Working on that article, having interviewed a few cheerleaders, I found the writing of such a lot less rewarding than I had hoped, and I didn't exactly have great expectations.

"Just write that they all said they sure hoped when they jumped in those short skirts, they had on clean drawers," Sarah said.

I so badly wanted to write that, but I didn't. Instead, I used their actual interviews where they wished for world peace and an end to cancer, and all the usual stuff that is like unanswered prayers.

But now Sarah was onto something and she wanted me to help her out. It was real journalism. Real investigative reporting. It was murder. And it had nothing to do with unattainable world peace.

I walked from the eatery to the alley where I had been hit by the garbage truck. It was dark down that alley, a perfect place to be mugged. I laughed. Me, mugged. I'm dead. But could I be hurt? Whatever the answer to that, I was determined to take a look.

It was funny how mysterious that alley seemed, considering the street lights and people walking along the sidewalk, talking, laughing, cars roaring and honking behind me on the busy street where I had been clipped by that dinosaur of a truck.

Pulling my phone from my pocket, I turned on the flashlight and went down there, walked farther into the dark. It felt like one of those exploratory bathyspheres drifting down, down, into places where the water pressure was beyond human ability to withstand, where the dark was so dark a shark might tremble.

Near the end, I stopped, stood looking at one of the alley walls, trying to figure how my attacker had run back here and disappeared. I shone the light on the brick wall, and there were chips of white in the red brick, like someone had used a mountaineer hammer. Which, of course, was ridiculous. But someone had made those gouges climbing.

I touched one of the marks, felt the wall crumble slightly between my fingers. Yeah, I was going to guess that was recent, way it powdered. Whatever had been wearing that hoodie had tossed it, went straight up this wall, like…well, like an insect.

This jived with what Sarah had discovered, and while I always thought she was onto something, I didn't think she was on to what she thought she was on to. Considering I was in a coma, had been in a cosmic waiting room, it was a lot easier to believe all manner of things now.

Bubbling with anger, I pushed my hand against the wall—

—and passed through.

I was like Casper the Ghost. I found myself standing inside a dusty foyer with a set of stairs winding upwards. Damn, I had one super power. Get anxious, and I could pass through walls. Yet, I was solid now.

I went up the stairs and came to a door that led to the roof, pushed it open with a loud squeak. Out on the roof, I looked around. There was serious light up there from all the street and building lights, and I could see clearly. Across the roof there was a string of clothes that led to the edge. Whoever had worn them appeared to have been peeling them as they went. On the roof of another building across the way, I could see a brown shoe. The space between the roofs of the buildings, that was some jump. Even more interesting, the building top across from me was higher than the one where I stood.

My attacker, and my guess, Sarah's murderer, was spry.

Sarah revealed her discovery to me about a week ago, and at that point, I thought she might have gone over the lip of common sense and plunged into the depths of madness. I knew something was up. I wasn't aware of what it truly was. Nor was I aware that I would be run over by a garbage truck and end up in a coma with a little man in a fedora talking to me. If that wasn't a big enough surprise, I could pass through walls. Were there other things I could do? Was Sarah in deadland, too?

I doubted it. I was in a coma. She was stone cold forever dead. She had undoubtedly passed into being one with the cosmos. Being part of nothingness might be something to look forward to. It was that ticket you paid to get there that was expensive, at least emotionally. I didn't like to dwell on the pain she must have gone through.

Day she died, she said she was going to look in a place where she was certain IT lived. That's what she called it, IT. I was supposed to meet her, but in the end, I couldn't. I texted her to tell her. My father had an important event to attend, and my mother and I were supposed to be there with him. He didn't ask much, but I think he wanted to show off his family, and me and Mom wanted to be shown off. The event would be full of the beautiful people. And by this time, I was finding Sarah harder to believe. She was onto something. But what she thought she was onto seemed unlikely, and I wasn't sure I wanted her crazy vibe to rub off on me. I was trying to fit in at what for me was still a new school.

I told her my situation, glad for the excuse to back off from her theories for a night. Maybe forever. She texted back that she was going anyway, that she had found its nest, as she called it.

Next day they found what was left of her up by the Hollywood Sign. Someone, or something, had cut out or torn out her spine, had taken the spine and her head with them. I couldn't decide if I should be happy I had stayed home or disappointed I failed to go with her. Had I been there, she might have had the help she needed to survive. Or, we might both be missing a head and a spine.

I decided not to let the use of my debit card worry me. I ordered an Uber. When it showed up, the fellow driving didn't look like a cricket in a hoodie, so that was some relief. I gave him an address a street down from where Sarah had lived.

When I got out of the car, I was in front of a mansion that was owned by a movie star who lived in Sarah's neighborhood. It looked like God's vacation spot. I stood there, taking it all in. Watched as every few minutes an open-top tour bus drove by, pointing out the house. The Uber driver hadn't seemed impressed. I don't think he cared about God's vacation home, didn't care if I was going to take a shit in the bushes. He was out of there so fast that the sound of the car rolling away and my closing the car door was near simultaneous.

L.A. was all about turnover.

I walked along the well-lit street and took a turn down a driveway. I veered off that, followed a path through some well-kept undergrowth that was thick and shadowy. Sarah used this route when she didn't want to go by the guard shack, interrupt one of her mother's parties which, she said, were nearly every night. Sarah called her home the Gatsby residence.

I had to push aside a board that was part of a six-foot fence. I wiggled through the gap and remembered I most likely could have just walked through the fence, using my newfound power.

But I did it old school. I looked at Sarah's house. It was not as elaborate as the house where I was let out, but it would do. It was not lit up like a floor show, way it usually was. It had taken Sarah's mysterious death to end party night. A few days more, who knew?

The backyard was less bright. I ran across it like a gazelle, heard a dog bark a couple houses over, and then I was climbing up the vine-covered trellis that led to Sarah's bedroom window. I pushed at the window, and though I nearly pulled a muscle in my back making it happen, the window slid up and I clamored inside. Where was that super power when I needed it?

The room was full of dead air. I turned on the little light on Sarah's desk. I had forgotten there was a mirror facing it, and I jumped when I saw my reflection. At least it was my reflection this time, not my buddy in the fedora. I sat down at her desk, looked through a scattering of notes.

I opened her desk drawer, and found what I was looking for. A small but thick black journal where Sarah kept her notes. She was so far above high school journalism it wasn't even funny. This girl was serious. She had shown me the journal before, read some of her notes to me, but when I opened it and looked at it now, there were a number of freshly written pages. I knew that by the date. The last one listed was the night she went to discover the nest. The night she asked me to go with her. Instead, I wore a very nice dress and shoes and was digesting shrimp and baked oysters at a party full of movie stars while Sarah was being torn apart, her remains dumped by the Hollywood Sign.

What Sarah had discovered, according to the notes, was that every ten years for a span of about three months, going way back to the beginning of Hollywood, back when California was just another desert, there had been a series of bizarre murders where bodies were ripped apart and the spinal columns and skulls taken. There would be a flurry of investigation by law enforcement, and when the killer wasn't found and the murders stopped, the victims would be, for all practical purposes, forgotten. Ten years after, the same thing. Sarah had concluded it was a cycle. The original thought was that these new murders were copycats. Could it be a family tradition, passed down from one relative to the next? Not likely. One monster to the next?

Maybe.

And we were now in a new period of murders. Six bodies and counting. Not including hers.

Sarah was obsessed with these murders. I went with her on jaunts through Hollywood to interview old detectives on what they knew, if anything, during their time on the force. And if not them, what their previous counterparts had known.

At a rest home, we spoke to a former cop who was pushing a hundred years old but had a remarkable memory for the case. He had to be interviewed between naps, many of them suddenly taken in mid-conversation. Told us to call him Junior. He sounded rational, until he didn't. He said he investigated the case and felt in his bones he had come close a few times, but never really discovered much that mattered. But his father, Andy Baker Sr., had.

Back in the late 1920s, when Hollywood was still young and the first murder was recorded, his father, a cop, had told him a curious story.

Andy had talked to a man whose young son, while climbing a tree with his friends, found a cache of dog and cat skulls with the spines attached, all of them gnawed on, in the higher boughs of a tree. The tree was near an orange grove and the skulls and spines were wadded amongst leaves, a spiderweb-like netting, paper fragments, along with torn and chewed cloth.

According to Junior, Senior Baker thought the animal bones and the murders might be connected somehow but couldn't prove it. Senior Baker also didn't think it was a coincidence about the animal bones being found near an orange grove not far away from where the human bodies had been discovered.

The orange grove had been the one detail the paper held back. Of course, it was California, so it wasn't all that hard to end up dead near an orange tree. But he knew it meant something, could feel it in his bones the way cops do. Even so, Senior Baker decided the idea of taking animal bones and oranges to his superior seemed like a good way to be shut out of the investigation, so he didn't. Instead, he set up his own stakeout across the street from the orchard, climbed into a tree there and waited.

The old man told the story like he had been there, instead of his father. Sights and sounds, smells, the whole nine yards. Only thing missing were sound effects. He said the grove was close to town and there was even a sidewalk that split the grove in half, and the sidewalk led downhill toward the city's bright lights. The breeze was steady and the smell of oranges wafted in the air. From this vantage the city looked different, cleaner, and he thought about what it might be like to live life as a bird. This thought entertained him for a while until the sun changed position and the evening air grew dry and cold.

It was coming up on nightfall. Baker needed to use the can and his snacks were almost gone. Just as he thought of calling it and heading home, a man dressed in a dark suit and a dark hat appeared on the sidewalk between the groves. He had a small white dog on a leash. Baker decided he would wait for them to pass, climb down, then stop by Musso and Frank's on his way home for dinner.

The man and the dog took their time as they approached the tree line across the way. The dog stopped to sniff every few feet for other dog deposits, until finally, seemingly satisfied with his position, the dog dropped into a crouch to do his business. In a strange show of solidarity, the man squatted next to the dog on the sidewalk. According to Baker, the instant the man's hand hit the pavement, gossamer wings burst through his suit jacket and out of his back, surrounding him like a chitin shield. The bug man scooped up the dog with an anterior leg and in one swift motion leapt into the orange tree overhead. Baker, confused by, but sure of what he'd seen, shimmied his way down to earth and onto the sidewalk.

It was about here that the recount by the old man began to get hazy.

Isn't that the way?

"And then what?" Sarah had asked.

"Dad said he ran over there, gun drawn. He confronted the man from down below, just as IT twisted off the head of that dog like a dreidel at Hanukkah. Before he could react, the thing was on top of him, slick with blood, slashing and stinging. Dad fired two rounds, but IT fluttered those big wings and took off in the direction of Mulholland Drive like a turbo jet, and disappeared into the night sky. I never believed him, not fully. Another detective, after dad retired, followed up on the story, but it came to nothing. Me, I touched on the case a few times, working in my spare time, but eventually I got the creeps about what I might find, and I hate to admit it, but I gave it up. You should, too. If you don't, one thing you should remember, passed down to me by my father, told to me by other cops who think they came close to this thing— You smell bananas, you run."

"Bananas?" Sarah asked. But the old man had closed his eyes and nodded off.

I pulled out my phone and used a search engine to look up mysterious, unsolved murders near Mulholland Drive over the years.

First thing that popped up was:

Suspected cult activity linked to graphic scene at Mulholland overlook.

I skimmed through the piece, found nothing out of the ordinary. Nothing about an exoskeleton, nothing about the smells of a gorilla paradise. The cops had labeled the men and animals murdered on Mulholland cult related. A cult that smelled like bananas and pulled dogs and bodies into a nest in orange trees. That seemed like a stretch. Of course, thinking it might not be a cult but something even crazier was also a stretch. Something about all of this tickled a place deep inside my brain, but I couldn't pull the memory to the surface.

As I sat there thinking and going over Sarah's notes, Fedora Man showed up in the mirror in front of me.

"Well, kid. What do you think?"

I startled and dropped the journal, papers flying everywhere. I hustled to pick them up and then reseat myself in front of the mirror. Fedora Man was still there.

"I guess I'm thinking this whole thing is crazy, but that the overlook on Mulholland seems to be a consistent piece of the puzzle."

"There you go, kid. You want to come back to your body and have a shot at Senior Prom, might want to get to cracking."

Fedora Man disappeared, and in his place was my face— white and strained looking. Being dead, no matter what form, wasn't good for your complexion.

The Uber dropped me off at the overlook next to a brown and white city plaque that read, "The City That Dreams Built." Someone had spray-painted the word *Broken* over it in bright blue letters. I walked over to the wooden fence, if you could call it that. It looked like the kind of fence an urban Dracula might have around his house.

I looked down over the sharp cliff below. That was not a drop you came back from. I was feeling nervous about the whole thing, and this was not helping. Cars were coming and going behind me down the twisting road, but none pulled in to join me. I stared across the valley toward the buildings lit up downtown, a sea of steel and metal and twinkling lights. Behind them were mountains with tiny specks of snow dappled across their peaks like powdered sugar.

From the map, I knew the overlook intertwined with Fryman Canyon Trail, a great winding path that cut through the Hollywood Hills and Studio City, eventually butted up against the back edge of Burbank. It was a perfect location, central to the city. I took note of that for the first time. The entrance to the hiking trail was a few feet to the right of the parking area. I surveyed the lot and realized there was room for only about ten cars.

The trail itself was shaded, lined with trees that had an unusual look about them. Some were growing sideways, directly from the edge of the mountain in sharp ninety-degree turns until their crowns overhung the path.

A great breeze came through, shaking their limbs, sending a flock of surprised night birds screeching into the air. Startled but undeterred, I made my way down the trail, hugging the inside of the dusty path as I edged along. I tried to take note of anything that could be considered out of the ordinary, anything that might resemble a hiding place or a den of sorts. Another twenty minutes had passed as I disappeared farther down the footpath. I felt myself growing tired and made my way to a downed tree trunk, took a seat. I was lightheaded, and I felt for a moment like I might faint. I tucked my head between my knees, tried to slow my breathing.

The sweet smell of bananas filled my nose. Suddenly, I realized the thing I'd tried to remember before. As a kid, we'd taken a school field trip to an apiary, where they raise bees. The night before, the school had sent out a notice not to bring bananas as a snack that day, as the smell was often associated with the pheromones of insects, and it could upset the delicate balance of the hive. The thought left as quickly as it came. I don't remember what happened next, other than a feeling that something wet and sticky had fallen over me.

When I came to, the smell of ripe bananas had been replaced by a rotten smell. I felt damp and exposed. I tried to sit up and was immediately propelled backward by something bound tight across my chest and legs. Piles of sticks and mounds of debris were scattered all around me. My head felt like someone had backed over it with a tractor tire. I laid there in a haze, tried to orient myself to where I was and what had happened.

I tried again to sit up, realized that plan wasn't going to work. I was able to turn my head far enough to see that I was suspended, held up as though in a hammock of twine looped through the trunks of the tall trees. I considered my ghostly ability. If it were to kick in without my intent, I could ghost through my bonds and drop to the ground.

I was not dangling over the cliff, but I was high enough that the drop would hurt, a lot, but wouldn't kill me. Unless I missed and rolled off the edge onto the jagged rocks. I tried not to think about that. What if I hit and kept going right through the earth. Did it work that way?

After a few more sideways glances, I realized I was one among many.

There were others suspended in the makeshift hammocks.

Mummified people, desiccated and dry as locust husks. In the moonlight that bled through a gap in the trees, I couldn't see them clearly, but I could see them well enough to know they were in varying stages of dry rot. They jerked and twisted in the cool wind as though still alive. There were dozens. The ones nearest me seemed fresher. I could make out the features and shapes of some; others had collapsed into themselves.

I couldn't make out any details of those strung higher in the trees, but it was clear they had been there for a very long time. There were so many I couldn't keep count. Not all were human. I saw a raccoon, dogs, one dangling from a leash. The cricket man was rich with snacks.

Way we were hung up, we were out in the open but couldn't be seen from below. The trees hid us. Why this place was so important to IT made sense. Concealment of bodies he could digest at his leisure, and he could hide here with no fear of development by the city. This protected land would always have a steady stream of tourists and hikers to feed off of. The idea that an acrobatic bug had grabbed me and brought me here without my knowing also made it clear IT had a natural, temporarily paralyzing toxin.

He might do a hit-and-run now and again, like he had with me, maybe venture out on a stroll taking heads and spines when he felt like it. Perhaps he'd hunted and killed Sarah more out of vengeance than hunger, tired of her tracking him, getting too close to the nest, but this was his primary method. Bag it and store it, eat it when needed. I was, for Mr. Cricket, a version of a McDonald's Happy Meal. Yeah. Mr. Cricket. I had decided.

Whatever drug had been stuck into me, it was starting to wear off. I could feel a bit of pain but not as much as I might have if a big part of me had not been in the hospital in a coma. I was sort of the doppelganger version of me. If I died in a coma, I would be done before Mr. Cricket could digest me, and if I died here, then I assumed I would never come out of that coma, just drift off into nowhere land, in that room waiting for eternity because I hadn't been able to destroy Mr. Cricket.

I decided to quit whining. I had been hit by a truck, knocked into a coma, spent time in purgatory, met a form of my subconscious that favored tough-guy talk and wore a Fedora. And now here I was a living dead partial ghost.

I could handle anything.

I tried to will myself to ghost out of my bonds, preparing for a smash landing or whatever may come, but…it wasn't working. Maybe I could walk through walls, but apparently that didn't apply to other uses.

"What you got here, sis, is a loss of ghost powers on account of you are just about dead-dead."

It was Fedora. He had taken the place of the mummified corpse that hung next to me. "Time is running out, and pretty soon you won't walk through walls, and you won't be here. Maybe there's some way you could take some good magazines with you. Something you don't mind rereading a lot."

"Screw you," I said.

Fedora went away and the mummified corpse remained in his place.

I was going to have to get out of this old school. I could move my hands and arms a little. I slipped my hand into my coat pocket, found the granola bar, then the bag of peanuts, the mini flashlight, but where the hell was the pocket knife? Had it fallen out of my pocket?

That would be typical.

I rooted around in my pocket with my fingers, and hiding behind the granola bar, lurking close to the bag of peanuts, I found it.

I was able to pinch the switchblade out of my pocket and, with a touch of my thumb, open it next to my thigh. I wiggled my wrist enough to cut at the bonds around me. Fortunately, the knife was sharp. My father had been given the knife because it had been used as a prop in some '50s delinquent movie he had written in the '90s. He had given it to me, though my mom did not consider it an appropriate gift, but—especially at this moment—I begged to differ.

I kept sawing and the bond snapped. I went after another. Then another.

And then there was a buzzing sound and the smell of bananas filled my nose.

Mr. Cricket was back.

With those web lines cut, my weight was too much for the webbing.

I fell. But not to the ground. I was left hanging upside down with my foot tangled in a wad of sticky lines.

The granola bar and the flashlight fell out of my pocket. I watched them pass by.

I heard a sound like bees buzzing, a stronger smell of bananas, and Mr. Cricket came into view, wings beating like a hummingbird. He was long and lean and looked insectoid, of course, and I guessed his body had to be light for those wings to carry him. His power was in his speed, stealth, and toxin. What had appeared to be a beard at first glance was a kind of fur. Its fingers were long and tipped with sharp nails. Its legs dangled in the air. Its large dark eyes were like great pools of poison.

It came at me.

I flicked out with the switchblade, caught Mr. Cricket across the face with a solid slash. Warm goo squirted down my arm.

Mr. Cricket buzzed away from me, wheeled, and came around at my backside.

I twisted myself on the line and faced him. Just above its rather nasty butt crack, a long stinger stuck out of it; he tried to stick me with it, to paralyze me again.

I sliced again at him, this time cut deep into the stinger. Mr. Cricket jerked in midair. One of his wings slapped me in the face hard enough to rattle the fillings in my teeth.

I slashed again. I caught one of his wings and pulled the knife through it. It was like running my finger through butter, that's how gossamer the wings were, how sharp the switchblade was.

Mr. Cricket tried to flutter around me. I was exposed, but he was starting to have trouble staying aloft due to the cut wing. Then the sticky line wrapped around my ankle snapped, and I landed on my back so hard it knocked the wind out of me.

I had sudden visions of lying on my back in the hospital bed.

Mr. Cricket buzzed down to straddle me, its clawed fingers gripped tight around my throat. I must have really put a snag in its stinger.

I jerked the switchblade up, still gripped hard in my hand, and drove it into one of the small eyes at the center of its head. It plopped out in a dark gooey wad and landed on my face.

Eewwwww.

I spat out what had gone in my mouth and stabbed whatever I could stab on Mr. Cricket. He sprang to his feet, wobble-stepped backwards, fell over. Then Mr. Cricket started crawling.

I eased to my feet, put the knife in my pocket. I saw a large limb lying nearby, picked it up. I made the back of his head my target, and went to work.

I don't know how long I beat Mr. Cricket, but let's just say when I was through, there wasn't enough of his head to stuff in a thimble.

I was exhausted. I thought of Sarah and wished things had turned out better for her.

I looked up through the trees at the light of the moon.

It was very bright. It made my eyes burn.

I snapped them shut.

Fedora whispered in my ear. "You ought to crack those peepers, sis."

I did. Still bright.

And then I knew. It was the overhead hospital light. I was in the hospital bed. The world was bright and white. I had done it. I had stopped Mr. Cricket, and what was left of my wandering soul was snapped back into the living me.

My parents' faces appeared above me.

"Hello," I said, my mouth dry as cotton, my voice weak as a mouse fart.

They smiled at me, reached out to touch me.

I knew then, I was going to be okay.

I smiled back.

LAST-KNOWN PHOTO

A SONJA BLUE STORY

BY NANCY A. COLLINS

I t's a dive, like most of the bars on this side of town—loud, dark, and pouring strong and cheap for the college kids who crowd the dance floors. I've been in so many joints like this they blur together—the graffiti-filled restrooms that smell of piss and bleach, the smeared mirrors behind the bars, the walls plastered with band flyers from *gigs yet to come* and *gigs recently past*. It doesn't matter what this particular establishment calls itself, or whether it books rock, blues, punk, goth, techno, disco, hip-hop, or country. All that matters is that it's a watering hole. And that watering holes attract lions, hyenas, and other predators. That's why I'm here. I'm a big-game hunter.

But what I stalk is far deadlier than any jungle beast— including the crazy naked ape that calls itself *man*. No, my preferred prey are things that exist in the shadows—that dwell in the flickering darkness at the corner of the eye. The creatures of myth and legend that humanity is convinced no longer—

"Excuse me, miss?"

I turn to look at the woman standing at my elbow. She seems to be in her mid-to-late forties, her face pinched and grooved by worry, her dark hair streaked with gray and pulled away from her face, which is bare of cosmetics. Where my leather biker jacket, tattered jeans, Doc Martens, and spikey hair make me one of the crowd, she is wildly out of place. I drop my vision into the *pretender* spectrum and give her a cursory scan. 100% USDA human.

"I'm looking for my son," the woman says, her voice tinged with equal parts anxiety, hope, and weariness. She must have been at this for some time, as she does not seem surprised by the sight of someone wearing mirrored shades after dark. "Have you seen him?" As she asks, she pushes an eight-by-ten flyer into my hand.

I glance down at the Xeroxed image of a young man, barely out of boyhood. His hair is carefully combed, and he is wearing nice clothes. Given the pose and lighting, it must be his high school graduation photo. The text above the picture reads: "HAVE YOU SEEN ME?" Below the picture are the words "$5000 REWARD" and what I guessed to be the woman's phone number.

"His name's Lonnie," she continues. "He disappeared while barhopping down here with friends over a week ago…"

"Sorry, haven't seen him," I reply, handing back the flyer. It's the truth. I have not laid eyes on the boy before—dead, alive, or otherwise.

"No, you keep it," she says, flashing me a weary smile, and I realize for the first time how much her son resembles her. "Maybe you'll see him somewhere?"

"Not impossible," I admit, and fold the paper into quarters and slide it into my pocket.

The woman nods a thank you and continues on her sad task, tapping on the shoulder of the next stranger leaning against the bar. I pay for my PBR tall boy and drop back into the crowd and pretend to drink it, but I never take my eye off Lonnie's mother. It is a watering hole, after all. It's only a matter of time before a predator shows up—not the kind I'm here for, but dangerous nonetheless.

The predator arrives in the form of a wiry man in his early thirties, who stabs at the image of Lonnie with a tobacco-stained finger. Lonnie's mother's demeanor abruptly changes, as hope and relief radiate from her face like light from an unshaded lamp. The wiry man motions to an exit I know opens to an alleyway that runs behind the bar. Lonnie's mom eagerly follows him as he cuts her from the herd. He pushes open the exit, motioning for her to step out ahead of him. He pauses long enough to cast a quick glance about the room, to make sure no one is watching, then smirks to himself as he follows his prey into the alley.

Ah, but you're sorely mistaken; *I* saw you, you son of a bitch.

I give it a beat before I follow them outside. As I step into the alley, I hear Lonnie's mother loudly proclaiming, "Let *go* of me!" There is anger and indignation in her voice, but also fear. They are halfway down the alley; the wiry man is tussling with his prey, trying to wrest her purse free of her grasp. She has already dropped the bundle of flyers, which scatter like leaves caught in the wind.

"Give up the money, bitch!"

"I don't have it *on* me!" she protests.

"Take me to it!" the wiry man says with a snarl, producing an ugly little snub-nose revolver from one of his pockets. That's when I make the call to take the hit.

"Hey! Let her go!"

The wiry man's head and hand snap in my direction and the gun instantly goes off. Lonnie's mom screams, her hands covering her ears. The bullet feels like someone putting out a lit cigar on my chest. And the lights go out.

Now the lights are back on.

I am on the ground, staring up at the sliver of night sky hanging above the alleyway. The force of the impact has knocked off my sunglasses, but I don't have time to look for them because I can hear Lonnie's mom pleading for her life. I rise like a marionette jerked erect by its puppet master. The wiry man has her pinned to a wall, pressing the still-warm muzzle of the gun to her head.

"You're gonna take me to where you got that money stashed, lady."

"But I need it to find my son—"

"*Fuck* your kid!" he snaps, banging her head against the bricks for emphasis.

Lonnie's mom opens her mouth to protest, but no words come out. Instead, her eyes widen in a mixture of surprise and horror as she sees me standing behind her attacker.

I strike as quickly as a cobra, simultaneously grabbing the wiry man's hair and gun hand, and peel him free of his victim as I would a leech. I squeeze his wrist, shattering it as easily as balsa wood, and the gun drops from his grip. He screams in pain and struggles in vain to free himself. But I am not done with him just yet. This man not only shot me, but also killed me—if only for a few seconds. He owes me a blood debt.

I flex my jaw and release my fangs, plunging them into the wiry man's jugular. His skin tastes of sweat, salt, and fear. I drink deep, but not all—just enough to repair the damage he has done to me. When I let go of him, he falls to the ground and stays there.

Lonnie's mother stares at me as I stand before her, revealed in all my monstrosity—mouth wet with stolen blood, eyes gleaming like those of a panther crouched at the edge of a campfire. To her credit she does not scream or faint. Instead, she simply asks, "What *are* you?"

"Willing to help you find your son," I reply.

"Drink this."

I set the cup of coffee down in front of Lonnie's mother before sliding into the seat opposite her. The diner is a twenty-four-hour greasy spoon that caters to the late-night party crowd, but it's early enough that only a handful of customers occupy the booths.

She mutely nods and picks up the mug with trembling hands, sloshing its contents onto the Formica tabletop. She looks up at me, trepidation and curiosity sharing space in her hazel eyes.

"My name is Sonja Blue," I say, trying my best to sound not-scary. "I know your son's is Lonnie. What's yours?"

She hesitates for a moment, then sets aside her coffee. "Imogene Strother. But I go by Genie."

"Pleased to meet you, Genie. No doubt you have *many* questions for me."

She shifts about uneasily, glancing around to make sure no one else is listening before leaning forward and whispering, "Are you what I *think* you are?"

"Yes," I reply with a nod. "But what I *am* is not exactly what you think that is. If you have to put a name to it—the closest is *dhampir*, neither living nor undead."

"Why do you want to help me?"

"Because a long time ago, probably before you were born, there was girl—younger than your son, but not by much—who disappeared under similar circumstances. Her mother spent years trying to find her, without any luck, despite the fact she had access to far more resources than you do. Eventually, she became so desperate she succumbed to charlatans, grifters…and worse. And, in the end, it broke her. No mother should suffer not knowing what's become of their child."

"No, they shouldn't," she agrees quietly.

"Do you have a more recent photograph of your son?"

She nods and dips her hand into her purse, retrieving her cell phone. She taps the screen, summoning forth an image from its digital depths, then slides it across the table to me. "This was taken by one of his friends on the night Lonnie disappeared. He'd just turned twenty-one earlier that week, and they were out celebrating."

I pick up the phone and study the image of Lonnie—slightly older, and with a different haircut than the one in his graduation photo—standing with one arm slung over the shoulder of a young man his own age, grinning into the camera. Both of them are holding up bottles of beer in a toast. Judging by the blitzed look on Lonnie's face, it was not his first beer of the night. I look past the young friends in the foreground, studying the people and décor in the background. I recognize it as Rackham's—a dive bar with pool tables, dart boards, and the occasional floating poker game. I also recognize a face in the crowd.

"I know this woman," I say, pointing to a blonde girl standing at the bar, looking over her shoulder in the direction of Lonnie. "Her name is Violet. Did your son's friends mention a girl?"

"Actually, they did," she replies, her cheeks coloring slightly. "His roommate Jordan—that's the boy who's in the picture with him—said Lonnie was talking to a blonde girl later that night. Then, when it was time to leave, they couldn't find him. Jordan assumed he'd gone home with her. When he didn't come back to their dorm room by the end of the weekend, that's when he called me; and I called the police."

"And what did they have to say?"

"They weren't much help. They didn't even want to take my missing person report; they assumed he was just another college kid out getting laid. It wasn't until he'd been gone a week that they started taking it seriously."

"I'm not surprised." I sigh.

"This Violet...is she a friend of yours?"

"Hardly."

"Is she—is she like you?"

"No. She's human. But the man she works for isn't. He's called The Banker. He runs a black-market blood bank that caters to the Ruling Class."

"Huh?"

"Vampires of high rank and influence."

"Like Draculas?"

"It's more complicated than that—but, yes, Draculas."

"Dear God." Genie gasps, putting a trembling hand to her mouth. "My baby—!"

"It's not as bad as it sounds. If the Banker has Lonnie, the odds are very good that he's still alive." I can tell by the look in her eyes that she desperately wants to believe me. I want to believe it, too. And it probably isn't a lie. "Is there anyone else here with you? Lonnie's father, perhaps?"

She snorts in derision and makes a face as if swigging spoiled milk. "That bastard is long gone, and good riddance! I wouldn't ask him for help, even if I knew where the asshole lived. I begged, borrowed, and stole to make sure Lonnie got an education. Luckily, he landed a scholarship; but that only covers so much. The money I raised for the reward is my life's savings."

"I see. Where are you staying?"

"At a motel on the edge of town. It's all I could afford. My car's there. I took an Uber into the city since I don't really know my way around."

"I understand." I get up and throw a twenty onto the table. "Come on. I'll drop you off at your room. It's almost midnight. If we're lucky, you'll have your boy back by sunup."

"I want to go with you."

"No," I reply firmly. "I understand how you feel, but where I'm going you can't follow. Nothing human can."

The first thing I notice as Genie unlocks the door to her motel room is the carpet's color, which was chosen to hide stains. The second thing I notice is that, save for the grudging nods to the digital age, such as the flat-screen TV bolted to the wall and the cheap cell phone dock/alarm clock combo on the bedside table, this room is no different from those I turned tricks in decades ago.

I quickly close the door behind us and throw both its deadbolt and U-bar lock before fishing the Glock out of the breast pocket of my leather jacket. I dip into my right hip pocket and retrieve its magazine, slap it into place, and chamber the first round. "Here, take this," I say, handing the weapon to Genie. "You stay here until I come back, understood? Shoot anything that comes through that door that isn't me in the head."

"But what if they're, you know, a vampire or a werewolf?"

"You've got nothing to worry about; the bullets are silver. Besides, take it from someone who knows; *everything* dies if you shoot it in the head."

After giving Genie a quick tutorial on how to sight the gun and switch off the safety, I make my exit, pausing long enough to make sure I hear her lock and bolt the door behind me. I check my watch. There's still enough time to hit the bars and find Violet. I didn't mention it to Genie, but I've been trying to nail down The Banker's base of operations for a few weeks now, with no luck. But thanks to the photo she showed me, I now have a decent clue as to where his lure is trolling for donors.

A half hour later I'm at Rackham's, but there's no sign of Violet. I move down the street to the Transcontinental, a metal dive famous for staying open later than its rivals and taking a lax attitude towards checking IDs and drug use in its restrooms. I circulate among the clientele, scanning the crowd for blondes.

Within a few minutes, I spot Violet dressed in a scarlet cocktail dress, sitting in a horseshoe booth and talking to a man in his late thirties with red hair and pale skin. He's dressed in a denim jacket with a Cannibal Corpse patch on the breast pocket. He has a mixed drink in one hand and his head is bobbing like a toy balloon on a string. Violet pulls a cell phone from her clutch purse and quickly texts someone. A couple minutes later, a tall man dressed all in black arrives at the table.

I step deeper into the crowd, careful not to be seen by her accomplice.

Together, Violet and The Banker's clerk slide the drugged death metal fan out of the booth. To the unwitting observer, they look like a young couple helping an inebriated friend get home instead of a pair of kidnappers. As they exit the bar, the clerk pauses to look around—whether out of habit or because he senses me is unclear.

I step behind a couple of partying frat boys and pull the shadows around my mind, blocking my thoughts. Although he lacks genuine psychic muscle, if he catches a "whiff" of my presence, then the whole night is screwed. To my relief, he continues out the door without a second glance.

I quickly follow them, exiting in time to see Violet and the clerk load their roofied victim into a waiting van in the parking lot. I hurry to my own vehicle and tail them, making sure to keep at least two cars between us. After ten minutes, the van pulls up to a block of two-story Depression-era warehouses that have somehow avoided being turned into loft apartments. The van goes around the back of the buildings, but I have a good idea of which warehouse it's headed for—the one marked "Royal Medical Supplies." Wow, how did I manage to miss *that?* Talk about hiding in plain sight.

I drive past the warehouses, only to circle back and park my car behind the dumpster of the business next door to the "medical supply" warehouse. There is a drainpipe handy, but I don't really need it in order to scale the outer wall. I dig my fingernails—as hard and sharp as a tiger's claws—into the brick face and climb up. Upon making the rooftop of the neighboring warehouse, I quickly scan my surroundings to make sure there are no guards or surveillance cameras before making the eight-foot jump between the buildings. I land like a cat and creep forward, searching for an entrance. I find it in the form of a small roof-hatch skylight that opens onto a room filled with plasma collection machines and centrifuges covered by plastic shrouds. So there really *are* medical supplies in here.

Using my switchblade, I force the lock on the hatch and drop down into the room below. I hold my breath as I land, expecting to be jumped by The Banker's clerks, but nothing happens. I stand up and look around; there's no sign of anyone, human or otherwise.

The Banker is either extremely overconfident or there's a security system I have overlooked. If that is the case, there is nothing I can do about it now.

I crack open the door of the supply room to discover a mezzanine overlooking the warehouse with a flight of metal stairs leading to the floor below. Although I can't see anyone, I can hear distant voices echoing in the open emptiness. A quick glance upward reveals an exposed ceiling with wooden and metal joists and beams. I exit the supply room and scurry up the nearest wall quick as a lizard and situate myself in a nice, shadowy corner that allows me an unobstructed view of The Banker's operation.

Below are dozens of neatly arranged hospital gurneys occupied by unconscious human "donors." They are a mix of relatively young males and females from every ethnic group. All of them are naked save for adult diapers, and they are attached to intravenous feeding and bleeding systems. Beside each donor station is a table bearing a blood collection scale constantly rocking a bag of blood back and forth to prevent coagulation.

I reach out and gently probe the mind of one of the donors with my own, testing as to whether their sleep is the result of sedation or psychic control. A young woman with dyed pink hair moans and writhes, as if struggling to escape something in her dreams. Suddenly, a whip-thin man with a long face and steel gray hair appears at the girl's bedside. Judging from the psychic energy he wears about his head like a dark halo, this is The Banker's Renfield. The psychic places his hand on the girl's forehead and she falls silent.

At least I now know from my brief contact with her mind that not only are the donors tranced to avoid tainting their blood, but they also aren't truly unconscious—simply incapable of movement and speech. They are aware of what is being done to them but are powerless to free themselves from this living nightmare.

The Banker's Renfield frowns and glances about. I feel a pricking at the corners of my mind, and I quickly cloak my thoughts. The psychic is extremely powerful if he can keep dozens of humans tranced—possibly even gifted enough to kill at a distance. I hold my breath as he continues to scan. The pressure in my head feels like I'm diving to the bottom of the ocean.

"Kitchener!"

The Renfield jerks his head in the direction of the voice and the invisible vise about my skull instantly disappears. "Yes, sir?"

The Banker appears, flanked by a pair of clerks. He wears the appearance of a white man in his early fifties—distinguished, well-groomed, and dressed in an expensive suit. I drop my vision into the *Pretender* spectrum and his good looks and easy charm melt away, revealing a walking cadaver with glowing red eyes, crooked talons, and sharp canines. He still has a nice suit, though.

"Violet has secured us a fresh donor."

"Has it been screened?"

"The results from the blood test should be ready momentarily." The Banker gives a humorless laugh as he fishes a cell phone from his breast pocket. "Ah! Speak of the devil!" The vampire's smile disappears, to be replaced by a scowl. "The new donor is clean of HIV, syphilis, hepatitis, septicemia, and malaria; however, it *does* have aplastic anemia. Worthless to me. What a waste of time and blood."

"I'll see to the termination, sir."

"There's no hurry," The Banker says with a grunt, returning the phone to his pocket. "It's too close to dawn to dump the body. It'll have to wait until nightfall. Just put it to sleep until then."

"As you wish, sir."

The Banker turns and heads toward a door on the far side of the warehouse, his clerks and Renfield trailing in his wake. Once the door closes behind them, I leave my perch and drop to the floor.

I hurry to Lonnie's side, as I had spotted him while eavesdropping on The Banker.

Like the other donors, he is naked save for an adult diaper and has a 16-gauge needle in his right arm connected to a blood collection bag. An automatic blood pressure cuff is wrapped around his upper arm, quietly hissing as it swells and deflates itself, controlling the flow of blood. A twenty-inch feeding tube connected to the IV stand next to his bed is run through one nostril and into his stomach. Save for being very pale and a newly grown beard that makes him look far older than twenty-one, Lonnie appears physically unchanged from the last photo taken of him.

I'll give The Banker this: he knows how to run a blood farm. Disconnecting Lonnie and getting him out of here undetected is going to be difficult, if not impossible; but I gave my word to his mother, and by that I stand. I have to try, even if this ends badly.

I grasp the nasogastric line protruding from his nostril and in one motion quickly pull the tube out as far as my arm can reach, then switch to my other hand and finish pulling it all the way out before he can gag. I grimace and toss the slimy tube aside, then turn my attention to the phlebotomy needle jutting from his arm. If I try to remove it, blood will spurt everywhere; and the smell will instantly alert The Bankers and his clerks, just like sharks in the water. I'm better off leaving Lonnie attached to the bag.

I drop the guard rails on the gurney and scoop up his motionless body, tossing it over my left shoulder in a fireman's carry while simultaneously snatching the blood bag from the collection rocker. Suddenly, a piercing electronic shriek rings throughout the warehouse. Shit! I should have *known* the fucker has pressure-sensors attached to the bleeding stations!

"*Poacher!*"

I turn in the direction of the shout to see The Banker approaching, flanked by his pair of clerks and the Renfield called Kitchener. Yep, I'm busted.

"You would steal from *me*?" The Banker growls, showing his fangs in ritual challenge. He motions to the psychic. "Get rid of this thieving trash, Kitchener!"

"As you command, milord," the Renfield replies, the dark halo about his head swelling like a storm cloud.

I give my right arm a sharp twist and my switchblade drops from its hiding place in the sleeve of my motorcycle jacket into my waiting hand. I throw it hard and true. The Banker stares, open-mouthed, as his human servant falls to the floor with a silver knife between his eyes.

The telepathic energy rising from the psychic's head explodes like an overloaded fuse, severing the neural leash holding the donors in bondage. Two score human voices cry out in pain, confusion, and fear as the captives emerge from their unnatural sleep, tearing blindly at the tubes invading their bodies. I feel Lonnie's body writhe against my shoulder, and I quickly return him to his slumber. This is no time for me to be distracted.

As I move forward to reclaim my switchblade, The Banker rapidly backs away, his handsome mask momentarily slipping to reveal the undead thing beneath. He turns to his clerks and hisses in a panicked voice: *"Stop her!"*

The closest of the two—the one I saw accompanying Violet at the Transcontinental—lunges at me as I snatch the knife from Kitchener's skull. I pivot to place myself between Lonnie and the vampire's claws and fangs, slashing with the switchblade. He shrieks in agony as its silver edge slices through his throat like rotten lace, releasing a torrent of black blood. The skin about the wound instantly putrefies, sliding away like melting wax. Within seconds, the wounded clerk is reduced to a skeleton writhing in a pool of foul-smelling ichor.

Despite witnessing what just happened to his companion, the second clerk tries to snatch Lonnie from my shoulder, only to find my switchblade buried in one ear up to its hilt. His liquifying brains leak from the corners of his eyes and run down his face like unholy tears as I yank free my weapon. As he falls to the floor like a broken puppet, I turn to face The Banker, who now cowers before me, hands upraised in supplication.

"I am no *poacher*," I say with a snarl.

"I-I beg your forgiveness, milady," he stammers. Despite his fancy suit and personal wealth, he is not a vampire of power. He is a lesser courtier; and one that knows he is outclassed. "It was a grievous misunderstanding on my part. You are free to take the boy. No hard feelings, right?"

"None from *me*, anyway," I reply as I reach out with my mind and touch those of the freshly awakened donors. *Get him.*

Suddenly, the warehouse fills with the sound of forty humans rising as one from their gurneys, sending IV stands and blood collection stations crashing to the ground. Their ragged voices clamor in pain, rage, and horror as they struggle to their feet. A handful collapse to the floor, their muscles too atrophied to support them. The others stagger forward, swarming The Banker like living zombies eager for their pound of flesh.

"*Take your hands off me!*" he shrieks, lashing out with his talons. Those closest to him drop to the floor, their throats slashed and bellies disemboweled, but it does not stop the ones behind them, or the ones behind *them*. While The Banker is stronger than a single human, he is not stronger than *thirty*.

They drag their captor across the warehouse floor to the door as he hisses and spits like a feral cat, striking out blindly with fang and claw. They remain undeterred, ignoring their own streaming wounds as they walk over their fallen comrades. I follow them as the sheer force of their numbers shatter the door frame and they spill over its threshold.

As they breech the anteroom where The Banker tested and cleaned his livestock before hooking them up to the bleeding stations, I catch a glimpse of the lure called Violet frantically struggling with the newly awakened death metal fan she had kidnapped earlier. She manages a single, piercing scream before the others overwhelm her like a human tidal wave and trample her underfoot.

One of their number—the girl with the pink hair—separates from the mob and darts over to a control panel set into the far end of the anteroom and hits a large red button with her fist. There is the sound of machinery engaging, followed by rumbling as a portion of the wall rolls upward, revealing the loading dock on the other side. And the dawn.

Upon seeing the lightening sky, The Banker wails like a banshee and turns his head to beseech me. "Milady! Sister, please... I beg you! Don't make me burn!"

"*I'm* not controlling them. This isn't my circus, and these aren't my monkeys; they're *yours*. Or *used* to be."

"I'll eat your soul in Hell, you thieving bitch!" The Banker shrieks, foam flying from his champing fangs as he is dragged onto the loading platform.

"Come now, *brother*!" I laugh. "As a banker, you should expect withdrawals!"

Before he can shout any more threats or curses, the surviving donors hurl their tormentor from the shaded protection of the dock shelter into the sunlight beyond its canopy.

Because the day is new, The Banker does not immediately burst into flame. Instead, his skin grows pink, then bright red—like a lobster being steamed alive—as huge welts balloon across his face and hands before exploding in gouts of grayish-yellow fluid. His eyes turn white as they boil in their sockets and his hair falls away from his scalp like cobwebs. He screams until his lungs collapse and he is reduced to a mummified husk, like an earthworm frying on a hot sidewalk. Yet still he writhes, jaws snapping at nothing as he blindly bites at the air around him.

The pink-haired girl jumps down from the loading platform and snatches up a nearby brick and, with a scream of angry triumph, brings it down on The Banker's denuded skull, crushing it.

Of the forty donors awakened by Kitchener's death, a baker's dozen survive. Confident their captor is no more, they flee, naked and bleeding, down the alley. Only the pink-haired girl pauses to look back one last time in my direction before disappearing into the sunrise.

Twenty minutes later and I am back at Genie Strother's motel—her unconscious son draped across the backseat of my car. I take a couple of minutes to disconnect him from the phlebotomy needle and blood bag before attempting to move him. I treat myself to a quick drink while doing so—waste not, want not.

Luckily, it's still too early for the housecleaning staff to be making rounds, and if any of the other guests happen to look out their windows to see me carrying a grown man in a diaper in my arms—well, it's probably not the first time that's happened here.

As I knock, I hear frantic movement on the other side and quickly step aside, narrowly avoiding the .38 slug that passes through the cheap door frame, immediately followed by Genie's frightened voice demanding, *"Who is it?"*

"Damn it! I told you to shoot at anything *but* me!" I snap as I kick open the ruined door.

"I'm so sorry! I must have fallen asleep; I wasn't thinking!" Chagrined, Genie automatically drops the gun. Her eyes widen as she sees her son cradled in my arms. "Oh my God! Lonnie! You found him!" She hurries to his side, covering his pale forehead with kisses while I place him on the bed. Upon seeing his bandaged inner arm, she turns to look at me with dread in her eyes. "Is he… one of *them*, now?"

"No," I say with a shake of my head. "He's been bled, but not bitten. He's still human. He's young; in time, he'll fully recover."

"And the kidnapper? The Bank Man?"

"He's permanently out of business," I reply as I place a hand to the side of Lonnie's head and touch his mind with my own. A second later, his lids flutter open, revealing hazel eyes identical to his mother's. He looks around the room, confused and fearful— until he sees Genie.

"Mom," he whispers, his voice raspy from disuse. "I had a nightmare…"

"That's okay, baby. It's over now," she replies, smiling through the tears coursing down her face. She takes his hand in both of hers and squeezes it. "Rest easy, sugar. We're going home soon."

I turn to leave, as I have done what I promised and there is no need to linger, only to feel a hand on my elbow.

"Your reward," Genie says, holding out an envelope.

I smile and shake my head. "I don't need it."

"I *know* you don't. But you *still* earned it. After you left, I kept thinking about what you said about the mother who lost her daughter. So I used my phone to Google a few things. And I figured out who you are—or, rather, who you *were*. Your father was a very rich man. You disappeared while on a trip with friends over fifty years ago…"

I stiffen and pull my arm free of her grasp. "Take the boy and go."

"Don't worry... I'll *never* tell," she assures me. And I'm sure she means it. "Not that anyone would believe me! I just want to let you know that I'll never forget you and what you've done for my boy."

"Yes, you will."

I watch from behind the mirror-tinted windows of my black Gran Torino as Genie helps Lonnie—now dressed in his own clothes and freshly shaved—into the passenger seat of her fifteen-year-old Camry. As she moves to the driver's side door, she pauses to search her purse. She frowns and digs deeper, but to no avail. Whatever she's looking for isn't there. She sighs in frustration and looks back at the motel room, then shrugs her shoulders and gets in the car. She drives past without looking in my direction and is gone, headed back to wherever it is she and Lonnie come from.

It wasn't difficult to wipe her memory of me and to construct a new one in its place—one where her son was the victim of human traffickers, and who managed to escape and find his way to her. It also made it necessary for them to leave as quickly as possible. So quickly, in fact, there was no time to waste looking for a lost smartphone.

I fish Genie's cell phone out of my pocket and tap the screen. Moms being moms, there is no password or biometric lock on it. Before removing the SIM card and flipping it out the window like a tiddlywink, I stare for a long moment at the window she'd left open: the Wikipedia page dedicated to the disappearance. I do not bother reading the text—what little there is of it. Instead, I focus on the black-and-white picture in the right-hand corner. It is a blurry snapshot, taken inside a crowded nightclub, of a sixteen-year-old girl holding a champagne glass. Behind her left shoulder hovers the outline of a man—or at least, something that pretended to be.

Beneath it is the caption: *Last-Known Photo of Denise Thorne. London, 1969.*

(In Memory of Louise Villeneuve)

KICKSTARTER BACKERS

A huge thanks to everyone who backed the
Dead Detectives Society Kickstarter campaign!

Abby Braunsdorf • Abe Scheppler • Adam J. Levine
Adrien PARTY • AEIOU & Sometimes Why • Aimee Hudson
Alex and Sam Rosen • Alex Dueben • Algie Lane III
Allan Burd • Amanda Headlee • Amy Claflin • Andrew Beirne
Andrew Byers • Andrew Kaplan • Andrew Martinez
Andrew Saxby • Andrew Wainwright • Andy Ramsay
Angie Booth • Anonymous Reader • Anthony Lagada
Alan Szymkowiak • Aphektos • Ariel Bermudo • Ashleigh Floyd
Aysha Rehm • Barry R. Hunter • Belanger Books
Benjamin Akers • Benjamjamin • Benny Lowery
Big Daddy Drew • BigGMonsterMan • Bill Bibo Jr
Bill Ginger • Bill LaMonaca • Bill Schafer • Bob Wiley
BOBBY ZAMARRON • Brad Kabosky • Bradley K. Taylor
Brcoley • Brian L. Black • Brian O'Pappy Booth • Brian Winger
Brian Yesowitch • bryan geddes • C-N • C. Cauthron
C. Louis Wolfe • Calliope Loula Daoundakis • Carolyn Rowland
Cathy Green • Charles Babbage • Charles W. McCurdy II
Christoff RDGZ • Christopher Helton • Christopher Saylor
Corey Redekop • Corky LaVallee • Craig Hackl • Cris Morris
Curtis B. Edmundson • Daldran • Dan Cruson • Danny Valentine
Darc Rose • David Capelan • David Dilkes • David E. Ray
David Lars Chamberlain • David Myers • David Nissen
David Seligman • David T. Griffith • David Tohtz • dbradical
Dennis Clarke • Denny Hager • Dino Buffetta Jr. • Dinsy Johns
Diron Anderson • Doc Wyatt • DocChronos • Dodie Sullivan
Dominik Plejić • Don Prentiss • Donald Cole
Donald McGowan • Donna-lyn Washington

Duane Swierczynski • Dylan Pucilowski • Ed Gosney
Ed McKeogh • Edward Boykin • Eileen M. • Elia Faz.
Elise "Warriorjudge" Simon • Elizabeth Taylor • Emily Luna
Emily Rousell • Eric King • eric priehs • Eric Schmidt
Erik Smith • Euan Murray • Eve Conte Seligman
FaSeanablyLate • Fidel Jiron Jr. • Francesco Tignini
Francesco Tignini • Francis Maconi • Fred W Johnson
Furry Foster Momma • Garrick Alvin Dietze • Gary Olsen
Gary Phillips • George Rivera • Gerry Green • Giusy Rippa
GMarkC • Greg Trosclair • gregory illig • Guénnaëlle Crunil
Guy Kendall • HaiKukture • HaiKulture • Hailey Claire Hull
Harris O'Malley • Heather Parsons • Heather Royston
Hostage_Jimbro • Ian Giggal • Igotz Delgado • Ivan Saldana
J Novello • J. HART • James 'Elfboy' Zieff • James Barron
James Caraballo • James Chambers • James Hellyer
James Johnston/aka Mr. Doom • James Kuhoric, Undead P.I.
James Palmer • James-Michael Roddy • Jason DeLong
Jason Forbes • Jason Grund • Jason Holtschneider
Jason Martinez • Jason Potter • Jason R Frei • Jason Rico
Jason T Blackstone • Jean Seby • Jeff Hinshaw
Jennifer K Ryan • Jens Ambiel • Jessica Coyle • Jessica Meade
Jim and Rhonda Lancaster • Jim Andrew Clark • JJ Lindsey
Jochem van der Steen • Joe Cobos • Joe Flood • Joe Jackson
John "AcesofDeath7" Mullens • John Averette Jr. • John Bennett
John Bowen • John Christopher • John Ellis • John G Bodnar
John Hanson • John M Creagar • John Nacinovich
John Palisano • John R MI • John Wolham • Johnnie Nemec
Jon Boese • Jon Terry • Jonathan Gensler • Jordan Theyel
Josh Viola • Joshua Hair • Joshua J Murphy • Josue Oyuela
Jp • JTS • Juan Morales Jr • JuanR • Judy McClain
Kal Powell • Karloff's Ghost • Kathryn McLeer • Kathy Bottarini
Kaushik Karforma • Kayla Brown • Keith Howell • Keith West

Kelly J Cooper • Kenneth Brian Beardsley • Kenneth Rouch
Kevin Halstead • Kevin Moreau • Kevin Wadlow
Kimberly Williams • Kirsten Kowalewski • krinsky
Kristen Helsel • Kristin S. • Kristina Meschi • Lamont Cranston
Larry Gelfand • Larry L Ostertag • Laura Snow • Leverett Butts
Lewis Chemasi • Linda Wilcox • Lindbergh E Hollingsworth
Lisa Kruse • Lisa McEwen • Lissette Buckley • Louis Schroeder
LUCIANO VAIROLETTI • Maramu • Marc McKenzie
Mark Slater • Mark W Wilson 67 • Mary Gaitan • Matt Stepan
Matthew Lazorwitz • Matthew Moran • Matthew P. King
Meg Smith • Michael Fraieli • Michael Fromm
Michael G Palmer • Michael Morse • Michael Niederman
Michael Nimmo • Michael O'Mara • Michael Shoemaker
Michael T Coyan • Michaela Weber • Michele Brittany
Mick Magno • Mick McGovern • Mike A. Rhodes • Mike Bunch
Mike Dubost • Mike Lazur • Mori Tate-Keech • Nathan Filizzi
Nick Breeze • Nick Fletcher • Nikolas P. Robinson
Nolyn Johnson • Pat St. Jean • Patrick Sharp
Paul Chapman-Farley • Paul Lucero • Paul Peet • Paul Popernack
Paul Rose Jr. • Paul Saunders • Peter W. Chan • Pip Scott
Prince Eric Vickers • PXLuzifer aka Nico
Pyndan & Roxy Wülffe • R.W. Wallace • Rachel L Peterson
Randall Beaton • Randall Beaton • Randy P. Belanger
Ravyn Bryce • Ray Schmidt • remlub navI • Rena Mason
Ric Bretschneider • Richard Garrett • Richard O'Shea
Richard Parker • Richard Thomas • Rick Hesseltine • Rick Siem
RIJU GANGULY • Rixhard Novak • Robert Belgrave
Robert Donovan • Robert Tkacz • Rodney Barnett
Rolf Laun • Ronald H. Miller • Ronald L. Weston
Ronald Shepherd • Roth Schilling • Rowan Stone • Rowan Stone
Russell Roberto • Rusty Smith • Ryan Power • S Ontiveros
S&M Cavanaugh • Sarah B • Sarah Waites • Scantrontb

Scott Casey • Scott Chisholm • Scott Gray • Scott Kane
Scott Pollard • Sean Con • Sean O'Reilly • Seth Alexander
Seth Bosley • Shawn Shultz • Sherri Mines • Shon Keely
Sierra Marie Hall • Sir Loin o Beef • Sirrah Medeiros
Skfisher87 • Slim Jim • Solomon Stone Romney • Sonnet Ireland
Stephanie Carey • Stephen Ballentine • Stephen W. Chappell
Steve Loiaconi • Steve Pattee • Steve Smith • Steve Thomasma
Steven Epperson • Steven J Sabatke • Stuart V • Susan Cierlitsky
Susan Jessen • Susanne Stohr • Tara Clarkson • Tarhan Kayihan
Terri Connor • Terry Sherwood • The Frankencast
The Kift's, Derbyshire • Theresa Derwin • Thomas C Raymond
Tim Majka • Tom Romero • Tom Wilkinson • Tony Anuci
Tony Ciak • Tony McCowan • Trevor "Ratenef" Chapman
Tucker Christine • Tyler Brunette • Tyler R Byers
Valentino Sergi • Vincent Darlage, PhD • Wade Felde
Will Lorenzo • William Dahlstedt • William DeGeest
William Graves • 'Will It Work' Dansicker • Zack Fissel • Zandor